HIDDEN ANGELS

BOOKS BY CAROLYN ARNOLD

DETECTIVE MADISON KNIGHT SERIES

Ties That Bind

Justified

Sacrifice

Found Innocent

Just Cause

Deadly Impulse

In the Line of Duty

Power Struggle

Shades of Justice

What We Bury

Girl on the Run

Her Dark Grave

Murder at the Lake

Life Sentence

SARA AND SEAN COZY MYSTERY SERIES

Bowled Over Americano

Wedding Bells Brew Murder

MATTHEW CONNOR ADVENTURE SERIES

City of Gold

The Secret of the Lost Pharaoh

The Legend of Gasparilla and His Treasure

STANDALONE

Assassination of a Dignitary

Pearls of Deception

Midlife Psychic

CAROLYN ARNOLD

HIDDEN ANGELS

bookouture

Published by Bookouture in 2025

An imprint of Storyfire Ltd.
Carmelite House
50 Victoria Embankment
London EC4Y 0DZ

www.bookouture.com

The authorised representative in the EEA is Hachette Ireland
8 Castlecourt Centre
Dublin 15 D15 XTP3
Ireland
(email: info@hbgi.ie)

ISBN: 978-1-83618-075-3
eBook ISBN: 978-1-83618-074-6

PROLOGUE

Orlando, Florida

The day was a scorcher. The thick air made it hard to draw a deep breath, and sweat was pooling at the back of his knees and his lower back. His T-shirt was sticking to him, and his sunglasses were sliding down his nose. But his reason for being there made his discomfort bearable.

The amusement park was crowded, working in his favor. People often let their guards down in places like this, thinking everyone was like them and looking for a fun-filled day. They failed to grasp the person next to them might have a different agenda. It's why pickpockets made a killing, more than making up for the cost of admission. But he wasn't after some cash or to steal anyone's identity. He was after the sweet innocence of a young girl.

He watched many of them, with their hair in ponytails, pigtails, or braids, skipping throughout the park. The heat didn't stop the good mothers and fathers from holding tight to their young one's hand. Wet palms, be damned. But at some point, they'd let go, and an opening would present itself. He'd be ready to pounce on that moment of weakness. And he had his eye set on one special girl.

He'd been following the family through the park, heard them talk to each other. American, subtle accent. Likely from Virginia or Maryland.

The girl was fair-skinned. Her brown hair in pigtails held by elastics with blue marbles. His favorite color. But she also had a bedazzled pink barrette clipped near her forehead, holding the baby hairs at bay. She was in a pale-blue jumper and low-rise socks and pristine running shoes.

What he was most attracted to was her spunk. The girl repeatedly swayed her father's and mother's arms, lifting them wildly in the air, despite them asking her to stop several times.

It will only be a matter of time...

He smiled, imagining the parents releasing those precious small hands. Just one careless consent to comfort over caution would spell the end of their happy little family and the beginning of his.

"Sadie, cut it out, please," the mother protested, but kept a hold on the girl's hand. The man had let go a moment prior.

"Ice cream!" The girl pointed excitedly at a vendor shack with a huge sign advertising the treat and loaded up with cotton candy, caramel apples, and twisty rainbow lollipops in the window opening.

"What do you think?" The man turned to the woman.

She flailed an arm as if to say, *why not?*

"Okay, let's do ice cream!" The father announced this with a burst of enthusiasm, but his smile faded quickly. He was likely more interested in seeking out a patch of shade and cooling down.

The man who was watching stepped past them with an "excuse me" and a smile at the girl. She smiled back, and his heart lifted. She was perfect. All the time he'd invested in tailing her would pay off. He'd make certain of it.

He reached the counter, and the teenager working there looked at him like she was bored out of her mind. Not that he could blame her. A person could only say "What can I get ya?" so many times before checking out.

He ordered two ice cream sandwiches with vanilla wedged between chocolate cookies. He stepped to the side and watched his target.

The mother was digging into her cross-body purse. The dad was keeping an eye on the girl.

"Don't wander off too far." An unsupported caution. He made no movement to catch up to her.

The girl didn't pay him any heed, and she was getting close to the vendor shack now. To him.

As if a blessing from above, the already intense crowds swelled more. He couldn't see the girl's parents, but he heard the father calling out, "Sadie!"

The girl emerged from the crowds a mere three feet from him. "Are you Sadie?"

"Yes." She eyed him with a leeriness that quickly disappeared when he extended an unwrapped ice cream sandwich toward her. "Is that for me?" she asked.

"It sure is, sweetheart." He dared himself to move closer and picked up the smell of her fruity shampoo. There would be no turning back now. They were meant to be together. "This one's for my daughter," he said, indicating the second bar. "Do you want to meet her?"

"Sure." Sadie looked up at him, her blue eyes piercing his and causing his sanity to briefly slip.

She believed his lie. This was very good. He reached for her hand, and the girl didn't hesitate to slip hers into his. He weaved them through the crowds and away from the shack. As he moved, he heard the girl's parents calling her name. If the girl heard them, she gave no indication, absorbed as she was in her treat.

"Good ice cream, eh?"

"Uh-huh." Not even paying him attention as her little tongue darted out to attack the vanilla ice cream.

He smiled as he continued walking with her toward the park's exit.

ONE

Woodbridge, Virginia
Tuesday, February 11

Amanda shuffled papers on her desk. They were all that remained of the case she and her partner, Trent Stenson, had closed two weeks ago. A dry spell when working in Homicide for the Prince William County Police Department was a good thing. Fewer calls meant fewer murders, but it was also unsettling. She was used to being called out to crime scenes on a regular basis, not sitting at her desk.

Selfishly, she wished she had more to challenge her, because then her mind would be too busy to torture her about Friday being Valentine's Day and the fact she had no one special to share it with this year. But being single was better than being paired with the *wrong* one. And she should know. She'd just come out of a serious two-year relationship. They'd ignored the distance growing between them until there was no way to repair it. But it ended peacefully and mutually. As the French would say, *c'est la vie*. It was this go-with-the-flow attitude she planned to adopt moving forward. Besides, it wasn't like she was all alone. She was part of a large family with six siblings, counting her half-brother, and Zoe, her adorable nine-year-old going on teenager at home.

"Time to go." Sergeant Malone, Amanda and Trent's immediate boss, swept into the opening of her cubicle in the Homicide warren at Central Station.

His words ran a shiver up her spine, and on impulse, she pushed the latest batch of papers away from her and wheeled out from her desk. Trent popped up in his cubicle, looking over the short partition that separated their workspaces.

Malone's words could mean only one thing. There was a body. "Boss?" One word, the implication clear. She was hungry for details and direction.

"There's been a standoff this morning at Herald Church," Malone began.

She'd passed that church many times in her short commute from home to work. She lived in Dumfries, a ten-minute drive from Central in Woodbridge. "A standoff?" She wasn't clear how this involved them.

"It started early this morning but was just cleared now."

His response didn't give her anything clarifying. "Were there casualties during the standoff?"

"Not exactly." Malone stiffened, and Amanda picked up on his sign of discomfort right away. She'd known the sergeant all her life. He'd been around the house before she had baby teeth. He was best friends with her father, the former PWCPD chief. He cleared his throat before continuing. "The hostage taker fired a round into the wall of the nave, and it exposed a body sealed behind the drywall."

Well, this is a first...

"A body in the wall?" Trent's voice came out with skepticism, arched with a question, full of disbelief.

"You hard of hearing, Stenson?"

"I'm not, sir. It's just highly unusual," Trent said, backpedaling.

"Unusual or not, this is your case now. Go. Check it out and bring me up to speed. I might pop by in a bit."

Amanda grabbed her jacket from the back of her chair and flicked off her monitor. "On it."

"Wouldn't expect less."

As she hustled down the hall toward the parking lot, she realized she could have asked for details about the victim. Male or female? Age? Nationality? Cause of death? But she'd be finding out soon enough.

TWO

Trent drove them to Herald Church, a centuries-old structure that likely dated back at least a couple hundred years. He was raised Christian in name only. His parents never dragged him to church on Sundays or enrolled him in Sunday school as a kid. As an adult, he respected religion and appreciated why some clung to its associated traditions. They offered comfort and familiarity amid the changing landscape of the world. He just never had a desire to attend mass or bend a knee in prayer.

He pulled into the lot as an ambulance was pulling out with its lights flashing. Once it hit the street, the sirens wailed. This place was bustling with police. Included among the few cruisers was a mobile command station marked with the PWCPD logo. It would have been used during the standoff. There was also a police-marked SUV, likely belonging to the lieutenant who was there for the hostage negotiation, but there was also an unmarked black sedan with government plates.

He parked next to it, and fed vibes were pouring off the thing. "The FBI is here? Malone could have mentioned that."

Amanda looked over at him. "Would it have changed anything?"

"I might not have come." He'd worked alongside feds before, nearly died in the process, but the experience taught him they didn't play well with others. Then again, this might only apply to Special Agent Brandon Fisher and Supervisory Special Agent Jack Harper. In all fairness, the others on their team hadn't rubbed Trent the wrong way. As for nearly dying, that was partially his own fault. He'd been young and eager to bring down a serial rapist and murderer and might have hastily gotten himself into a bad situation. His pride and need to prove himself playing a role. It would have been nice if the FBI were more open to his viewpoints though. They liked to assume authority. To think about reporting to them again...

Amanda smiled. "You would have come. Besides, if you're worried about who is in charge, don't be. The body is in a Prince William County church. Our turf, our body."

He loved how she had a way of seeing right through him. "True."

They got out of the car as a woman was leaving the command vehicle. She was tall, blond, and in her late forties. She pulled sunglasses from a pocket and put them in place, all while looking around, gauging her surroundings. Her gaze, he would swear to it, fixed on him and Amanda, though it was hard to tell for the dark-shaded lenses. She'd clearly flagged them as new arrivals but didn't show any concern about their presence.

Officer Wyatt ambled toward him and Amanda. "Guess you two got the luck of the draw."

"Guess so," Amanda said. "What can you tell us?"

Trent admired how she often got right to the point at a crime scene. He found it in such beautiful contrast to the otherwise kind and gentle aspects of her nature. She wasn't soft by any means, but she was sensitive, an endearing quality he saw as benefiting this line of work. The academy cautioned new recruits to bury emotion, keep objective, and remain detached. But in his opinion, something could be said for taking things to heart, making them personal, showing fellow feeling and compassion.

"Not much to say that you probably haven't heard already. There was a standoff, and the perp—"

Amanda held up her hand, a gentle smile on her lips. "About the body specifically."

"It's in the wall." Wyatt offered a sarcastic smirk.

"Nothing else?" Trent asked.

"Nope. Crime Scene's been called, as well as a medical examiner."

Both were stationed a thirty-minute drive away in Manassas.

"So you have nothing to offer on the deceased?" Amanda pressed.

Wyatt shrugged. "I'd say the body's been in the wall a long time."

"Why do you say that?" Trent asked.

"You'll see for yourself soon enough."

Trent looked at Amanda and shook his head. "Any reason to believe the body's connected with the standoff?"

"You would be best to talk to her for more details." Wyatt butted his head toward the blond FBI agent. "But not from what I've gathered."

"Please just tell us what you know." Trent was happy to put off talking to the fed for a while. Besides, he'd prefer to be armed with some knowledge before approaching her.

"The priest was held at gunpoint," Wyatt said. "Don't ask me for the details. See the FBI agent."

"And why is she even here?" Trent asked.

"She's with the Crisis Negotiation Unit and was called in to help."

"The PWCPD has officers trained in negotiation," Amanda pointed out.

"They do, but the HT wasn't responding to their efforts. And I guess a lot of them are on vacation right now."

"The HT?" Amanda asked, cutting into Trent's thoughts. "Oh, hostage taker. Just took me a sec."

Wyatt laughed. "That's right. Sorry. I just talked to her for a few seconds, and I already sound like her. Federal agencies love their acronyms."

From the sound of that buildup, Wyatt was enamored with the federal agent. *Where's the thread to sew his lips to her butt?* Trent had idolized the feds until he worked with some. "What was the hostage taker's name?" To hell if he was going to use the acronym.

"One sec." Wyatt pulled his notepad and flipped the pages. "Cameron Cofell, twenty-three."

"And the hostages?" Amanda asked.

"Just the one. The church's priest."

Trent looked at Amanda but asked Wyatt, "His name and the reason for holding him hostage?"

"Again, you'd be best to talk to her." Wyatt pointed a finger at her this time, and the action captured the woman's attention. She started walking toward them.

Just great...

"Thanks," Amanda told Wyatt as she turned to bridge the distance too.

Trent followed with reluctance. The lyrics of a classic rock song rang through his head. "Once Bitten Twice Shy." Though it might be a tad dramatic to let one experience influence his view of the FBI. Besides, years had passed. He'd changed, and it was just as likely that Brandon Fisher had. He'd been a rookie back then too. His ego and need to prove himself could have affected his behavior. Brandon must possess some redeemable qualities anyhow, because Amanda's best friend had been dating him for a while now, and he had shared some insights into serial killers when he and Amanda had encountered their first.

"Special Agent Sandra Vos with the FBI's Crisis Negotiation Unit." She lifted her sunglasses and held out her hand toward him. Amanda cut in and shook it when he didn't.

"Detective Amanda Steele, and this is Detective Trent Stenson," she said, gesturing to him.

"Nice to meet you both."

"We were hoping you could tell us more about what happened here today. We're aware a gun was fired during a standoff which hit the wall and led to the discovery of a body. If you could give us some background, such as what led up to this, that could help our investigation," Amanda said, her voice expectant.

"Sure. The incident started this morning around three AM, when the HT broke into the priest's living quarters and took him into the church. The priest's assistant called nine-one-one when he heard screaming. He lives in one of two apartments in the rear of the church."

"I take it the second apartment belongs to the priest?" Trent asked.

"That's right. We've come to understand that Cameron Cofell—"

"The HT," Trent interjected and regretted his conformity instantly.

"Yes. He woke the priest, that being Father Alan Linwood, and led him from his bed at gunpoint into the church."

"And his reason for doing this?" Trent asked.

"He wanted the priest to confess to holding secrets of child abuse."

"The priest abused him?" Trent asked, though he suspected there was more below the surface of her statement.

"No. He says his parents did, and confessed as much to the priest, who didn't take any action."

"Has anyone conducted a welfare check on the parents?" It seemed like a valid question. Cameron may well have targeted them first, before coming after the priest. Unless Trent was missing something.

"They both died in a car accident three years ago."

"If the priest learned of the abuse through a confessional, he'd be within his rights to break that confidentiality," Amanda chimed in.

"Exactly the viewpoint of the HT. Obviously, I can't say if Cofell was abused, but he's certainly a troubled young man. He also has a criminal record. He was sent away for sexual assault two years ago and given one year and court-ordered therapy for three. He's been living in a halfway house since he got out and struggling. He just wanted the world to know the truth, or *his* truth anyway."

An ambulance was leaving when Trent and Amanda were pulling in, and no one was in the back of a squad car. Cameron could have been hauled off already. "Is Cofell okay or...?"

Vos nodded. "Physically, yes. Mentally and emotionally? It's questionable, but it'll take someone with a different degree than any I have to officially determine. But he didn't have a death wish. He surrendered peacefully after the gunfire."

"I suspect it wasn't easy to stop SWAT from rushing in," Amanda empathized.

"You'd be right about that. Those guys are trained to act and use force. Just a different tactic to what I implement, which is peaceful resolution through dialogue."

Trent admired that she acknowledged her limitations and wasn't ego driven. "And where is Cofell now?"

"He was taken into custody by the PWCPD."

Trent nodded. The more they spoke to Vos, the more Trent found his respect growing for her. She struck him as intelligent and grounded. "I'd say it's likely Cofell was abused. It's a cycle that sadly seems to repeat itself." Trent's aunt had been with an abusive man for ten years. It took his murder for her to be freed from his clutches, but his childhood had been a rough one.

"It does," Vos agreed. "We reached out to Cofell's therapist, Beverly Campbell, but as expected, she refused to answer our questions about him."

They must have woken the doctor, but it proved they'd done all they could to drill down and get answers. Again, his respect notched upward. "You said his parents were dead. What about other relatives?" Until they knew the identity of the person in the wall, they needed to gather all the information they could. It was sometimes hard to say what might factor into an investigation.

"He has an uncle, the mother's brother, but we couldn't reach him."

"Could we get his information from you?" Amanda asked, clearly of the same opinion as Trent.

"Sure. Sean Olsen, sixty-five, lives here in Woodbridge." Vos recounted this without consulting any notes, and she didn't give the impression the recall was hard work. She recited a phone number for him too without referring to anything.

Trent pulled out his notepad and scribbled down the man's information. He had a good memory, but he wasn't interested in testing its limitations. He found recording things helpful. If it wasn't old-school with pen and paper, he was pecking notes into a department-issued tablet.

"The priest admit to knowing about the abuse?" Amanda asked.

"He's not saying," Vos said matter-of-factly.

"Do you have any idea if there's a connection between the hostage taker and the dead body?" Trent just got to the point, interested in her take. After all, she'd been talking to the man for several hours.

"If there is, the HT never gave any indication. During our talks, dead bodies and death never came up. Not even his own.

Sometimes those who feel down on their luck or hopeless consider suicide as their exit plan," she elaborated. "Cofell never expressed that desire, which helped my efforts to convince him surrendering peacefully was what he wanted. This drastic measure was just about exposing the priest."

"At least no one was hurt, and Cofell is now in custody and safe from himself," Amanda said. "Actually, how did the priest fare?"

"Father Linwood should be just fine, but he was grazed in the arm by the bullet. He's been taken to the hospital for treatment."

That explains the ambulance... "It could have been a lot worse. Has anyone asked the priest's assistant about the body in the wall?" Trent steered the conversation back to his reason for being here.

"Chet Solomon. The information officer working the standoff with me spoke to him pertaining to the abuse, but the body came after Cofell's surrender, so I'm not sure if Chet was asked about it." Vos looked around and directed their attention to a man in his thirties standing with PWCPD Officer Brandt. "Your colleague might have asked him, though I'm sure you'll find that out soon enough."

"Thanks for everything," Amanda told the agent.

"Don't mention it. Here's my card." Vos handed it over to Amanda, put her sunglasses back in place, and added, "Call if you have questions after I've left," before walking away.

"She was nice and helpful," Amanda said.

"Not bad. For a fed." Trent smirked.

THREE

Amanda had every intention of talking to the priest's assistant, but that would have to wait. Crime Scene arrived, and they were tailing them up the front steps of the church and inside. She told Officer Brandt to keep Chet on scene until they spoke.

While she'd passed this church many times, she'd never stepped through the doors. Not that she went to any places of worship. Since losing her husband, daughter, and unborn son almost ten years ago, she still hadn't reconciled her relationship with God.

At least the investigators were familiar. She and Trent had a good relationship with CSIs Blair and Donnelly, and they were assigned to most of their cases. If Amanda gave it any thought, she'd wonder if they were always working. Though that was much like her. The badge held a lot of power and dictated much of her time. The first twenty-four hours of an investigation were crucial, and she'd gone all night in previous cases scraping together all the possible leads she could. These long shifts often came at a high cost. They had played a role in breaking up her previous relationship. Logan had accused her of putting her work above family and home life. She could see his point, but she'd be nothing without Zoe, who she had adopted over three years ago. The light of her life and reason for getting up each day. They'd be fine without Logan like they had been before.

She entered the nave and took in the rather elaborate structure. Colorful stained-glass windows took up huge sections of wall space and depicted scenes from the Bible. The artistry was incredible. The pulpit and grand altar behind boasted a ten-foot-tall statue of Jesus with his arms open. But none of this captured her full attention. It wrestled with the shattered hole in the drywall.

As she moved closer, she realized that when the bullet had struck, it had chewed into the board as a mini explosion. The result was a three-inch opening in an irregular shape.

Staring out into the nave was a dried-out eye socket. The bullet would have just missed it by one to two inches.

"Nothing creepy at all about this," Blair mumbled as she set down her collection kit and pulled out a hi-res digital camera.

Yeah, nothing... Just that this person was encased in the walls of this church while the congregation worshiped and belted out gospel songs.

An officer was standing by waiting for the word to cut into the drywall. He had a drywall saw in hand and was shifting his posture, looking rather uncomfortable, though Amanda could hardly blame him. He'd probably been delegated to the post since the discovery without any say in the matter.

Blair took some pictures, the flash blooming out and casting light along a spread of the wall. She reviewed the shots she'd taken on the small screen of the camera. "Huh. This would work better with more light."

She and Donnelly set up a couple of floodlights in the area, directing their bulbs at the wall.

Blair took more pictures and checked her work. "Yes, much

better." She put the camera away and set a tarp on the floor with Donnelly. It was placed immediately in front of the wall to catch any potential forensic evidence.

Blair nodded to the officer to start ripping at the drywall. "But go slow and easy."

"Yes, ma'am." The officer tentatively and narrowly dipped the tip of the saw into the hole and worked the blade to the right. He only penetrated deep enough to catch the drywall, careful to avoid hurting the remains behind it.

The suspense was enough to toss Amanda's stomach and had her thankful she hadn't eaten since breakfast. It was now after noon.

Minutes passed like hours while the officer cut into the wall. Every few moments, he paused and pried a rectangle cutout he'd made from the studs. It was like disassembling a jigsaw puzzle, though an image was taking form rather than disappearing.

First, another dried-out eye socket. Then ears, full face, a neck, a beaded necklace, a right shoulder, a patch of clothing...

Trent brushed up against Amanda's arm, and she jumped. The contact was unexpected. It was like he'd reached out from the beyond. He mouthed an apology.

An impromptu, reverent silence for the victim had a hold on them all.

The officer finished with the last piece, and when he removed it, the image was complete. He excused himself.

In front of them were the mummified remains of a young female wearing a dress, two blue jelly bangles on her wrist, a neon-beaded necklace, and a pair of Mary Jane shoes.

"She's young," Donnelly said, while Blair snapped more pictures.

Call it a hunch, but nothing about this case was going to be easy or straightforward. Someone out there must be missing her, losing sleep worried about her safe return. But who was she? How long had she been inside the wall? Who put her there? How did she die?

So many questions needed answers.

FOUR

Amanda studied the image in front of her, and none of it became easier to accept even as the seconds passed. The body was wedged between two studs. With decomposition, the remains had slumped down, angling to the right. The bullet was lodged into a stud a mere inch from the side of her face. If it struck farther away, would she have remained undiscovered?

"I think she's been in there a while," Trent said.

"Me too. The condition of her body and her clothing would suggest that." The bangles and beaded necklace looked like pop jewelry from the eighties. The sunflower-patterned baby-doll dress, late nineties. Mary Janes were mostly timeless. Not being a fashionista, Amanda couldn't tell when this style was popular. Even if she had a better handle on fashion, it might not help pinpoint when the girl was put in the wall. The clothing and jewelry could have been purchased at a thrift store. At any rate, the outfit wasn't well color coordinated with the yellow, blue, and neon green. "The ME will be able to determine how long she's been dead." Working in Homicide and seeing her fair share of bodies, she appreciated things weren't always as they looked. "I imagine the original walls were lath and plaster. We'll need to find out when the wall was redone. It should give us a time frame."

"We can ask the assistant," Trent said.

"One small mercy," Blair cut in, hunched beside the pieces of removed drywall. She stood when they looked at her. "Nothing on the backside of the drywall suggests she tried clawing her way out."

"So she was dead when she was sealed inside," Amanda concluded.

"Also the bullet entered the wall on a slight angle, just missing her," Donnelly said as she set up a laser to map out the trajectory of the shot.

Could her death have been an accident? Her disposal at the hands of panicked and desperate parents? Perhaps they lacked funds for a proper burial or feared falling under suspicion. But even that scenario was inexcusable. Amanda's redhead temper moved in and had her blazing. The girl couldn't be more than sixteen years old. Whoever did this would pay for what they did.

"We've arrived," Hans Rideout announced as he stepped into the nave with his assistant, Liam Baker. As he got closer to the wall, he stopped and stared.

"It's unsettling, isn't it?" Trent said to him.

The medical examiner didn't respond for a few seconds. "It's fascinating to me, really. Tragic, of course, as she's clearly quite young. But the wife and I went to Westminster Abbey during our trip to London a couple of years ago. Suddenly, in a way, it's like I'm back there."

Amanda looked at everyone else, and their faces were marked with confusion too. "Not sure what you're trying to say," she said to him.

"Oh, I'm not trying to say anything. That church has over three thousand buried within its walls and grounds. There's a shrine for some royal, or otherwise notable person in British history, tucked into every corner. Most of the monuments are quite elaborate with much symbolism and others include sculptures representing grieving family members. Many are rather macabre. The one that made the greatest impression on me depicted a husband in battle with the Grim Reaper to save his wife. Of course, he lost that battle, because behind that elaborate work is the crypt where her body was entombed."

How lovely... The thought passed through. The detour wasn't much of a distraction from the darkness of here and now. Both were rather disturbing.

"How fascinating," Donnelly offered when no one else commented.

"Yes, quite. Now, let's see what we have." Rideout gloved up and stepped next to the body. "The clothing suggests female, but I don't like to make assumptions on that alone. The shape and size of the jaw confirms it for me, though. No more than seventeen, I'd say. Being in the wall has affected decomposition, but I'd still say she's been in there for at least twenty to twenty-five years. I'll know better once I've conducted more tests on her back in the morgue." He looked over his shoulder. "Liam, set out our tarp and help me get her out, would you?" As a seeming afterthought, Rideout turned to the CSIs. "Assuming you're finished with your photographs?"

"We are." Blair hastened to wrap up their tarp with the drywall and debris and secured it in a large evidence bag.

Everyone stepped back to allow Rideout and Liam more room to work.

Liam laid down a black tarp on the floor, and the two men worked to gently hoist the body from the wall.

Watching the deceased being liberated filled Amanda with a mixture of sorrow and determination. Rideout's words weren't far from her mind. *Twenty to twenty-five years...* Had her parents waited for her return all this time, or had they long since given up?

Her body appeared fragile, like it would snap and break with the slightest provocation. No one spoke as the young woman was set on the tarp.

Once she was in place, another impromptu moment of silence.

After a few moments, Rideout kneeled next to her, careful not to interfere with the tarp, and looked at her more closely.

"No pockets in this dress, so I'd say she was left without ID, at least in the usual places."

Little Jane Doe in her Mary Janes...

While Amanda's heart ached, she squared her shoulders and stood with confidence. She'd take this pain and wield it as a superpower, something she was often forced to do when the victims were children. Maybe it had to do with her being a mother that made such injustices harder to handle. Their elders were there to protect them, shelter them as best they could. But her career as a cop taught her not everyone could be trusted. Monsters were real and preyed on the weak and vulnerable. Her mission to take them down and save future victims was what fueled her forward. "Well, she didn't put herself in there. Any clear sign on cause of death?"

"Hmph." Rideout sank back onto his heels. "I'm not comfortable concluding COD here, but I will say that her body looks rather beaten up." He drew circles with his fingertip around her eye sockets and indicated some other dark splotches of skin.

Amanda had expected to simply hear Rideout's regular spiel. That he'd need to transport the body back to the morgue. That was what she'd been prepared for. But this detail gave the darkness more distinction. Made it harder to face. This poor child had been a victim before her death. Before her entombment. Even if Rideout was able to figure out how she'd died, would Amanda be able to find who killed her after two decades? Was that person even still around?

FIVE

Amanda led the way out of the church with Trent trailing close behind. The parking lot had emptied out. The command vehicle, the FBI sedan, and several cruisers were gone, leaving just the vans from Crime Scene and the Office of the Chief Medical Examiner and two squad cars. Chet Solomon was seated in the front of one with Officer Brandt.

She hustled toward them. Poor little Jane Doe had waited long enough for justice. There would be time to process what she'd seen later.

Brandt and Chet got out of the car when she and Trent reached them. The priest's assistant looked much younger up close. Probably mid-twenties.

"Give me a minute," Brandt told the man and hurried over to Amanda and Trent. "The guy's got a clean record. And, for what it's worth, he doesn't know about the body in the wall. Speaking of... anything you can share about that?"

"Likely a teenage girl, in there for twenty years, possibly more," Amanda said.

"Damn."

"Yeah. So I guess it's our job to bring this guy into the loop.

Would you make the introductions since he knows you? That might be more comfortable for him than us just walking up." A relaxed subject was more likely to talk openly. Information might even slip out that wasn't intended.

"Yeah, of course." Brandt took them to the man. "Chet Solomon, this is Detective Steele, and Detective Stenson. They have some questions for you." Brandt met her eye as if to ask if that was all she needed from him. She nodded.

"Mr. Solomon, I can imagine this has been an upsetting day for you," she started out, genuine in her empathy but also paving the way for honest and open communication.

"You have no idea." Chet rubbed his forehead like he was soothing a migraine. "It feels like it's been longer than a handful of hours, that's for sure."

"We understand you're the priest's assistant," she said, letting the disparity about the time go.

"Yes, but more accurately, the lay pastoral assistant," Chet clarified.

"What does that position entail?" Amanda asked.

"Much the same for any assistant providing support to a higher-up. I work alongside Father Linwood to ensure the care of the congregation and that church operations run smoothly. I'd like to go see the father, if I could. I understand he was injured."

"Father Linwood was grazed by a bullet, but he is receiving treatment," she said. "We just have a few more questions for you. After that, you'll be free to leave." There was no reason to suspect Chet. He would have been a child when the teenager was sealed inside.

"I'm not sure what else I can tell you," Chet rushed out. "I've never met the man who held Father Linwood hostage. I don't want to comment about what transpired."

"We'd like to discuss another matter," she said, though she might circle back around to asking more about Cameron Cofell and his accusations. She didn't like coincidences, even when events seemed as unconnected as these two. Guy holds up a priest in his church, only to reveal a dead body in the wall with a wayward bullet. That alone was so wild a notion, it sounded like fiction.

"I don't understand..." Chet narrowed his eyes and shifted his gaze from her to Trent.

"The body of a young woman was discovered in a wall of the nave." There was no delicate way of putting such a grisly find.

Shock loosened his jaw, letting his mouth fall open, but his body stiffened. Raised, squared shoulders. Ballooned chest as if his lungs froze midbreath. Deadpan eyes. "A woman..." Chet repeated, capsulizing the horrifying part.

She was surprised that none of this had gotten back to him. "That's right. No older than seventeen." She spoke slowly, observing Chet as she spoke. He provided comfortable eye contact but otherwise gave the impression he was numb to what was being said. This she could understand. The news was unbelievable for her, and she'd laid eyes on the body.

"How did she... She got in there somehow. How?" He eventually spat out the question.

"We were hoping you could help us answer that," Trent said, speaking up for the first time.

Chet rubbed his palms together, a nervous tic. "I had nothing to do with it, if that's what you're—"

"Not at all, but we noticed that part of the nave is drywall," Amanda began. "I suspect the original was lath and plaster going by the rest of the building's architectural features." The spires, the bell tower, and the stained-glass windows all told of its age. "Do you know when the wall was done, or why it was updated?"

"I'm sorry, but I don't. You'd do good to talk to Father Linwood about that."

Amanda didn't care for people trying to shuffle them along. It made her guarded and suspicious. "As the father's assistant, I'd have thought you'd be aware of such things. Even if you heard about it after the fact," she added. Based on Rideout's initial assessment on time of death, Chet wouldn't have been around. But she'd heard of cases where mummified remains presented older than they were.

"Well, I haven't been with the church that long."

"How long?" Trent asked.

"Three years. I'm from out of town and moved here when the assignment began. I live in a small apartment at the back of the church, next to Father Lindwood's residence."

Which Vos had told them. "Who was in your position prior?" *Or more to the point, twenty-some years ago...*

"I'd prefer you ask Father Linwood about that."

"We will," she told him. "You said you never saw the man before, but does the name Cameron Cofell mean anything to you?"

"That's who...? Well, it's been a while since I've seen him."

"He wasn't an active member of the church then?" Trent asked.

"No, but his folks were up until their deaths."

Amanda nodded. That much made sense and aligned with what Special Agent Vos had told them. Cameron's actions were prompted by confessions to the priest. And just like Chet, how could Cameron Cofell have any connection to the girl in the wall? He certainly wasn't old enough either. His choosing this church and shooting that wall must all be a coincidence, whether she liked it or not. "Could we get a list of congregation members dating back twenty-five years ago?" She worked off the long end of Rideout's initial assessment.

"It would all be in the archives, though I'm sure Father Linwood would like a warrant."

"We can get one. Thank you for your help." Amanda handed him her card.

He took it. "I thought when I moved from the city, it would be peaceful here. But only God can save us."

She walked away letting him have his beliefs and what offered him solace, but for her, she'd learned a long time ago that smaller towns didn't make for less crime. Given all the cases they worked she sometimes wondered if there was more.

SIX

Amanda and Trent found out what hospital Father Linwood had been taken to for treatment and set out after pulling a brief background on him. It didn't tell them much except that the priest was seventy-one and single. The latter was something they could have guessed. They never saw Malone before leaving the church, but she called him on the way to give him the update. She had him on speaker so Trent could hear everything being said.

"What I'm hearing is you don't have much yet," Malone stated after she shared what they had. The statement struck as an accusation, and a wave of defeat rolled over her.

"We are just getting started. We're going to speak with the priest at the hospital. Hopefully he can shed light on what took place in that church. Even perhaps identify the girl," she added.

"Keep that pie-in-the-sky outlook, Steele. It suits you."

Does it though... She had been trying all sorts of new things since she and Logan parted ways. Adopting a more positive outlook was one, right up there with living in the flow. "Okay, well, we're here now, so..."

"Bye." Malone ended the call, and minutes later she and

Trent were walking down the linoleum hallway toward the priest's room. The soles of Trent's shoes periodically squeaked against the floor, and the sound was the only thing popping her out of her pessimism. It was a fallback setting, but who was she to believe she could find Jane Doe justice after so long? Twenty-some years in a wall classified this case as cold as they came. And those were not her specialty, though she had solved some older investigations as they linked to current ones. All might not be lost...

Trent pointed at the number plaque next to the door. They'd arrived.

She rapped her knuckles on the doorframe and ducked her head through the doorway. "Alan Linwood?"

"Father Linwood, thank you. But come on in." The man appeared shrunken on top of the bed, buried beneath a mountain of white sheets topped by a thin, blue blanket. He struggled to sit straighter as they entered the room. A white bandage was wrapped around his right upper arm where the bullet would have grazed him.

"Stay where you are, if you're comfortable," she told him kindly.

"I'm fine. It's the doctors who are all worked up. They say my arm is gonna be fine, but now they're worried about my heart. Something about its irregular beat. It's why I'm stuck with a room and a bed, but it's nothing. It's that poor boy's soul that's in danger. I keep praying that he can be saved and find forgiveness in the kindness of our Lord."

Amanda recoiled at the mention of *our* Lord. Trent must have sensed it coming from her, as she caught him glance over through her peripheral vision. She wasn't good at keeping her spiritual views from those around her. Not that she sought out the opportunities, but when they arose, she often said more than proper decorum would allow.

"Come, children of God, we can pray together."

Clearly the priest wasn't skilled at reading people, or he chose to overlook the change in her energy. "That's not why we're here." Fast, hot, sharper than she intended. "Let me take a step back and introduce us."

Linwood angled his head, taking Amanda back to the last time she'd visited her family's graves. A sparrow had sat on her husband's stone, tilting its head and watching her closely. A loving observer, not one who seemed to be scrutinizing her.

She cleared her throat. "I'm Detective Steele, and this is my partner, Detective Stenson."

"Please to meet you both. Are you here to discuss that misguided young man?"

"No, Cameron Cofell isn't why we're here. Not exactly anyhow." Technically if he hadn't fired his gun, they wouldn't be standing here now. "When his bullet hit the nave wall, there was something behind it."

Linwood regarded her blankly. "Okay," he dragged out. "And what was there?"

"The body of a teenage girl," she served directly.

"What?" The priest's response set off a series of machines attached to him. Ear-piercing beeps. The heart monitor danced wildly.

Trent ducked into the hall but popped back into the room when the machinery fell silent a few moments later. Linwood was quick to calm down again. But maybe they should have let more time pass before coming to speak with him. He'd been through an ordeal, and they were there with horrific news. She may not be religious, but she didn't want to be responsible for killing a priest. She also wasn't superstitious or someone who believed in Karma, but she didn't want to test it either. "I apologize for upsetting you. I didn't mean to startle you... Father Linwood." She wished it wasn't so difficult for her to address him by his title, but saying it out loud flashed her straight to the past when a man with a collar took her hands and told her God had three more angels. She was hurting so badly the statement had soured her against religion and God. "I just wanted to get to the point of why we're here."

"Well, you certainly got that point across." Linwood bunched up the sheets and blanket with his unscathed arm and pulled them closer to himself. "But what do you think I could possibly tell you about a body behind the nave wall?"

"How long have you been the priest at Herald Church?" she volleyed back.

"Thirty-seven glorious years."

Amanda found the adjective noteworthy. *Glorious*, yet according to Cameron Cofell, he oversaw a congregation with members who deserved to be put behind bars. Covering up such behavior, if that's what he'd done, was as good as condoning it in her mind. She'd let that go. For now. "Since the church is older, most of it is lath and plaster but where we found her, it was drywall. Why was that area renovated?"

"The plaster was cracked and falling apart beyond the point of repair. The whole thing was gutted and stripped to the bones."

Poor choice of words... "When was that renovation done?"

"Oh, some time ago now. Easily twenty years or more."

Cementing Rideout's initial assessment about Jane Doe's time in that wall...

"But you're not sure?" Trent asked.

Linwood tapped his head. "This noggin is pretty good but not *that* good." He smiled, and it had Amanda breathing easier. That and seeing that his coloring was returning to normal and the bright red was leaving his cheeks. "The records would tell us though."

"And that's something we could look at?" Linwood's assistant thought the priest would request a warrant for the congregation list. It was possible this would be different.

"Sure thing. If you can get me one of those warrants, I'll make sure Chet hands that right over."

She resisted groaning. "What was the extent of the renovations?" She curbed the fear there may be more victims yet to uncover.

"It was just the nave walls."

"Who did the renovation?" Someone working on the project had likely put that girl in the wall.

"Volunteers. God always supplies. Some even came from out of town."

"We'll need their names," she said. "Is that something you can provide us?"

"As much as I want to cooperate with the police, there's no list I could hand over even if you obtained a warrant requesting one."

Trent raised his eyebrows. "Surely, there are current congregation members who might have worked on the construction?"

"There might be. But it was a long time ago." Linwood passed his gaze to the window, where shadows were being cast by small birds flying past outside.

"It was," Amanda agreed and waited until she regained his attention before continuing. "And I'm sure as a priest, you're protective of your congregation."

"They are all God's children."

Amanda let him have that. His opinion, to which he was entitled, but it also bled right into where she planned to go next. "You likely know all of them so well."

"I do my best." There was leeriness in his tone, and he wasn't doing well hiding it.

"Then you'd have known if any teenage girls went missing?" It was possible Jane Doe wasn't directly associated with the church. She might have been connected to one of the out-of-towners, or someone taking advantage of a construction site.

Though taking things that far gave her a headache. Where would she and Trent even begin?

"I would have, but none did. That's why all of this is so strange."

"Do you remember anyone wearing blue jelly bangles or a neon-green beaded necklace?" It didn't even need to be Jane Doe herself.

Linwood met her eye, a light in his. "No, I do not, but I'm not into jewelry."

"Maybe one of your congregation members has an eye for such things?" she asked, trying to pry some names out of him. "We are talking about getting justice for a murdered teenage girl here."

Linwood stiffened. "If you're implying that one of my flock had something to do with her death, you couldn't be more wrong. I didn't put her there, and I have faith that none of my congregants did either. I'm not going to give you names so you can harass my flock. God put them under my care, to protect them."

Amanda wasn't judge and jury but if Cameron Cofell's claims were true, Linwood had failed to protect its youngest members. "We will not be 'harassing' anyone, but we do need to ask some questions."

"Not going to happen, Detective. I'm sorry, but I'm not pointing a finger at anyone who supports the church or has in the past."

"Then you won't tell us who was in Chet's position before him, or dating back to the time of the renovation?" Her negative opinion affected how she'd phrased the question. She'd teed things up for him to turn her down.

"Not without a warrant."

"I find it shocking that you're holding back after what took place today," Trent said, his gaze intent on Linwood.

The priest waved his good arm. "Cameron Cofell has

always been a troubled soul. He claims I keep secrets. I hold confessionals, and I respect the sanctity of that arrangement, as should be the case. Cameron doesn't seem to understand that. Now his parents' deaths, that cast a shadow over the congregation. Two God-fearing individuals were taken from us, but as I remind the bereaved, we are not to question God. We must believe He has a plan."

Amanda had about enough talk of God and his plans for a lifetime. "Yet, Cameron went to the lengths he did, just because he was *troubled?*" She had a hard time buying there wasn't anything untoward happening. Linwood hadn't even denied knowing about the abuse at the time or now. In fact, what he'd just said about the confessional booth felt like an admission. He had known that Cameron was abused as a child. But how did that help them figure out what happened to the girl in the wall?

Linwood pinched his lips tightly together, emphasizing his jowls.

"We were told Cameron wanted you to admit to knowing about the sexual and physical abuse he suffered at home. That's why he held you hostage."

"Whether I did or not, I will not say. Should I get a lawyer?"

Still no denial, but something else hit her. The allegation against this priest was he'd heard and forgiven sins of sexual abuse, but what if his involvement didn't stop there? What if the priest himself participated, or was guilty of his own separate misdeeds? What if Jane Doe was one of his victims who threatened to speak up and he killed her and put her in the wall? He was being rather elusive in his responses and barricading his congregation. Though it could be a front to protect himself from further scrutiny. "It's fine, Father Linwood, we'll leave for now. Thank you for your kind cooperation."

"Bless you, child."

Amanda let out a low growl once she cleared the doorway, then said, "That man makes my skin crawl."

"All the talk of God?"

"Not just that, but I think he knows more than he's telling us." Linwood was no wilting rose either. His heart might be acting up, but he wasn't weak.

"Oh, he does. For one, churches keep a record of everything. And I mean *everything*. A note of every service held, who gave the sermon, any special visitors. I'd be surprised if there isn't a list of volunteers who worked on the walls."

"All right, but we can't force him to talk. My fear is he's harboring more secrets than Cameron accused him of."

"You think he knows about the girl and her murder and burial?"

"Why not?" Amanda replied. "It's even possible he's the one responsible."

"The priest a killer?"

"I'm not saying he is, but it might explain why he's being so shifty. Not that we can do anything about this suspicion right now anyhow. The guy's holed up in a hospital bed. We can't exactly drag him down to Central. Besides, we don't have enough for that."

"Nope," Trent conceded, "but we have more than enough to support a warrant requesting the congregation list. Father Linwood says there isn't one for renovation volunteers, but it doesn't hurt to go in armed with a court order for that too."

"And even if Father Linwood's claims are true about the volunteer names, we might find a chatty parishioner who can give us some."

"Fingers crossed that someone remembers a teenage girl with blue jelly bangles."

SEVEN

Warrants for the names of congregation members, previous assistants, and renovation volunteers came rather effortlessly. In regards to the construction, the church was to hand over any associated records. But there wasn't much for a judge to deliberate in a situation like this. It seemed rather straightforward that someone with access to the church during the renovation was behind the girl's murder and entombment.

Trent drove them to the church and noticed the time just before he shut off the car. *5:15 PM.* "If you need to get home to Zoe, I can handle this. It's not too late for me to turn around, drop you at Central, and come back. I have no problem doing that."

Amanda set a hand over his, and he pulled back.

"Sorry, I shouldn't have touched you. But Zoe's fine. I made arrangements for her tonight."

"If you're sure? I know how important it is that you spend time in the evenings with her."

There was a stretch of silence, then she said, "I appreciate you saying that, and you're right, but Jane Doe's been waiting for justice twenty-some years, and I don't want to make her wait a second longer if I can help it. I'll make it up to Zoe."

He admired that gung-ho quality about Amanda, but sometimes wondered if she didn't take too much on her shoulders. That she didn't demand more from herself than was reasonable. "All right then. Let's see what we can accomplish tonight."

Amanda didn't say another word but got out of the car. He could sense that sticking around to work the case and not going home was eating at her, but he'd given her an out. All he could do now was respect her decision and carry on.

The van belonging to Crime Scene was gone, but two squad cars remained. The officers assigned to them would be on site to lock down the area and preserve the crime scene. It would allow him, Amanda, and CSIs to revisit the scene, even obtain new evidence, without its integrity being called into question.

He and Amanda walked around the church to the residences and knocked on Chet Solomon's door. The assistant answered before they had to knock a second time. He was flushed, and his hair was sticking up in the back. Clearly, he hadn't found his way to visit Father Linwood at the hospital or if he had, it had been a brief visit between their chat with the priest and the warrants coming through.

"Detectives? I don't have anything else I can tell you."

"We come armed with warrants," Amanda said, getting to the point.

"Then you spoke with Father Linwood?"

"We did, but he wasn't giving us any names, and he couldn't remember the exact year of the reno," Trent put in.

"What do the warrants cover exactly?"

"One is for the congregation list, dating back twenty-five years; one is for all records associated with the renovation, including volunteer names; and there's one for previous assistants' names," Amanda laid out.

Chet took a deep breath. "All right, then. Let me grab my coat, and we'll go to the church office to see what we can find."

"But that's on the property...?" Trent asked, thrown a bit by the coat comment.

"It is, but with the nave being a crime scene, it's still locked down. Officers have told me that I'm to access the church from the front and clear any business past them should I need to go inside. One minute..." Solomon left, presumably for his coat, and returned a few seconds later wearing an olive-green puffer jacket.

Officer Wyatt was standing vigil at the front of the church, like one of those royal guards outside Buckingham Palace. Only he responded to their presence with a "good evening" and a glance at Solomon. Trent shook his head at the mental picture he'd conjured, attributing it to Rideout's talk about London.

"We just need to access the church's office," Amanda volunteered, though Wyatt showed no signs of blocking their path.

"Knock yourself out." Wyatt didn't move, but there was plenty of room to get past him and through the door.

Stepping inside, the discovery from that afternoon flooded Trent's mind with images. They layered on top of each other. Snapshots of Jane Doe's face, jewelry, positioning, and small stature. He might not be quite as affected as Amanda at seeing child victims, but it didn't mean it didn't hurt. There was no fairness in a young person exiting the world.

The air had a dense quality that lingered where death had been. But here, there was an unexplained lightness as well. It was like the girl's spirit was relieved that she was finally found and freed from her hidden place.

"We need to head over there." Solomon jabbed a finger to a doorway at the right of the nave and headed off in that direction. They entered a small room with a table and a rack of robes. "The office is just past the robing room."

Trent knew the robing room was where the priest got ready,

and it was likely that Solomon was the one responsible for ensuring the robes were cleaned and laid out. The space was only a few steps wide, so they quickly arrived at a doorway that spilled into a modest workspace with a wood desk, filing cabinets, and a few chairs.

Solomon slipped behind the desk. "I've worked on digitizing church records since I came on board. Everything here was old-school." He gestured toward a large book that was spread open on one of the filing cabinets. "It's how Father Linwood is used to doing things, so I still handwrite records into the book, but I have approval to key them into the system afterward. It took a bit of work to convince him that an electronic backup offered a level of security for the church records. You said that you wanted the congregation list from twenty-five years ago?" He leveled his gaze at Amanda as he rolled the chair in closer to the desk.

"That's right," Amanda said.

"Also, is there any way of flagging those who might still be active with the church?" Trent asked.

"That shouldn't be a problem either." Solomon tapped away on his keyboard and clicked his mouse a few times. Soon after, a printer in the corner of the room whirred to life. It started kicking out papers, and the assistant walked over and retrieved each one as it shot out. When the print job finished, Solomon stapled the list and handed it to Amanda. "You'll notice a column noting a Y or N for whether they are current members. Another column shows when they first joined the church."

"This is excellent. Thank you, Chet," Amanda told him.

"As I said, I had no problem handing any of this over, as long as Father Linwood was in agreement."

Clearly, the priest's approval holds more sway than a legal warrant... "Chet, would this list include the names of Father Linwood's previous assistants?"

"There's just the one that was my predecessor. Daniel

Barron. His name will be on the list, but he was with Father Linwood from when he started here thirty-seven years ago."

Since this Barron character was around back when the girl was put in the wall, they'd need to track him down and have a talk with him. "And where is he now?"

Solomon frowned. "He died just before I came on, but if you're considering that Daniel might have been behind the body in the wall, he wasn't."

The hairs rose on the back of Trent's neck. "What makes you so confident?"

"Before coming to the church and devoting himself to God, he lived a rough life on the streets. He got hepatitis from a needle and with his already-weakened system, he ended up with asthenia."

"I'm not familiar with what that is," Amanda said.

"Me either," Trent admitted.

"I wouldn't have heard of it if it wasn't for Daniel. To start, it can be a temporary or permanent condition. For Daniel it lasted right up until his death. The illness manifests in several ways. Daniel had isolated weakness in his arms and legs and was prone to tremors, and his movements were slow. But since physical strength isn't necessary for this position, Father Linwood took Daniel under his wing. I'm just saying there's no way he could have..." Solomon met Trent's eyes, leaving the rest unsaid.

Trent tapped the tip of his pen to the page, leaving a series of little dots. If what Solomon was telling them was true, they could eliminate the previous assistant as a suspect.

"We appreciate you telling us all this," Amanda said. "Are records associated with the renovation in there?" Amanda flicked a finger toward the large book that Solomon had pointed out earlier.

The assistant shook his head. "If they were, I would have entered them. But the fact is I don't remember anything like that. Let me search the system for some keywords such as 'reno,' 'construction,' that type of thing."

"That would be appreciated," Amanda said, passing a glance at Trent. He wondered if she was thinking what he was, that Solomon was far more cooperative than his boss.

"One second..." More keyboard tapping. "There's nothing coming up with any of those, but there might be something else I could try."

There was no way that all records of the renovation would simply disappear. Even if there wasn't a list of volunteers as Father Linwood told them, the church would have had to buy supplies. "What about an accounting system? There should be invoices for construction materials that the church needed to pay for."

Solomon paused his tapping on the keyboard to look up and offer a sly smile. "Great minds, they say. That's exactly what I'm looking into now. With the project being so long ago, any hard copies would have been shredded by now, but Father Linwood is meticulous with the bookkeeping. He's also a stickler for consistency, so he's been using the same system forever. Thankfully there have been a lot of software updates since the program first came out. It offers quite a bit of flexibility and searching options. There should be something in the archives, but I can do a system-wide search, not limiting it to any specific year. Let me see what I can find." Solomon tapped his chin, then barraged the keys again. Sat back. "Nothing. Hmm."

"There must be some way of pinpointing exactly when the construction happened," Trent began. "I mean short of asking church members."

"Ah-ha!" Solomon's eyes lit up. "I think I might be on to something." More typing on the keyboard. "Yes. Okay, so the church receives donations in various forms, including for products or services, but regardless of which kind, a monetary value is assigned and a tax receipt issued. One of these was sent to Gray's Building Projects twenty-three years ago in the amount of thirty thousand dollars."

Trent had heard of the man and his company. Amanda had contacted him in a previous investigation. The value of the donation receipt seemed exuberant for materials only. Despite volunteer labor it must have included an allocation for what professional labor would have cost. "That could be what we're looking for."

"I think it just might be," Chet agreed. "Robert Gray isn't what I'd call an active member of the church, but his wife attends regularly. Hopefully all of this helps."

"More than you know. Thank you," Amanda told him.

Trent had expected Solomon might be standoffish and difficult. That couldn't be further from the truth. "Yes. Thank you, Chet." He held out his hand to shake the assistant's.

He looked at Trent's palm like it was a foreign entity but eventually took it and shook. "You're welcome. I'm sure Father Linwood wants the answers as much as we all do."

Trent wasn't so sure about that, though his viewpoint about the priest might have been altered by Amanda's suspicions of him. Regardless, they left Solomon armed with potential leads, including an immediate starting point. Trent got behind the wheel and started the engine. "Robert Gray? What are the chances?"

"I was thinking the same. Hit the gas."

EIGHT

It had been a while ago that Amanda had spoken to Robert Gray, so she had Trent pull up a quick background check on him in the onboard computer. Robert was sixty-two and lived just a few blocks over from Amanda. As Trent drove past her street, her heart swelled thinking of Zoe. She'd be home with her aunt Libby, who graciously came their way so Zoe could be tucked into her own bed. Right now, Zoe was likely watching TV or playing in her room. Did she wonder why Amanda was late or had she just resolved that Amanda was unpredictable? It hurt to think she might give the girl reason to doubt her importance in her life. If only there was a way to make up for lost time, but the thought was futile. Tomorrow wasn't a guarantee. Or the next minute.

Amanda flipped through the congregation list in the passenger seat. "So there's thirteen pages here, but it's not quite as bad as it sounds. It looks like it's close to double-spaced, so there's that."

"That's a start."

She took out a pen and circled active members from twenty-three years ago, as it was assumed the construction happened then. Something Robert Gray should be able to confirm. "It looks like there were seventy active members at the time of the renovations, including Doug and Winnie Cofell."

"Then they were part of the church for a while. But how many members have since left? Any way of seeing when people parted ways with the church?"

"I see your point. It would take a certain type of person to kill and entomb the girl in the wall and continue to pray there on Sundays. In that case"—Amanda thrummed the pen against the printout as she studied it—"it looks like eleven, but none left close to that time. Three are marked deceased though. The Cofells and Daniel Barron, the former assistant."

"Who I think it's safe to say couldn't have done this."

"Based on what Chet Solomon told us. Getting a second opinion of him wouldn't hurt. The Grays might even be able to tell us about him."

"All right. Still though, the church is good at retaining its members. If we talk to ones who were active then and still are, we're left with fifty-nine people."

"Or from here we focus on those who left over the years. That's just ten." Amanda shook her head. "Though, as I said, none of them are glaring on the page either. It's not like anyone left within a year of the renovation. The closest was five years later."

"Then there's the volunteers who came from out of town," Trent said, clearly caught up with what lay ahead of them. "That's assuming we can even find out names."

"Right."

"Not a good time to mention them?"

"It would never be a good time." They had enough people to talk to already without adding more to the list, but she reminded herself solving a case was about taking one step at a time.

Trent parked in front of a modest two-story home.

"Well, there's no time like the present to knock off two members from the list." She did notice that despite Chet saying that Robert Gray didn't attend regularly, he was still listed as an active member along with his wife, Tasha.

They got out and rang the front bell. Its melodious chime summoned a response. Footsteps padded toward them, and a shadow was cast across the sidelight.

The door swung open and a woman in her sixties, likely Tasha, Robert's wife, was standing there. She held the door, and her long slender fingers and manicured nails with bright polish nabbed Amanda's attention.

"Tasha Gray?" Amanda asked, holding up her badge.

"That's me. Something I can help you with?" She let her gaze travel from Amanda to Trent.

Amanda gave the brief introduction and added, "We'd like to speak with you and your husband about your association with Herald Church. Is Mr. Gray home?"

"You caught him on one of those rare nights." She added that latter bit more as a mumble, and it zapped guilt through Amanda. Did Zoe think that way of the nights Amanda made it home on time from work? Like it was some freak occurrence, tantamount to spotting a unicorn?

"Could we come inside?" Trent said and passed a side-glance at Amanda.

"Sure." Tasha stepped back and let them into the home.

It was beautiful and open-concept with mid-century design elements. An exposed winding staircase tailed up to the right of the entry. A large hallway ran through the middle of the home to the kitchen in the rear. Amanda spotted cabinetry and a counter. She drew her gaze back and noted the sunken living room to the left. "Is there somewhere we could sit?"

"In here." It was offered with a huff. Amanda got the sense their arrival had interrupted something. Tasha motioned for

Amanda and Trent to go on ahead, before turning over her shoulder and bellowing, "Robert, get down here, please."

A man responded from upstairs. "I'm in the middle of—"

"The police are here." Tasha came into the room shaking her head.

Amanda and Trent each sat on a chair, and Tasha lowered onto the couch.

Thumping on the stairs announced Robert must be on his way. A handsome man soon graced the doorway. He stopped there, taking them in. Just as Amanda was sizing him up. She'd only spoken to him on the phone during the previous investigation. He was a striking man with deep dimples that left their mark even with his resting expression, and his dark hair was threaded with silver, giving him a distinguished look.

"Move it, Rob. They're detectives wanting to discuss the church."

"Yes, sorry we had to come during the dinner hour," Amanda began.

"No apologies needed. We eat late like the Europeans," Robert said, inching into the living room and eventually sitting on the other end of the couch. He narrowed his eyes on Amanda. "You sound familiar."

"Detective Steele. We spoke during a previous investigation."

"Investigation?" Tasha clenched the collar of her shirt. Again, flashing her bright nails.

Robert turned to her. "You know the one."

Tasha crossed her legs. "Oh, right. Yes, I do. How unfortunate that was."

"That it was," Amanda agreed. That case had involved another teenage girl as a victim. She had been killed and posed at her prom. Touching closer to home, she had been the older sister of Amanda's niece's friend.

"Does this have to do with what happened at the church? I

heard about it on the news." He took out his phone and scrolled on it. "Looks like there's a new article now." He got up and showed her the screen.

The article was entitled "Herald Church Condones Sexual Abuse in Its Members." The media certainly didn't waste any time dispensing bad news. She wasn't touching this one. "What did you hear?" She wanted to clarify if it was just the standoff or the discovery of the body too. She was also curious what had been disclosed about the latter.

Robert returned to the couch. "Just that there was a hostage situation at Herald Church, and a body was found in the wall." He put it out there tentatively, like he wanted Amanda to verify the report.

"I couldn't believe it when Rob told me," Tasha put in.

"Well, the remains are what brought us here," Amanda said.

"I'm not sure I understand why," Tasha said.

Amanda looked at Robert. "Were you or your wife involved with the construction work on the church twenty-three years ago?"

"Ah, yeah, they removed the lath and plaster in the nave and put up drywall. I donated all the necessary supplies," Robert told them. "Wait, is that where the body was found?"

He'd just confirmed the timing of the construction, which meant that's how long Jane Doe had remained sealed behind the wall. Amanda made brief eye contact with Trent, who subtly nodded. "That's correct, Mr. Gray," she confirmed. "The remains were that of a teenage girl."

Robert sat back. "Wow. Well... I had nothing to do with that. As I said, I supplied the materials, but I didn't have time to pitch in on the work itself."

"You never have time," Tasha muttered and added, "I made apple pies and brought them to the volunteers doing the work. Some of the other ladies in the church also brought treats, and we set up a coffee and tea station."

"Sounds lovely." Amanda acknowledged the woman's contribution. She'd feel heard, and it would encourage her to speak openly. "To the point, we believe this girl was placed into the wall cavity during the time of construction. How long did the job last?" She directed this question to Tasha.

"It wasn't too long," the woman said. "A couple of weeks, three tops. People worked as they could on weekends and after their jobs."

"And Father Linwood gave them access to the church?" she asked.

"Or his assistant. That was Daniel... What was his last name now?" Tasha scrunched up her lips. "Barron, yes, that's it."

"And what was he like?" Trent put in.

"Kind, timid. He came from a rough past, and it never fully let him go."

"How do you mean?" The subject of Daniel had come up so effortlessly, she rolled with it.

"He was physically weak. He got sick from a contaminated needle, shooting up heroin. It weakened his autoimmune system and caused him to have tremors in his arms and legs. He didn't have much strength at all."

Amanda passed another glance at Trent. They had their second testimony, and as far as she was concerned there didn't need to be any more mention of Daniel Barron. "So the reno volunteers were let into the church each time they arrived to work on it?" She found the thought of that inconvenient, though the priest and his assistant did live on site.

"Actually, I think Daniel or Father Linwood might have made some copies of the key too, so they wouldn't be disturbed if people wanted in at different times."

"Do you know of any teenage girls with the church who disappeared or all of a sudden stopped attending?" She'd asked this question with her eye on Robert, who kept adjusting his position on the couch as if he were uncomfortable. Was it the subject matter itself or because he had something to hide? Though she didn't imagine Tasha extended her husband much leash.

"It's church. Sometimes people just stop coming." Tasha darted a quick look at Robert, but she was quick to go on. "Life comes up or any other slew of excuses. I'd need more information to jog anything loose. We are talking about a long time ago."

"What about a girl who wore blue jelly bangles and a neon-green beaded necklace?" she asked.

Tasha winced. "You wouldn't happen to have a name?"

Amanda shook her head. "Her identity is one of the things we're trying to figure out."

"That poor dear. Nameless and encased in a wall for over two decades. I wish I could be more helpful."

"Do you remember who worked on the project? Names?" Amanda leveled this question at Tasha. She'd at least hung around the site.

"Oh, we are talking twenty-some years ago. I remember Pete Rose was there, but he and his wife are still good friends of ours. Little harder to stay in touch these days though as they moved to Wisconsin."

Amanda glanced at Trent, and he was tapping on the tablet.

"Pete Rose, like the famous ballplayer?" Trent asked.

Tasha pointed at him and smiled. "Exactly like that. But this Pete couldn't hit a ball to save his life."

"When did they move?"

Tasha scrunched up her face. "Say ten years ago."

It didn't seem that the Rose family had hurried out of the county at least. "Why did they move?"

"He got a job offer from a Fortune 500 company that he couldn't refuse. He's still with them too."

The career opportunity was unlikely a lie since the families were still in touch. Still, she'd pull a background on the Roses for due diligence. "How long have you been members of Herald Church?"

"Look at you with all these tough questions." Tasha began. "But this one's easy. I was baptized there as a baby, so all my life."

"And you?" Trent asked Robert.

"Since I married Tash, so thirty years."

"You've both known Father Linwood for a long time then," Amanda said. "Today a young man accused him of holding confessional secrets about sexual and physical abuse. Can you see him holding on to that or turning the matter over to police?"

Tasha narrowed her eyes. "Why would he go to the police? If the priest broke his silence, it would violate the sanctity of the confessional booth. Then what would be left?"

Trent lowered his tablet. "The abuse could have been stopped. An innocent boy was—"

Tasha put up her hand. "Supposedly. Accusations were made. Not confirmed."

Seconds ticked off. Amanda wasn't touching it.

"I suppose so, ma'am," Trent eventually said.

Tasha flailed her arms. "All I'm saying. People can claim any number of things. It doesn't mean they're true."

"We're not arguing with you there," Amanda said, wedging back in to wrap things up. "Well, we appreciate you both taking the time to speak with us. Please call if you remember any other volunteer names after we leave." She stood and extended her card to Tasha.

The woman snatched it. "I won't. By that I mean, I doubt I'll remember anyone. But if I do..." She held the card up and followed them to the door. Robert lingered in the background. Tasha added, "I heard it was Cameron Cofell who barricaded Father Linwood. Not from the news but through the church grapevine. That boy was always a tortured soul. Most of the time he just had this blank stare."

Amanda nodded, not knowing what to say in response. Trent didn't speak either. That changed once they got in the car.

"Blank stares, tortured soul, troubled. Yet no one bothers to do anything about it, even ask if the boy's okay. Instead they all look the other way. They're all responsible in my book." Trent started the car and did up his seatbelt with a distinctive click. "Cameron's behavior speaks to abuse. I don't doubt for a second that he was a victim. And, honestly, I'm irritated by Tasha Gray's defense of Linwood and the confessional booth. The way she was so defensive and self-righteous about it makes me curious what she's copped to over her lifetime."

"I'm with you, Trent. I mean, we're talking about a boy being molested and abused, and she's still defending priest confessions."

"Even if it's self-serving, I might never wrap my head around how some people think and what they'll justify."

"I gave up trying to unravel people a long time ago. Well, aside from trying to think like a criminal from time to time. A necessity of the job."

"I get what you're saying." Trent started typing on the onboard laptop. Amanda watched the name Pete Rose come on screen, followed by Trent clicking on his basic background. "Just for due diligence," he said.

"Great minds. So what are you seeing?" She eased farther back into the passenger seat.

"Looks like a recap of what we just heard. Address in Wisconsin. No criminal record."

"Might not have been caught for anything."

He tapped in the wife's name next. "She's clean too. All right, who's up next?" He looked over at her.

"Oh." She grabbed the list from the backseat and drew a line through the Gray and Rose families. "How about Clay and

Mable McFarland? They're listed as active members now and twenty-three years ago."

"Okay. You sure you don't just want to focus on the ones who left? It's a smaller list."

"It is, but we could also miss something. There were only ten members who left since the renovation, none right away. Maybe we're looking for a current member who did this back then and was never bothered by their secret."

"They could have also hung around to ensure she stayed in that wall."

"There's that too. But anyone around back then might have something to offer the investigation. You agree?"

"Yeah, even though that makes our to-do list bigger again. You said Clay and Mable McFarland?"

"Yep."

Trent tapped away on the keyboard again. "The McFarland family lives in Woodbridge. Shall I get us there?" He nudged his head toward the windshield.

"You shall."

NINE

Clay McFarland took Amanda and Trent to the living room while his wife, Mable, saw to a finicky toddler in the background. Amanda eased onto an overstuffed recliner, and Trent sat on a wingback chair.

"That's our granddaughter Renee," Clay said. "She just turned two last month, and she's doing her best to live up to the stereotype for her age. Mable will be back once she gets the girl settled."

"Oh, would you stop?" Mable came into the room. "Cut the girl some slack. She's just not used to being away from her mother. This is her eighth night in a row."

"Our daughter and her husband thought it was a good idea to take off to Mexico for a couple of weeks," Clay offered.

"And they deserve it." Mable wiped her brow and dropped onto the couch. "Sorry for all that rigmarole, but she's down now, and I can talk."

Amanda loved the buzz that kids added to a home. They made it electric, giving it an unmistakable pulse. Some might see it as chaos, but she found it invigorating and rejuvenating. Not that raising a child wasn't hard work. It was certainly a round-the-clock job and one that lasted a lifetime. "You might have heard what took place at Herald Church today?" So much had been jammed in, it was hard to believe it was still day one of the investigation.

"Oh, we heard about poor Father Linwood being held at gunpoint," Clay said.

"Yeah, by that lunatic Cameron Cofell." Mable spat the name as if she were disgusted that it had come off her tongue.

He'd been described as different things, but this was the first for *lunatic*.

"We wanted to deliver flowers to Father Linwood at the hospital, but we arrived after visiting hours. We had to leave them with the on-duty nurse. Hopefully he got them." Clay turned to his wife.

"Whatever that boy was thinking, I'll never know," Mable said, drawing a deep breath afterward, going a bit red in the cheeks, and clearly about to set off on a tangent. "And after all Cameron was given. The Cofells loved him like he was their own."

"*Like* their own?" Amanda asked.

"He was adopted. Winnie was in her late thirties. A baby was never going to happen for them. They did everything they could for him."

Good parents loved their adopted children as if they were their own flesh and blood. The bond was real without line or distinction, just like it was with her and Zoe. But that aside, this was the first time they'd heard anything about Cameron being adopted. Though did that matter? Really, their priority for coming here was Jane Doe, not the standoff. As far as the law was mostly concerned that case was closed, less the legal hoops including trial and sentencing. That would take more time. There was no question that Cameron had held the priest at gunpoint. No mystery left to solve. But what Mable said clung like a barb, and made Amanda curious, if only for the briefest of detours. The FBI agent had told them that Cameron was living in a halfway house. It was either court-ordered or because Cameron had nowhere else to go. But that wouldn't make much sense. When the Cofells died a few years ago, their estate should have passed on to him. "Did he inherit when his parents passed?"

Mable shrugged.

"We'd have no reason to know what happened with their money. I don't suspect they had a lot in the bank, but that old farmhouse they lived in was paid for," Clay said. "Doug inherited it from his grandfather. It had to have been worth somethin'."

Yet Cameron was living in a halfway house... Amanda shut all these thoughts down, put her focus back on the girl in the wall. She was their case, not Cameron. "Well, we actually came here to talk about the other thing that happened at the church today," she began and waited.

"Ah. The body?" Clay eased in.

"I can't get over it," Mable blurted out. "First poor Father Linwood is held at gunpoint, then his church is damaged... Only for that to lead to the discovery of a body inside the wall."

Amanda would bite her tongue. While she empathized with the priest facing a loaded gun, she certainly didn't view him as *poor* anything. That likely was bolstered by the fact she didn't see him as an innocent either. His trespasses remained to be seen, but he wasn't off her radar. She'd also hold off on disclosing it was a teen girl for now. "That's right. We understand that the two of you have been members for a long time."

Husband and wife looked at each other. He answered, "Thirty-five years or more."

"So you were around when the renovations were done to the nave? When the lath and plaster was replaced with drywall?" she asked for the record.

"Yep, and what a messy job that was." Clay let out a whistle.

"You helped with the project?" Trent jumped in.

"No, no, not me. I'm good with plumbing and some minor electrical, but I don't have any experience laying board or muddin'."

"Who else helped with the job?" Amanda asked.

"Well, it's been a while, but a buddy of mine from out of town helped. He wasn't a member of the church, but he was a muddin' wiz. Couldn't even tell where there was a seam. He'd put it on smooth like butta. I tried to get a key for him from Father Linwood, but he refused on account of Andy not being from the church. Even though he was giving up his personal time, after work, no less, to help out. And he gave a few other volunteers keys. Of course, they were adding to his coffers."

"To the *church's* coffers, and it's about time you let that go, Clay," Mable said, exasperated. "Holding grudges gives you wrinkles and isn't Christian."

"I'm trying."

"You'll need to forgive him," Mable said. "Forgiveness isn't my husband's strong suit."

Clay rolled his eyes, but thankfully his wife didn't seem to notice.

"What's Andy's full name?" Trent looked up from his tablet, and he briefly met Amanda's eye. She wondered if he'd caught on that Clay had inadvertently answered another one of their questions about access to the church. They needed to find out who was given a copy of the key.

"Andrew Blake," Clay said.

"And where does he live?" Amanda asked.

"Here in town," Clay said slowly. "Don't be telling me you think someone who worked on the reno killed that person and put them in the wall?"

"Dear Lord." Mable crossed herself, and Clay followed suit.

Clay's assumption of murder didn't strike Amanda as odd. It was an obvious conclusion anyone with a brain would draw. "We're just gathering information. Do you recall anyone specifically who received a key?"

Clay thrummed his fingers on the arm of the couch. "Hmm. Oh, Doug Cofell did, but that's the only person I can think of. I do remember that Andy was ticked off Doug had one when he didn't. At the time, I defended Father Linwood. But Andy's point was Doug wasn't working as much as he was."

This might not mean anything, but that icky feeling was back in her gut and churning up the acids. Was it merely a coincidence that Doug Cofell had a key to the church and was helping during the renovations? Or did it indicate something more sinister? The couple was accused of abusing Cameron, but had they hurt another child before? Though from what the McFarlands just told them, the Cofells didn't have any other children. Amanda must be getting carried away, tired, and trying to make sense of the evil she came face to face with today. Surely, Doug Cofell having a key came down to pure coincidence. "The body found was that of a teenage girl."

The McFarlands looked at each other but said nothing.

"Around the time of the renovation, do you remember if any teenage girl from the congregation suddenly stopped attending?" Amanda asked.

"That was a long time ago. What has it been...?" Clay turned to his wife.

"Twenty-five years, give or take?" she guessed.

"The church records show twenty-three," Trent said.

"And I appreciate it might be hard to remember that long ago, but what about any girls who wore blue jelly bangles or neon-green bead necklaces?" She directed this question at Mable. Stereotyping, but women typically did pay more attention to those sorts of things. Even more so when the other person here was a sixty-something man.

"At one point, weren't all the young ones wearing those jellies? The bracelets, the shoes... I'm sure there were jelly earrings."

Amanda would take her word on all of that. The craze passed before her teenage years.

Mable nodded then shook her head. "Sorry, though, I can't say any girl stood out in particular. And I don't recall one who disappeared."

"I understand. Well, thank you for taking the time to talk to us." Amanda got up, passed off her card, rolled through her regular spiel, and headed for the door.

She and Trent got into the car, and he typed *Andrew Blake* into the onboard computer.

"He's just a few blocks over from here," he said a few seconds later. "Wanna go, then call it a night?"

"I want to go, but I'll hold on calling it a night until I hear what he has to say. He could break the entire case wide open. Then we'd have to slap cuffs on someone before I could sleep."

Trent laughed. "Fair enough."

He got the car moving, and she said, "I find it strange that no one remembers her. How can a young girl just disappear and no one take notice?"

"Do you need me to answer that?"

"I do actually." For whatever reason, her mind was blank.

"You're not going to like it, but Doe might not have been a member of the church or associated in any way. She could have been linked to a volunteer, or some rando on the street saw an opportunity and got inside late at night."

"Okay, I don't even want to consider that last suggestion. But you raised a good point. If this person went in late at night, why wouldn't they have woken up Father Linwood or Daniel Barron? Clearly, they can hear what's happening in the church from their living quarters. It was the yelling that alerted Chet Solomon to the standoff early this morning."

"Remember, people sometimes worked in the evening. Linwood and his assistant could have gotten used to that. Even if they heard something, they'd be likely to let it go. That, or Linwood was involved."

"While I appreciate you trying to fire some ammo at Linwood, this one's not hitting."

"Well, the more I think about him, I don't care for him. He certainly doesn't give off a warm and fuzzy vibe. I didn't go to church often growing up, but my family attended mass on Christmas and Easter. The priest I knew was a gentle spirit, kind, a real people person. I guess Father Linwood's shields might be up after what he's been through today, making him defensive."

"Whatever the case, he certainly seems shut off about Jane Doe. I'm not even sure if he cares at all. Same about Cameron Cofell."

"That judgment might be a bit harsh. The father has gone through a lot and the congregation is his flock, a charge he takes very seriously. He doesn't want any of them to be wrongly accused."

"I believe the word he used was *harassed*," she said drily. "And there's no denying that, in the least, he let Cameron Cofell down. I don't think anyone with an ounce of intuition would miss the red flags that he was abused."

Trent shook his head. "And Cameron might not be the only person he let down. Jane Doe?"

"Hard to answer that yet." Their conversation came to a natural conclusion, and her mind wandered.

Are there more bodies to be found in Herald Church?

TEN

Amanda watched the minute change over on the clock on the dash, making it 8:05 PM. This happened just as Trent pulled into the parking lot of Andrew Blake's apartment building. They decided to speak with Clay McFarland's friend before other church members because he'd be more likely to offer an alternate viewpoint. Not being a part of the organization, a sense of loyalty wouldn't hold him back from speaking his mind.

"Blake's in unit three-oh-five," Trent told her as they headed toward the building's main door. They found it was a lockout, with names or initials alongside a panel of intercom buttons. Only one showed *AB*.

Trent hit the button and, shortly later, a man's voice came through the speaker.

"Hello?"

"Andrew Blake?" Trent said.

"Who's this?"

Amanda nodded for Trent to continue. She took the man's response as confirmation of his identity.

"I'm Detective Stenson. I need to talk to you about Father Linwood and Herald Church."

No verbal response but the door buzzed, indicating Andrew had released the lock. Trent held the door for her, sweeping his arm for her to go through. "After you."

"Thanks. Why tell him you wanted to talk about Linwood?"

"From what Clay told us, I don't think he's a fan."

"Because he didn't give him a copy of the key?"

"Might be that. Might be more to it."

"Blake still helped with the renos."

Trent shrugged. "As a favor for a friend?"

They took the elevator to the third floor and gauged the numbers on the doors and determined they needed to go right.

Amanda knocked on 305, and the door was opened a moment later. The smell of warm buttered popcorn smacked her in the face and had her stomach growling. They'd been going nonstop today, and she hadn't even noticed she was hungry until this onslaught of aromas.

"Andrew Blake, we're Detectives Stenson, and Steele," Trent told the man.

He was in his early sixties and wearing thick-lensed glasses that made his eyes appear huge. "Come in."

Amanda accepted the invitation, struggling to put the popcorn out of mind. A more difficult task when he took them to his living room and a heaped bowl of it was sitting on a coffee table next to the couch.

"Want some?" Andrew lifted the bowl, extending the offer to both of them.

Trent declined, and she should too. Focus on why they were there. But she was always telling Trent to accept offerings of hospitality because it set the person they were questioning at ease.

"And you?" Andrew put the popcorn right under her nose. "Take what you like. Don't be shy. Dig right in."

She must have been easy to see through. "Ah, sure, but just a small amount. Thanks." She grabbed a mittful and instantly regretted that she had. It was hard to come off with authority while tossing popcorn into her mouth or crunching on kernels. Hopefully, Trent would read her thoughts and continue taking the lead on this one. After putting a few on her tongue, she sank into a sort of heaven where salt and butter collided and exploded in delicious pleasure. All other concerns melted away with it. *Yeah, Trent's got this!*

Andrew sat down on the couch, crossed one leg over the other and nestled the bowl of popcorn in the triangle he'd made. She and Trent remained standing as there weren't other places to sit. "I must say, I am curious why you want to talk to me about Father Linwood. I assume it has something to do with the guy being held at gunpoint today. Still not sure how that brings you to me though."

"We're not exactly here about the hostage situation," Trent said as Amanda continued to munch away.

"Well, the news also said something about a body being inside a wall in the church. That would have even less to do with me. But you did say you wanted to talk about Linwood. A little deceitful, don't you think?" Andrew scooped a palmful of popcorn and put it into his mouth.

"Not really. We'd like to hear your view of the man. You must have something to say about him, or you wouldn't have let us in the building," Trent said.

Andrew chewed and swallowed the last of his mouthful. "All right, I'll play along. I heard the allegations against him, and let me say nothing much would surprise me. I thought you were here to start building a case against him."

Amanda gulped what was in her mouth and felt the lump of popcorn travel down her throat. "Allegations of what, exactly?"

"Sexual abuse. Not saying he participated, but that he let it go on in his church. In my opinion, awareness without action makes a person just as guilty as the one doing it."

"Unfortunately, the law doesn't see it that way," Trent said.

"We understand that you helped the church some years back with renovations they did in the nave. They took out the old lath and plaster and installed drywall. Clearly you have no respect for Father Linwood, so why do it?"

"I love drywallin', but mostly I did that for a friend. He loves that church. Thinks the world of Linwood too." The last part came with an eyeroll.

"That was enough to compel you over there after working all day?" Amanda was finally free to participate. She'd practically inhaled her mittful of popcorn. It was surprising she didn't choke on it.

"I was part-time then but searching for something full-time. Pitching in on the church reno just kept my skills up."

"We heard you're great at applying mud," Trent said.

"Now I know you were talking to my pal Clay. He goes on about that any chance he gets. It's probably because he tried to get into construction, but it didn't suit him."

"Was work done late into the night?" If it was a matter of routine, Father Linwood or his assistant were less likely to be disturbed by the sounds of construction.

"If you consider ten o'clock late. They wanted to get the job over as fast as possible. I remember that."

"How long did the project take?" she asked.

"Three weeks, thereabouts. I was there for about a week." He extended the bowl toward her again, but she shook her head. If she gave in, she'd just mow down the entire thing.

Amanda just had the disturbing thought now, delayed as it might be, that Andrew Blake might have inadvertently sealed Jane Doe in the wall. "Did anyone else do the mudding?"

"It was just me."

"And you worked on it during what hours?" Trent asked.

Andrew narrowed his eyes. "Seems curious you'd care about that."

"Please just answer Detective Stenson's question," Amanda said.

"Would have been from seven until ten at night, after my paying job. I'd mud whatever had been that day."

"And the right side of the nave, about midway... Do you remember what day you mudded that?" she asked, not sure where that would even get her.

Andrew laughed. "You're kidding, right? This was a long time ago. I'm doing good to remember the things I did yesterday."

She studied his face, but his expression was relaxed, and he was making comfortable eye contact. She got no sense of deception from him. She smiled at him. "Fair enough."

"I've been patient and played along, but why are you so interested in that job— Oh." He flung the popcorn bowl onto the coffee table. "These questions have to do with that body. It was found in the nave, to the right, midway up? And you think that I... That I had something to do with it?"

"No one has said that, but did you?" She volleyed that back without a trace of judgment but in a no-nonsense tone.

"Did I?" It was like the man was asking that of himself. Next thing, he shot to his feet and placed a hand over his stomach. "Dear Lord Jesus! I'm going to be sick. That person was stuffed in there, drywall on top of them, then I... then I..." He covered his mouth and belched. Thankfully the popcorn didn't make a reappearance.

Amanda glanced at Trent. If Andrew Blake was putting on a performance, he deserved an Oscar.

Andrew dropped his arm. His eyes were wide and wet. "If I had known, I'd never have..."

"I see this is quite a shock to you," she said.

"Ah, yeah."

"But if you could please sit again," she said. "We do have more questions for you." Once he sat down, she continued.

"Can you give us the names of other volunteers you worked with?"

"Man, I wish I could, but it was a long time ago. And I was working alone for the most part. Though there was this one guy, a member of the church, and he had an attitude. Impatient person."

"Clay said you got annoyed with someone over access, that they had a key for the church, but you didn't? Do you remember their name?" She didn't want to suggest Doug Cofell.

"It was a man. What was his name again...?" Like earlier, this sounded like he framed the question for himself. "Dave, Don... *Doug*! Last name was Coffee, Coffin... *Cofell*." His eyes widened. "Hey, that was the name of the man who held Linwood hostage. A relation?"

"It was his son," Trent said.

"Now it's all coming together. The claims of sexual abuse and finding out that Doug fella was his dad... Nothing would surprise me. That Doug guy had bad juju coming off him in waves."

"Why do you say that?" she asked.

"Some things can't be quantified. It was just an icky feeling I got being around him." He peered into her eyes. "I'm sure as a cop you have good instincts and have run into this before."

She nodded. "I have."

"Me too," Trent put in.

"Well, then. There wasn't anything definitive, just that gut feeling."

Speaking of, hers was telling her Andrew Blake was genuine with nothing to hide. "That wraps things up for me. Detective Stenson?" She looked at him.

"All I have." He slipped his tablet into a sleeve, and they saw themselves out.

In the hall, she said, "Blake tells it how he sees it. I like that in a person."

"Takes out all the guesswork anyhow. He's certainly not a fan of Father Linwood or of Doug Cofell. Bad juju... I haven't heard that one in a while."

"Huh. I'd suspect with so many adopting new-age thinking, we'd hear more of it."

"Whatever the case, we can mark Andrew Blake off the suspect list. But where does that leave us?"

"Do you need to ask? Are you forgetting about one long congregation list in the car?"

"Right, but there's no way we can tackle all that tonight. And I think you need food before you collapse. The way you kept lusting after that bowl of popcorn." He laughed.

"Very funny. But true." She smiled. "To be honest, I entertained a brief fantasy about a cow's ass."

"About what now?" He started choking.

She shoved his shoulder. "Just that I could do a big, juicy steak. You know, take a chunk out of a cow's—Never mind."

"Okay... the steak part I understand, but you want a *chunk out of* what now?"

"Cut it out."

"How about we get ourselves some steak and knock off some more names from the list?"

"Kill people? No thanks. A chat with some? Sure." She winked at him. "As for that offer of beef, I wish I had the strength to resist." She should, but it was hard to turn him down. Her stomach was certainly begging her to accept, but her mind was wandering. She found herself briefly getting lost in his eyes when she had no right to do so. He was in a committed relationship, and whatever attraction she felt for him needed to be ignored.

"So is that a yes or..."

"I accept. Yes, please, get me steak." *In my belly...* She could hear Zoe saying it in her head. All it took was Logan recycling that movie line once. Zoe still brought it up now and then.

"You got it." Trent got them on the road.

She sat shotgun, guilt-tripping about Zoe. Surely, more visits to congregation members could wait until tomorrow. If she went home now, she might even get there before Zoe fell asleep. "Actually, Trent, could you take me to the station?"

"Sure, is everything all right?"

"It is, but how about we call it a night?"

He looked over at her, mouth slightly gaped open. More shock than judgment. "Sure. No steak then?"

"Sadly no. But raincheck?" She wasn't sure why she'd added that latter bit. It made it sound like he'd asked her on a date. "I'll just grab a bite to eat at home," she was quick to add.

"Whatever you wish."

"Thanks."

As he took the familiar turns to Central Station, her mind jostled images and conversations from the day. Yet no matter how she reframed them, none brought her any closer to identifying Jane Doe.

ELEVEN

Amanda was recovering from whiplash after the events of last night. She knew at some point her little girl would grow up, but she didn't expect it to happen at the age of nine. From the moment she adopted Zoe, they carried on a tradition that Zoe had with her biological mother. It was that of reading to her before bed. Amanda was excited that she'd made it just in time last night, only to be turned away.

"I'm too old for that now." Zoe had then offered up her cheek for a goodnight kiss.

"Are you mad at me for being home late?"

"Nope. But please respect my wishes." Zoe chuckled and brushed the back of Amanda's hand with her fingertips.

Respect my wishes... It was curious where she'd picked up that line, but it could have been from anywhere. "All right, big girl. Nightie night."

Zoe had groaned, and Amanda laughed as she left the room, pulling the door most of the way shut. She left it open a crack of two inches, and Zoe didn't protest.

It was now nearing eight thirty Wednesday morning, and Amanda was at her desk still thinking about those precious moments with Zoe. And that line... *Please respect my wishes...* Had Zoe heard that from Logan too? It sounded like something he might have said when he got on his high horse about her job with its unpredictable hours. But he never understood the demands or her dedication to the badge. It wasn't work a person could simply turn off. Even in bed, her girl sleeping in the room next to hers, her mind was working.

I'm too old for that... Another thing Zoe had said. This phrase had ping-ponged around in Amanda's brain last night and hampered her ability to fall asleep. It was eventually what had her getting out of bed and grabbing her relic of a laptop. She'd brought it back to her bedroom.

Jane Doe's outfit was bothering Amanda. While Mary Janes were timeless, like with everything in fashion, certain styles were attributed to different eras. A quick Google search had told her the ones on Jane Doe were the 1920s style, a tribute to the flappers of the day, and they were popular with the punk rock and goth cultures of the late nineties and early 2000s. The age could match up with Jane Doe, but the bangles, necklace, and flowery dress predated her. Maybe Jane Doe dressed out of the norm for a girl her age twenty-three years ago. It was possible she was a bit of a rebel, dressing how she wanted to. The ensemble could have been purchased from a thrift store. It may also have been handed down. The latter could suggest siblings. But both could suggest a financially poor upbringing.

No one they spoke to yet had known of a girl who had gone missing from the church. Was she a runaway who had encountered her would-be killer? That could explain why no one knew of her.

"Good morning." Trent entered her cubicle with a Hannah's Diner coffee.

"You're the best. I dropped Zoe at school and came right in. Thanks again." She took a tentative sip, a quick test to tell if it had cooled enough to gulp. Not quite yet.

"Don't mention it." He walked to his cubicle and started to take off his coat. "Actually, should I leave this on? We have other congregation members to speak with."

"We do. We'll get started in a moment, but let's savor our coffee a minute."

"Who are you?"

"Just wanted to discuss Jane Doe a bit with you. I did some more thinking about her outfit."

"It was rather eclectic."

"You noticed?"

"I'm not hard of seeing, but having two sisters who are both a little fashion crazy probably fine-tuned my eye."

She remembered Trent mentioning that one of them was an influencer on social media. She couldn't remember what type of product she primarily promoted, but given what Trent just said, something in fashion was likely. "Well, then I don't need to tell you that everything she wore wasn't typical of a girl her age twenty-three years ago. Was she a rebel or did someone dress her?"

"And was she clothed like that just for her burial? To make a statement of some kind?"

"Not sure about that. She was put in a wall. I'd say the killer never wanted her to be found. My thinking is she may have come from a home that wasn't that well-off financially. The clothes could have been from a thrift store or hand-me-downs. Which I realize could suggest an older sibling."

"And that would beg answers to other questions. To start, we can't seem to find one person that noticed Jane Doe was missing. How is that even possible?"

"She could be in Missing Persons," she countered. "There's just no way for us to find her there. Without identifying markers and a place to focus the search, we're at a dead end."

"And this path keeps getting darker."

"Welcome to Homicide."

"So just to be clear, you're suggesting she was kidnapped or somehow found her way to Woodbridge where she encountered her killer and was put into the church wall?"

"Uh-huh."

"Which still leads us back to someone in the church being a murderer."

"Correct again." She got up from her desk and was about to grab her coat when her cell phone rang. The caller's ID had her sitting down again. "It's Rideout," she told Trent and answered on speaker.

"Amanda, it's Hans."

He rarely stood on formality, but she picked up on something in his voice she didn't care for. "Good morning. Trent's here too. Do you have something for us?"

"Hey, Trent. I came in early this morning, wanted to get started on this dear child. She's been in a wall for long enough, and it's time to get her justice."

"I feel the same." She had a lot of patience, but the nervous energy rising in her chest threatened to wipe it all out.

Rideout continued. "I've only finished with the prelim. I've done X-rays and taken measurements, and other external tests. I've bagged her clothing, and it will be sent to the lab for processing. One never knows what they might find that will be useful. I also ran her prints. Nothing came back with that. Now DNA can be viable for testing for hundreds of years, but that all depends on the environment. With the girl entombed she was kept under stable conditions. There wouldn't have been any major fluctuation in heat or cold. The space would have also had little to no oxygen, zero sunlight. So I'm pleased to say her DNA was viable, and I received an instant hit from Missing Persons."

It was like the ground fell out beneath her. Her stomach came into her throat. "Who is she?"

"Sadie Jackson from Hagerstown, Maryland." He slapped that out as if he expected them to recognize the name.

At least they could ditch Jane Doe. "Sadie Jackson." Saying it didn't spark anything for her.

"Either of you recognize the name?"

"No," Trent said. "Should we?"

"I suppose you're both too young, but Sadie Jackson made nationwide news thirty-one years ago. She was eight years old when she was kidnapped from one of the big Orlando, Florida, theme parks."

Amanda had taken Zoe to one last August. Malone encouraged her to take another vacation more recently, but she wasn't in any hurry now. "Over three decades ago, but we found out the wall was done only *twenty-three* years ago."

"Which makes this more tragic then. Where was she during those other years?" Rideout asked.

Amanda mumbled, trying to work out the math, but she was trying to process all of what Rideout had told them. *Maryland, Florida, kidnapped, eight years old...*

"Save yourself the headache," Rideout edged in. "With what you just told me, she would have been sixteen years old when she was put in that wall."

Amanda laid a hand over her heart. *Sweet sixteen...* It was devastating to think of all Sadie had suffered in her short lifetime.

"It gets worse," Rideout cut in.

"How could it possibly?" A stupid question. With this job, there was always a *worse*.

"Those X-rays I mentioned revealed a lot. Due to them, I feel confident in saying she was beaten to death. Lots of broken bones. Cause of death was likely due to internal bleeding. Specifically, one of her ribs was broken and punctured her lung. But it wasn't just perimortem injuries I found. There was indication of healed bones too." A long pause. "And there's more."

Amanda pinched her eyes shut for a second to brace herself for what was coming next.

"The X-rays tell me that she gave birth. Based on the healing of the tissue surrounding the bones, I would say probably within months of her death."

"Murder," she seethed while resisting the urge to throw her phone at the wall. "Let's just call it what it is. Some sick frick—" She snapped her mouth shut, hating herself for losing control of her emotions.

Trent put a hand on her shoulder, and it worked to calm her. *Some.*

"Was anyone ever suspected in the abduction?" Trent asked.

"I'm not really the one to ask about that. Nothing was publicized about it. You might best talk to the FBI with any questions about the investigation."

She had a couple contacts within the Bureau. Brandon Fisher's number was in her phone, and Special Agent Vos's card was in her coat pocket. "So whoever took Sadie kept her for eight years and got her pregnant. She had a baby and was killed not long after. I got that right? Oh, and while they held her, they repeatedly beat her?"

"You heard it all," Rideout stated somberly.

"What happened to the child?" Trent asked.

"I'm afraid only God would have that answer. No birth record listing her as the mother."

"How could you expect there would be? Could be under another name, though." Every time she listened or opened her mouth, things became progressively worse.

"Well, that's all I've got for now, but I knew it couldn't wait. Oh, the girl's parents are still in Hagerstown. I'm assuming you'll want to pay them a visit."

That's all? He'd detonated a bomb and now he was off. "We will. Thank you for calling." She ended the call, chilled while her anger burned hot. She googled Sadie's name on her computer, and several results filled the screen. She clicked on the first, entitled "The Search Continues for Sadie Jackson". She was taken back by the face of a bright-eyed eight-year-old. The sight of her wide smile stabbed Amanda's chest. The caption under the photo read, *Photographed by Sadie's mother the day of the girl's abduction*. She glanced over her shoulder at Trent. He shook his head. "We need to find out everything about this case," Amanda stamped out. "The circumstances surrounding her kidnapping and anyone considered a suspect. I think it's clear that whoever put Sadie Jackson in the walls of Herald Church was also her kidnapper."

"That or she had the worst luck of anyone on the planet."

"I'd say she had bad enough luck as it is, but knowing her identity is the strongest lead we've had yet. We're going to start by talking with her parents though. They've waited long enough. And before you say notification could be passed off to the PD in Hagerstown, the parents might also be able to tell us something about that day that never made it on the record." She grabbed her coat and led the way to the lot. Stopping for one breath, one second, would have everything sinking in just that little bit more. She wasn't sure she could withstand that.

TWELVE

Amanda's phone rang not long after they left. Malone. She'd skipped updating him before leaving Central. Her mind was set on getting to the Jacksons. It was the better part of a two-hour drive to Hagerstown, Maryland. It was a heartbreaking revelation to find the couple was in the same home where they had lived with Sadie.

"Where did you two take off to?" Malone said. "I was told you both practically ran out of the station. Get a solid lead?"

Amanda and Trent looked at each other. She had the call on speaker, so Trent had heard every word. "You could say that." She recapped the details they'd learned from Rideout and added they were on the way to Hagerstown. He didn't say anything when she finished. "Are you still there?" she prompted.

"I'm here. I remember that case. It stayed in the papers for the longest time, but she was never found."

For good reason... It was sickening to think that girl was stuffed in the wall for the last twenty-three years. And before that held who-knows-where. Every day must have been sheer hell for her and her parents. "Then you're familiar with the case. What can you tell us?"

"Just that she was taken from a Florida amusement park. If I remember, video surveillance from the park caught a couple leaving with her, but the picture was never shared with the public. I can only guess the resolution wasn't that great. Technology has come a long way since then. You might need to speak with the FBI, as it was their case."

"I planned on that. But if they have video, surely, they saw what direction these people headed after they left the park."

"I can't speak to that, but nothing was made public. As the months went on, updates hit less and less, until the girl faded from the news."

A knot pitted in Amanda's stomach. The girl was taken, abused, raped, and the rest of the world just carried on with their lives. "You said it was a couple though? A man and woman or...?" This changed the course of the investigation. She'd assumed a sole man was responsible. But transporting a dead body would be heavy work. Lessened if two people were involved.

"A man and woman," Malone confirmed. "Rideout is absolutely positive the remains were Sadie Jackson?"

One would think a woman would have stood up for the girl. There were a lot of sick people out there. Reprehensible. Degenerates. She shook aside her thoughts. "Rideout doesn't say anything unless he's certain."

"All right. Well, keep me posted on everything. The parents might have something to say that will click all these years later. Stranger things have happened."

"That's what we're hoping." *Sometimes visiting the past is the only way to move forward...* Hopefully that would prove true this time. Even still, the Jacksons deserved closure and to meet the detectives investigating Sadie's murder. Malone ended the call, and she pulled Vos's card and punched in her digits. At least this agent was familiar with the situation. If she called Special Agent Fisher, she'd need to run through everything from the top. Vos answered during the second ring. "It's Detective Amanda Steele," she told the federal agent. "Detective Trent Stenson is on the line too."

"Yes, from Prince William County PD. How is your investigation going?"

"Let's just say it's taken an interesting turn. The body belonged to Sadie Jackson of Hagerstown, Maryland. Are you familiar with the case?" The Bureau was a big world. This case was also thirty-one years old, cold by any definition, and likely housed in some filing cabinet in the basement of the J. Edgar Hoover Building. She flicked Vos's card in her hand. It looked like she worked out of the Washington Field Office. Same city, different address.

"The name doesn't sound familiar. When was this?"

"Thirty-one years ago. Probably long before your time." Vos looked to be in her mid-to-late forties. "But we're hoping you can access the case files and share them with us."

"I'll do my best."

Amanda hadn't expected Vos to respond so quickly or favorably. "That would be wonderful. I realize there was a lot publicized at the time, old news articles I could look up, but..."

"They provide a small fraction of the picture. Only what's been censored and they've been cleared to say," Vos said, reading Amanda's hesitation spot on.

"Exactly."

"I'll start getting everything together when I get off here and give you a call once it's ready. Shouldn't be more than a few hours or so. You caught me at a good time. You can come pick it up or I could meet you halfway, if that's easier."

Amanda was impressed by Vos's cooperative spirit. "That

would be great. Among everything, there should be a video that showed the couple leaving the park with Sadie."

"If it's there, I'll pass it along. To think this started thirty-one years ago, and such a sad, tragic ending to her story, but at least she can finally be properly laid to rest and her parents given closure."

Amanda's heart pinched at the tender way Vos emphasized how big of a deal closure was in and of itself. "There is that."

"Though we clearly want to make whoever took her pay for what they've done," Vos added in a cool manner that had Amanda wondering if she was a mother too.

"That we certainly do." Amanda found herself smiling, bonding with the agent she'd only spoken to twice. She left her cell phone number with Vos, thanked her, and ended the call. "You might have a hang-up with the FBI, but I rather like Sandra Vos."

"I admit she seems great." Trent made a turn off the highway, following the promptings of the GPS toward Hagerstown.

"She does." Amanda quickly added Vos to her contacts, then said, "When we revisit the congregation list, we should focus on couples."

Trent shook his head. "Great idea, except one half of a couple could be with the church, and the other a nonbeliever. Even then, we could still miss the mark. The kidnapping duo might be from outside the church."

"Unassociated volunteers," she lamented, hating that he had a point. "All right. We'll pin visiting more church members until we have more to go on."

"I don't think we have a choice."

"Leaving that for now, a woman being involved with Sadie's kidnapping could explain the clothing. She could have passed hers along to Sadie." Amanda's heart opened with each repetition of the girl's given name. It was restorative after referring to her as Jane Doe so many times.

"Very possible. Rideout said he passed the clothing along to the lab, so they'll be processing it closely. If there is DNA from another contributor, they should find it."

"Let's hope our luck changes, and it leads us right to the people who did this to Sadie."

A little over an hour later, Amanda sat up straighter as Trent pulled in front of a gray brick bungalow. Two large windows framed by black shutters looked out to the street, and an over-hang sheltered the front door.

Neither of them said a word as they got out of the car and headed up the walkway. Being here with the news they had to deliver weighed Amanda's steps.

There was a welcome board next to the front door and a welcome mat. Redundant but also so incredibly ordinary. Resilient. Kind. Despite suffering so much, the Jacksons spread joy in such a simple way. Its impact had Amanda taking a deep breath.

She rang the bell and listened closely for movement inside the home. She had called ahead, keeping things brief. Just said that she was from the PWCPD and had news about Sadie. Would they be home to talk. They said they would be. Amanda admired the resilience of their marriage, being able to endure thirty-one years of anguish and uncertainty. Statistically, most couples divorced after the death or disappearance of a child.

The front door was opened, and a man stood there, a woman looking over his shoulder.

"Colin and Rosemary Jackson? I'm Detective Amanda Steele, and this is Detective Trent Stenson." She provided their first names to intentionally set the Jacksons more at ease.

"Yes. Please come in," Colin said, and he and the woman shuffled backward to let them enter.

The entry was a tight space, encroached on by a large

sectional couch to the immediate left. Amanda and Trent wiped their shoes on a mat set inside the door.

"I hope it's all right if we leave our shoes on." Amanda preferred that, so if she and Trent needed to leave in a hurry, they were ready to go.

"That's fine," Rosemary said quickly, probably eager for an update on her daughter. Though the fact Sadie wasn't here must have told her the news wouldn't be good.

"If there's someplace we could sit down…?" Trent prompted the couple.

"Of course." Colin led them through the home to the dining area off the kitchen, where there was a small table. "Will this be all right?"

"It's good," Amanda said. "Thank you." Once everyone sat down, she continued. "As I told you over the phone, we have news about Sadie. Regrettably—"

Rosemary gasped and reached for her husband's hand, which he cupped in both of his.

"I regret to inform you," Amanda picked up, "that Sadie was found dead yesterday morning in Woodbridge. DNA has confirmed it's her."

"Woodbridge?" Colin said.

Amanda nodded. "It's a town in Prince William County, Virginia."

"Oh my God." The mother clasped her mouth.

"Ah, what was she, ah, doing there?" Colin's voice was hoarse, and his eyes were full of tears, but he was clearly doing everything to hold himself together for his wife.

This next bit would be harder to share, but the Jacksons deserved to know. "She was found behind an interior wall of a church. We believe she was entombed there for the last twenty-three years." Amanda laid out the overview, knocking off the main points in a swift manner. *Ripping off the Band-Aid…* Sticking to the facts helped her stay detached and occupied her mind. Otherwise, her thoughts could drift and jeopardize her emotional balance.

"I don't understand. Twenty-three years ago? When she was sixteen?" Rosemary bunched her forehead as if she had a headache. "Where was she before that?"

"We're still investigating," Amanda said.

"She was such a sweet girl. Why would someone do this?" Rosemary palmed her cheeks, but no tears had fallen. Her shock and horror at hearing the fate of her daughter was tangible. The lack of theatrics, wailing and screaming, likely only kept at bay by a flood of adrenaline. Confronted by horrible loss, many became instantly numb, transported to an adjacent reality that cushioned them from the harshness of reality.

To say anything, to surmise why the people took her, would be a best guess without knowing the identities of the couple.

Colin moved his chair closer to his wife and wrapped his arm around her. "We... *we* always thought or held out hope that she'd come home to us. It's why we've lived here all these years, just so she'd be able to find us."

"I can understand that, and we both wish we came with better news," Amanda said. "We're very sorry for your loss."

The Jacksons folded into each other. A few moments later, they pulled back, and Colin cleared his throat. "How did she die? Who...?"

Amanda shook her head. "We are doing all in our power to find out who did this to her. She mostly likely died from internal bleeding due to physical injuries she sustained." That was a gentler way of putting it than *due to a beating she'd received...*

"She probably fought back, possibly making things worse," Rosemary said, straightening her posture. "She was born with a strong will. She always knew what she wanted and would tell you." She sniffled now. "That's what happened that day. She wanted ice cream, and Colin and I got distracted searching for change. We should have just charged it to a card." This bit she threw in with a glance at her husband. "By the time we got ourselves together, hordes of people were everywhere around us. We lost sight of Sadie. We couldn't see h-her." Rosemary's voice fractured, and she twisted the collar of her shirt.

That moment must have been utterly horrifying. Then the ensuing days, months, even years would have been riddled with guilt and regrets. The *what ifs*.

"That must have been terrifying," Trent empathized.

"There are no words." Colin rubbed his forehead. "Do you think the people who took her held on to her for eight years before killing her?"

"It's most likely," Amanda said and braced herself for what she had to tell them next. "Our medical examiner is also positive that Sadie had given birth."

"She'd *what*? She was only a child." Rosemary clamped her mouth shut and bit her bottom lip.

Colin bunched up his face and smacked the side of his fist against the table so hard, it rattled the chandelier overhead.

Amanda had seen it coming and was prepared, but Trent flinched some, and Rosemary hiccupped a startled sob. Neither of them rushed to ask about the child. They may have been processing the shock.

"If you find these people, that man," Colin seethed, "I'd like five minutes alone with him."

Amanda could understand that response but couldn't condone it. "Sadly, that wouldn't undo anything or bring Sadie back."

"He raped my baby girl!" Colin broke down then, tears streaming down his cheeks as his chin trembled. "And I'd swear on a stack of Bibles that if he ever crosses my path, I will kill him with my bare hands." He drilled his gaze into Amanda's as he made this pledge, and it raised the hairs on the back of her neck.

"Colin, please." Rosemary set a hand on his forearm, and Colin shrugged her off. She heaved a sob.

"I'm sorry, Rosie. It's just our little girl, ya know."

Amanda looked away as the couple hugged again. She wasn't even able to face Trent, though she felt him watching her. She had to rein in her emotions, try to dismiss the fact they'd just ripped apart the Jacksons' hearts. Her own eyes beaded with tears. She blinked them back, determined to be strong and unassailable, their raft in the storm. She gave them a few moments, then softly cleared her throat. They parted from their embrace.

"I apologize for needing to ask," Amanda began, "as I'm sure you've answered this question a million times over. But did you happen to notice anyone following you that day? Maybe just the glimpse of a face you saw a couple times or more?"

"Ask whatever you want, but you're right. We answered that question many times in the months afterward," Colin said. "It started with the Orlando police and then the FBI. Not that I bemoan the process for one moment. We considered everything and responded thoughtfully. Rosie and I hoped that all the talk would eventually jog something from us that helped them find our girl."

"Then it would have been worth repeating ourselves over and over," Rosemary said.

Colin continued. "But eventually, it all just became too much. Hopeless. Like it didn't matter what we remembered, what we said. None of it made a difference. Sadie was gone. But in response to you, no one stood out. How could *one* when there were so many faces? It's a tourist destination, and the place was teeming with people."

"We understand there was a video that captured a couple leaving the park with Sadie. I take it you were shown this?" Surely they had been as word of its existence was made public.

"We watched it. Nothing about those people stood out to us," Colin said.

"They've haunted my nightmares since though. For the last thirty-one years." Rosemary added that last bit in a low voice, almost comatose. "And to think she was less than two hours away for the last twenty-three years." She was now staring at the table, her gaze blanked over.

"Is there any family we could call to come be with you?" Amanda needed out of there, and the Jacksons needed time to assimilate what they'd just been told.

"No, we'll be fine," Colin said. "We appreciate you coming here to tell us in person. At least now we have some answers."

"When will we get her body so we can have a proper funeral for her?" Rosemary deadpanned, clearly embedded in her protective shell of shock.

"You would need to discuss that with the medical examiner, Hans Rideout." Amanda wrote his number on the back of her business card and gave it to Rosemary. "Just so you have a way to reach him, but I will have him call you."

"Thank you."

Amanda affectionately brushed her hand down the woman's upper arm, and Rosemary crumbled. She yanked Amanda to her and cried into her hair. It took every ounce of Amanda's willpower not to break down herself. This woman's grief was pulsing from her and crashing into Amanda in steady waves. But she resolved to protect her own heart, putting up a breakwater between herself and Rosemary's grief.

"Rosie, they probably need to get on their way," Colin said.

Rosemary pulled back and leveled her bloodshot eyes at Amanda. "Sorry to hold you up."

"It's no problem at all," Amanda told them. "There are qualified counselors out there who can help you, if you wish. Many of them are provided as a free service to families of crime by various counties. Call me if you want me to arrange any of this."

Rosemary nodded. "I will."

"Take care." Amanda backed onto the front step, and when she turned away from the house, she could finally breathe again.

Trent walked close to her side. "We did a good thing back there."

"Then why doesn't it feel like it?"

THIRTEEN

After leaving the Jacksons, Amanda struggled to regain her focus. Shedding the energetic residue wasn't easy. She'd been managing fine until she'd made the mistake of touching Rosemary's arm. That alone was too intimate a gesture. Then Rosemary pulled her in for a hug. This case threatened to jeopardize her emotionally if she didn't watch it.

"How are you doing over there?" Trent looked at her. She didn't want to face him but did anyway. She needed to toughen up and snap out of the hold of that notification.

"I'll be fine." She smiled at him, but swiftly put her gaze back out the windshield. It had started to rain, one of those cold February drizzles, and the wipers squeaked as they made every other pass. It was like the weather was taking cues from her mood and the Jacksons' grief.

"You will be, and so will they. We just gave them closure after years of doubt and uncertainty."

"But they had hope. Now that's gone."

"You can't convince me that deep down, in their hearts, they didn't expect this outcome."

She shook her head.

"I noticed they never asked about Sadie's baby," he said.

"I'm relieved they didn't. We don't have anything to tell them on the matter."

"It might have been too difficult to think about right now."

"Considering this baby was the result of a man forcing himself on their daughter."

"My point. And there's also the fact that this baby would be in their twenties by now. The Jacksons would have missed out on their grandchild growing up as they had their daughter. That alone would be a lot to process."

"Many emotions to balance, that's for sure." *An under-statement.*

"How about we stop for a bite to eat?"

"I'm not too sure I could stomach food right now."

"What about coffee? Maybe a donut?" He bobbed his eyebrows.

She laughed, despite her mood. "It seems like you might want a sweet treat."

"Why not? Besides, I think it would do us good to take a step back for a few beats." He peered into her eyes.

"Sure. Why not?" She mimicked him.

"All right then. I remember seeing a coffee shop on the way here. It's not far."

They drove for another five minutes before Trent turned into the parking lot of a bakery. When she got out of the car, the sweet smell of confections had her stomach growling. Just something small, not too heavy, wouldn't be the end of the world.

She wasn't four feet from the car when her phone rang. It was Special Agent Vos. "That was quick," she said to Trent.

"Is that Vos already?"

She nodded and answered without putting it on speaker because they were in a public area.

"Getting my hands on the files turned out to be rather easy," Vos told her. "Did you want to meet somewhere?"

"You name the place. We're just on the outskirts of Hagerstown, Maryland, at the moment."

"That's about an hour and a half from Washington. It's about the same, fifteen minutes more, for you to get back to Woodbridge. How about I just meet you at your station?"

"Are you sure? You must have a lot on your plate."

"Always, but if the information I dug up can help you solve a thirty-one-year-old mystery, bring justice for a little girl, I can justify a drive."

"If you're sure..."

"I wouldn't say it if I wasn't."

Amanda was impressed by Vos's dedication and work ethic. "Incredible, then. Let's say two hours at Central?"

"See you then." Vos was the first to hang up.

"I'm going to guess we're on the move now," Trent said.

"Gold star goes to you. Vos already has the Jackson files for us. She's meeting us at Central in two hours."

"Then I still have enough time to pop in and grab myself a coffee before we hit the road."

"That you do. I'll take one too and that donut."

He turned to her. "Really?"

"It sounds rather good to me now." After speaking with Vos, her spirits were lifted. The ugliness of the notification had faded into a shade of acceptance.

"All right then." Trent smiled at her as they entered the bakery.

As she stepped into the warmth of the shop, Amanda inhaled deeply. In this moment, she resolved to let the Jacksons' grief propel her forward. Whoever had taken Sadie would pay for what they did.

FOURTEEN

Amanda dropped off two dozen donuts she'd bought on a whim and put them in the lunchroom at Central. Based on the satisfied groans of a few officers who had already bitten into one, her decision was a complete win. She considered selecting a donut for the agent, but wasn't familiar with her tastes. Or even if she ate gluten. Malone flagged her down on the way to her cubicle, and she entered his office.

"How did things go with the parents?" he asked her.

The question wasn't about how the Jacksons handled the news. It was about whether they ascertained any leads from talking to them. She responded based on the former, as if she were naive. "It was a tough notification, but at least they have closure."

Malone angled his head. "Any leads?"

"No, but we're expecting FBI Special Agent Vos to turn up any minute with the case files on the Sadie Jackson investigation."

"Oh?" His eyes got large. "She's coming here?"

Trent popped into the doorway, holding up his index finger. "The main conference room."

"I'd say she's here. Go," Malone told her. "Keep me in the loop."

"Will do." Amanda found Trent and Vos sitting at the table in conversation. She'd caught the tail end of it, but the words "they have a lot to process" and the tense energy suggested they'd been discussing the Jacksons. On the table were a few banker boxes, marked *Sadie Jackson* and the year she was taken.

"Special Agent Vos, thank you for coming and bringing all of this." Amanda gestured to the haul.

"Don't mention it. Like I said, I hope it helps."

"I don't see how it couldn't," Amanda said.

"Me either," Trent put in.

"Would you like water or coffee? Tea?" Amanda asked.

"I'm good. Any more coffee today, and my gut might rot right out." She flashed a fleeting smile. "So I didn't have time to familiarize myself with all of this personally, but I did speak to the lead agent who worked this case."

"Who is that?" Trent had a notepad in front of him and wrote as Vos told them the name.

"Leslie Foster. He's retired now, but he said he'd welcome your calls if you had any questions." Vos pulled out her phone. "Should I text his contact info to you?" She looked pointedly at Amanda.

"That would be great." She set her phone on the table, and a few seconds later it chimed with the information. "Thank you."

"Don't mention it. I have a teenager too, and I suppose this has me thinking about her safety. The world can be a scary place."

So Sandra Vos is a mother... "Which we get an up-close and personal look at on a regular basis."

"Sadly, that's the truth. We might as well get started here." Vos clasped her hands on the table. "Sadie Jackson, age eight, was taken from the amusement park. All of this you know. Also about that video that captured her leaving the park with a couple."

"Is that video in here somewhere?" Trent swirled his pen in the direction of the boxes.

"No, but my colleague from the Science and Technology Branch will be pulling it from the archive server and sending it over. Her name is Lakisha Hester. Where should I have her send the email?"

"You can have it sent to me," Trent said and provided his email address.

"I'll pass that along, but please allow her until the end of day tomorrow to get it pulled together before you follow up. Her hours can be all over the place."

"That's fine. I think we'll find a way to keep ourselves busy." Amanda understood things took time, and they wouldn't be twiddling their thumbs.

"That's never a problem." Vos offered a smile. "There were thousands of tips called in, and the Bureau did their best to follow every credible one. But since calls were already flooding in, the director made the decision not to publicize any still shots of the couple from the video."

The unspoken implication seemed to be *credible* was an assessment made on limited information and instinct. Mining the tips could reveal a valid one that was originally dismissed, but she understood the real-life limitations. "Manpower and money."

"You got it. I was told the video wasn't very clear either. The couple's looks are rather vague and generic. We are talking thirty-one years ago so technology wasn't where it is today. There should be still shots as pulled from the footage in these boxes. Pictures of Sadie are in there too. These would include ones shared through the media nationwide during an appeal to the public. That's what had the phone lines ringing off the hook with callers from all over the United States."

Recalling Sadie's bright little face had that ache returning in Amanda's chest. "Any of these calls from Prince William County?"

Vos shook her head. "I took a quick look before I came here."

That answer was a double-edged sword. If such a tip had been overlooked, it would be devastating. But the absence of one left them without direction.

Vos continued. "Agent Foster told me there was also footage taken from throughout the park. Lakisha will get you those videos as well. But the poor quality is something that unfortunately applies to all of it. Limitations in technology back then hindered this investigation. But we were able to confirm this couple followed the Jackson family for a while through the park. Since the place was crowded, the Jacksons didn't notice. For the most part they were holding the girl's hand and keeping her close. They said they let themselves get distracted for one moment."

"Looking for change to buy her ice cream." It was tragic how such a small thing resulted in Sadie's kidnapping. But that's all it took for life to change. One blink of an eye.

"That's right. You did some research?"

"The Jacksons told us that much," Amanda admitted. "Once they had scrounged the money together, they looked up and she was gone. The kidnappers took advantage of the crowds to walk off with her."

"Exactly what we believe happened."

"Who were considered as prime suspects?" Trent asked.

"No one was considered *prime*. Relatives, friends, and acquaintances of the Jacksons were heavily investigated and cleared, both by looks and alibis. Foster considered the possibility the couple kidnapped her for ransom or was hired to do so by someone close to the family."

Amanda couldn't see how the latter would fit with the girl's fate of assault and rape. Typically in ransom situations, kidnapped children were the strongest means of leverage. It wouldn't do the kidnappers any good to harm them. They certainly didn't hold on to them for eight years. There was also something else that stood out. "Why though? The Jacksons didn't strike me as having money. No ransom requests came, did they?"

"No, but it's just one example of how thorough this investigation was. Sadly, as we speculated then, and have confirmed now, Sadie was taken across several state lines making her movements that much more difficult to track."

Amanda was tossing around Vos's earlier words about the couple being hired to kidnap Sadie when a dark thought hit her. She might have been quick to dismiss one aspect. There was evidence of rape... "Could these people be tied up with a sex-trafficking ring?"

"It was considered. Oftentimes these predators take young girls and teens from outside of their areas because their abductions are less likely to tie back to them."

A few years ago, she and Trent, with the assistance of other PWCPD officers, took down a sex-trafficking ring in Prince William County with a reach to Washington, DC. Was Sadie Jackson an early victim of that very same organization? "Trent and I got an up-close look at one of these rings."

Vos scanned her eyes, then glanced at Trent. "The one that brought down Congressman Davis?"

"The very same," Amanda said.

"Wow, that's incredible. Well done."

"If only a million more weren't still out there." It was futile to believe eliminating all these monsters was even possible. But it was highly unlikely an organized ring would bury one of their girls in the walls of a church. Then again, often the worst kind of evil hid behind claims of being God-fearing.

"Well, I'm sure you know this, Detective, but in this line of work you must take the wins you can. There will always be sick people in this world."

"A cynic yet a realist. I respect that." An honest compliment.

"I like keeping things real." Sandra smiled. "In the end, though, a sex-trafficking ring was seen as less likely."

"Based on what?" She was curious about their conclusions.

"To start, her age. Though these perverts cater to all types. The case was examined by the FBI's BAU. That's the Behavioral Analysis Unit."

"We're familiar with it." Amanda glanced at Trent, knowing that was where his *buddy* Brandon Fisher worked.

"Based on their assessment, statistically when a girl Sadie's age is taken by a couple, it's more likely they lost a daughter or were unable to have children of their own. The couple from the video was estimated to be in their early thirties."

"Still, normal people don't go out and take someone else's kid," Trent put in.

Vos held up both her hands. "No argument here."

"When was the last time someone actually looked at this file?" Amanda asked.

"Ten years ago."

Which was still too late to help Sadie... "Is there anything else we should know?"

"That's all I got from Leslie Foster. I have no doubts you're likely to uncover far more from digging in." Vos got up and tucked her chair under the table.

For some reason, the conclusion of this meeting stamped home the finality for the Jacksons. Amanda easily recalled their broken expressions when she and Trent left them, the way the mother reached out and hugged her as if searching for the strength to take her next breath. "Since the Jacksons live in

Maryland and the case was originally FBI, I was wondering if you have victim counselors you could send out to them."

"Absolutely. I'll get that arranged. You have my word on that."

"Thank you." Amanda got up and shook the agent's hand. Like the first time, Vos had a firm, confident grip, and kept eye contact throughout.

"You're welcome, but thanking me isn't necessary. I hope you get these people."

"Me too," Amanda said.

Vos left the room, and Trent looked at Amanda. "Should we dig in?"

She woke the screen on her cell phone, and it was four fifty. She had a decision, and tonight it seemed an easier one to make. "Actually, I should probably call it a night."

Trent stopped all movement. He'd just removed the lid from one of the boxes. "I understand."

She knew he would, but she didn't need his approval or understanding. "I should at least get home to Zoe for dinner one night this week."

"Hey, I totally get it."

"I'll see you tomorrow first thing?"

"You got it, but if you don't mind, I'm going to stay and work some on this. I'd at least like to find that photograph of the couple. Even if it doesn't really tell us anything."

"If you're willing to do that, wonderful." She wanted to catch a look at the mystery couple too, even if it was out of focus. A part of her wished she'd see it and magically gain clarity. But she also knew if she saw them before heading home, their fuzzy images would beckon her to stay.

"Consider it done. I'll stay until my eyes cross."

"Well, that's not necessary." She surprised herself by giving Trent an out. Could it be she was starting to understand and appreciate some work-life balance? Though she shook that aside. Making the decision she had tonight didn't mean she had things under control. If anything, the opposite. Evil things happened, and no matter how hard she worked, she could never stop all of it. And sometimes she needed to step back and breathe.

FIFTEEN

Trent dug into the files the moment Amanda turned her back to leave the room. He should have joined her in calling it a night. He had plans to Netflix and Chill with Kelsey tonight, but she'd understand. Or would she? It was just two days from Valentine's, and he hadn't arranged a thing. He could blame it on this case, but the holiday came the same time every year. Work had been slow recently too. He'd had time to book her favorite restaurant weeks ago and plan some sort of grand romantic gesture. It wasn't a good look, especially as it was their first Valentine's as a couple.

Two minutes... That's all it would take to make the reservation. He pried his gaze from the boxes and looked up the site for the restaurant on his phone. He called and waited impatiently while it rang four times. Just when he was about to give up, they answered.

"Chez François."

Kelsey's palate was much more refined than his. He was happy with a burger and a beer, or steak and a glass of wine. Her favorite culinary pleasure was fine French cuisine. When she'd found out he'd never had escargot or frog legs, she started talking about how they needed to start saving for a trip to France. Laughing off her suggestion with the admission he didn't know any French had done little to curb her enthusiasm. "You can let me do the talking," she'd said. He didn't remember what transpired from there, but thankfully the matter got dropped and they'd gone on to something else. He didn't have the heart to admit he wasn't a fan of flying and didn't see a voyage across the Atlantic in his future. Going to this restaurant would be a stab at compromise. He might even stick those *things* in his mouth. "I'd like to reserve a table for two for Friday night."

"What's the date for that Friday, monsieur?"

Is this guy for real? "Ah, this Friday, the fourteenth."

There was a prolonged silence, then, *"Dans deux jours?"*

"I don't speak French, but I'd like a table for Valentine's Day."

More static followed by an arrogant snuff of derision. "You must be joking, *monsieur*. Practical joke, *oui*?"

This guy was inching wildly close to being verbally throttled. "Listen, you either have a table or you don't."

"Ma non, impossible." The word rolled off his tongue as ampos-eeb-le. "I could happily reserve you a table for the Friday three weeks from now. Will that day work for you?"

Trent became a touch feverish. "Are you sure there's no availability for this Friday? It would mean a lot to my girlfriend to eat there."

"Oui, monsieur, as it means a lot to those who thought ahead and booked months ago."

Months ago... Even though the news was delivered at the point of a dagger, it alleviated Trent's conscience. There's no way he could have known he'd need to book that far in advance.

"Monsieur?" the man prompted with a huff of impatience.

If not for Kelsey, he might tell this man to take the table three Fridays from now and put it where the sun didn't shine.

He thought of the future, how dinner there in three weeks might make up for his failure to come through on Valentine's Day. "I'll take that other reservation."

"*Très bon*. Name, *monsieur*?"

Trent left his name and number, and the man sounded pleased when he said, "*Voilà!*" before hanging up.

"Unbelievable," Trent mumbled to the dead line. He'd be letting Kelsey down on Valentine's Day, and now he needed to tell her the investigation was keeping him late tonight. A white lie when he could have cut out. The reason he hadn't was to stop Amanda staying out of a sense of obligation. She deserved a full night with Zoe. He picked Kelsey's number from his contacts.

"Hey, handsome," she answered, cutting the second ring short.

"Hey, beautiful." It was the way they spoke to each other, their "couple" thing. "So, I'm calling because I have bad news about tonight."

"Oh?"

Just one word with no emotion or judgment attached. Just simple, pure curiosity. It was an aspect of Kelsey's personality that he adored. "I need to work a bit longer tonight, so we're going to need to push our plans. Possibly call for a raincheck."

"That's fine. It was just some TV and popcorn."

"And wine, which you love."

"I won't let your absence stop me from pouring a glass, but it was my night to pick the movies. Don't tell me that has something to do with your canceling?" she teased.

He wasn't too proud to admit that he liked a good rom-com from *time to time*. He drew the line at musicals. "Your picks will just roll over to next time."

"I'll hold you to that." Her smile traveled the line. "I take from talk of *roll over* and *raincheck*, you're not sure when you'll be home?"

"Yet, I'm the detective." Trent looked at the spread of boxes. He'd helped Agent Vos carry in two of them, and they had heft. "I suspect late. I wouldn't suggest waiting up."

"All right then. I'll miss you. But at least we have Valentine's Day to look forward to."

"That we do." He nearly choked on the words and ended the call thinking he wouldn't be winning an award for being a good boyfriend anytime soon. There were times when he wondered what Kelsey saw in him. Not that he had low self-worth. Most people would describe him as good-looking, but more importantly, he valued honesty, respect, responsibility, and compassion. What he couldn't offer was culture or money. Kelsey was well-traveled, worldly, and wealthy. His roots were humble. Yet, she never made it seem like these differences mattered to her. He wondered if that might change over time.

There was a knock on the door of the conference room, and Trent looked up to see Malone.

"Amanda go home?"

"She did."

"Huh. How did it go with the FBI agent?" Malone stepped into the room, and Trent gave him the overview. When he'd finished, Malone was looking deep in thought. *Worried* might even be a more apt description. "Well, do what you must and head home. I don't need to tell you the department isn't a fan of paying out overtime."

"I understand." And he did. He sacrificed his night with Kelsey and might not even earn a buck in compensation. But if he found something in all this paperwork it would be worth it.

"Night." Malone tapped the doorframe on his way out.

"Night," Trent echoed, and got to work.

SIXTEEN

Amanda had the most amazing night with Zoe. Since she'd missed out on pizza night, which was everyone else's Taco Tuesday, when she'd arrived home, she announced it was Pizza Night the Second. It had been met with rave response. Zoe had squealed and jumped up and down around her. They both ended up on the couch folded over in laughter. When it was time for bed, Zoe let her read *a little bit* to her before she groaned and said, "I really am too old for this now." Amanda's argument that lots of adults read every night didn't have any impact. Zoe argued that they didn't have people read *to them*. Point made.

For the hours she was with her girl, she was able to push thoughts of Sadie and the Jacksons out of her mind and really be present. The only time that bubble popped was when Malone had called to check on her well-being after hearing she'd cut out early. While she appreciated his concern, she wished he'd waited until the next day to talk to her. But as a friend of her father's from before her birth, he was as much family as he was her sergeant. She assured him she was fine, and sold herself that belief. And Zoe had set about healing her, even though she was unaware of her skill.

That sweet, special girl...

Amanda was still smiling at the memories on the way to her desk the next morning, a tray with two coffees from Hannah's Diner in hand. One for herself, and the other for Trent. She had dropped Zoe off at school and still had plenty of time to hit the coffee shop. Though calling it that didn't seem to cover it anymore. Their menu had expanded quite a bit since the owner, May Byrd, was joined by her niece and Amanda's friend, Katherine Graves, who had a knack for online advertising. Her efforts were so successful, they'd taken on some full-time staff to help with increased business.

Amanda shrugged out of her coat, and her gaze landed on her desk. Sitting on top of her notepad was a small stack of photographs. The one on top was rather fuzzy. Absentmindedly, she reached out and hung her coat on the hook next to her, set down the coffee tray, and picked up the pile of pictures.

In the top one, little Sadie was holding a man's hand and an ice cream sandwich to her mouth with the other. A woman was at Sadie's other side, but clearly with the man. This shot captured her reaching over and playfully batting his shoulder. It struck as a sickening display of victory.

"Good morning." Trent came in, and she was pleased to see that he was empty-handed.

"Here you go." She plucked one of the cups from the holder and handed it to him over the partition.

"For me?"

"For you. I appreciate what you did last night." The fact he had stayed late so she could justify going home meant the world to her.

"Work *our* case?" He narrowed his eyes, scrunching up his forehead. "Just doing my job."

"You know what you did for me. Thank you."

He held her gaze and said, "You're welcome." He let a few seconds pass, then said, "I see you received my gift?" He nudged to the photos in her hand.

She lifted them up. "I did. They really aren't that clear, as they told us." She looked at it again. A man and woman of average height and average looks. The woman was wearing a souvenir shirt from the park. The shape of the mascot's head was all that gave it away. It was understandable why the FBI hadn't wanted to publicize the photograph.

"None of the rest are much better, unfortunately."

She shuffled through the others, picking out the forms of the man and woman at a distance behind the Jacksons. The background imagery changed, and it confirmed they had been following them. What was it about Sadie Jackson that had made her a target? It was no doubt a question that the FBI had bounced around for years, one mystery that was never solved. If it had been, Sadie might still be alive. "We need to make what we have work. I have every intention of identifying these people and putting them behind bars for the rest of their lives."

"And I plan on being right there with you."

"Did you have anything else to share with me from the files?"

"I mostly sorted the contents of the boxes into categories. The tips and investigative notes attached to each in a pile, another with the written list of evidence and accompanying photographs, and a third stack of suspects who were questioned regarding her disappearance. I read some of these, and of what I did, it was clear none of them took Sadie."

"Well, Vos said everyone was cleared. What do they have for evidence though?"

"Videos that we have coming, and the photographs from them that you're holding. There was also a notation of what Sadie was wearing that day. That being white shorts, a blue T-shirt, marble-beaded elastics, a pink barrette, and blue jelly bangles."

Like the ones she was entombed with... The rest of the description brought the photo she'd seen online back into clarity. "She was with the same people from the moment they took her. They held her and kept her secret from the world."

Trent nodded. "And it's most likely they were associated with the church."

"Right, so if they were in their thirties then, by the FBI's best estimate, they'd be in their sixties today. We could use that to narrow down the list of members tied to the church twenty-three years ago." She set the photos aside and grabbed the list. "We need to pull the backgrounds on the remaining members, paying no heed to whether they are couples or not. As you said before, only one half of the partnership may have been involved in the church. It's more work but..."

"We do what we have to do."

She nodded, pleased that she was paired with such a hard-working partner. She'd had a string of partners before Trent but none of them stuck for various reasons. In her career, she'd observed not everyone was wired with the *sacrifice* mentality. Some in law enforcement viewed the work as their day job. The good cops saw it as their *calling*. Like she did. Like Trent did.

She dropped into her chair and ripped a few pages from the printout and gave them to Trent. "Just the ones I circled," she told him.

"You got it."

She got to work on her names and stopped cold on the Cofells. Doug and Winnie. The situation at the church that led to Sadie's discovery was due to their son's actions. He essentially accused them of abuse. *Sadie's body told that story...*

Was Amanda searching for a link that wasn't there?

She brought up the backgrounds on the Cofells despite knowing they were dead. Their records confirmed they died three years ago in a car accident. Both had been in their early sixties. The skin at the back of her neck started tingling. That would place them in their thirties when Sadie was kidnapped.

Amanda looked at their photographs on file with the Department of Motor Vehicles. They were both nondescript, of average looks and average height, per their noted measurements. The woman had blond hair with a silverish glow in her license photo opposed to the darker hair of the woman with Sadie and the man leaving the park. But this didn't rule her out. The way many women colored their hair, it was hardly conclusive. The man's hair had also lightened with age. But the shape of their faces was very similar to the video surveillance photos from the park. Could it be that the Cofells were behind Sadie's abduction and murder?

She looked over at Trent's cubicle but decided to set aside her suspicions and carry on with pulling the rest of the backgrounds. But no one else on her list stacked up the same. "Ah, Trent. How are you coming along?"

"On the last one, but so far, nothing helpful. How did you make out on your end?"

"Much better, I believe. Come take a look." She had placed the photographs of the Cofells side by side on her screen. When Trent joined her, she held up the clearest picture of the couple who had taken Sadie.

"Huh." He turned to look at her, and she faced him. Their noses were close to touching. "Sorry," he said and pulled back. "That could be them. Who are they?"

"Meet Doug and Winnie Cofell."

"Huh." Trent crossed his arms, letting out the guttural sound for the second time in less than a few seconds. "But they're dead."

"They weren't thirty-one years ago."

Trent bobbed his head.

"I realize that the chances of this are astronomical," she said, "but Cameron claims his parents abused him. We've talked about it, and we believe him."

"Then it just so happens that Cameron holds Father Linwood at gunpoint in Herald Church, where Sadie's body is inadvertently discovered behind a wall in the nave. Where the Cofells were long-time members."

"And Doug had a key." Excitement raced through her.

"But if the Cofells took Sadie," Trent said, "where does that leave the investigation? They are dead, far outside the realms of human justice. If they did this, though, I hope they're burning in hell right now."

If one existed, it was the least they deserved. But none of this changed things for her and Trent. "We need to build a case, see if the evidence incriminates them. And I say we start by talking to Cameron to find out everything he knows."

"You think he knew about Sadie, and about her being in the wall?"

"I'd say no because of his age, but we still need to speak with him."

"I get that."

"There's also the matter of the Cofells' estate. It had to go somewhere. We find out who inherited and see if any of their things are still kicking around. What we find could either remove our suspicions or confirm them."

"Let's get started."

SEVENTEEN

Cameron Cofell was being held in the cells waiting for his arraignment. The officer in charge down there warned Amanda and Trent that Cameron wasn't talkative. Amanda insisted on giving questioning him a go anyhow. While he was being brought to an interview room, she paced in the neighboring observation room. Every few steps she'd look through the one-way mirror, expecting Cameron to be escorted through the door any minute. After what felt like a long time, he finally arrived.

He'd only been in a cell two nights, and yet he looked haggard, as if he'd been in there months. His hair was disheveled, and his fierce green eyes contained a storm. A trace remained of his natural good looks. Square jaw, firm lips, and the hint of dimples.

Amanda took all this in as she sat across from him in the interview room. He barely flicked her, or Trent next to her, a glance.

"I'm Detective Amanda Steele." She provided her first name to set Cameron at ease. The more relaxed he was, the more likely he was to talk with them.

Not a look or so much as a grunt.

"This is Detective Trent Stenson," she said. "We have some questions about your parents, Doug and Winnie."

Now he lifted his gaze to take her in. His eyes scanned hers and danced over her and landed briefly on Trent. "I've said everything I feel like sayin'."

"We appreciate talking about them and the past must be difficult for you." She could only imagine that it would be. Thankfully she wasn't pulling from personal experience on this one. "But we believe you."

He didn't say anything but continued the strong eye contact.

"They weren't good parents, and I'm sorry that you had a rough childhood." Her sentiment was genuine, and Cameron must have felt that.

His posture softened a little, and he shrugged. "It wasn't your fault. *You* had no idea."

Amanda picked up on the emphasis. While she might have been in the dark regarding Cameron's suffering, others weren't and had done nothing to step up and save him. Namely Father Linwood. She opened a folder she'd brought in with her and pulled out the photograph showing the couple leaving the Florida park with Sadie Jackson. She set it in front of Cameron. "Do these people look familiar to you?" She tapped a fingertip to each of them in turn.

He glanced at them, and she expected him to say something about the image being fuzzy, but he reacted quickly. He swept the photo off the table.

Amanda glanced at Trent. *Strong reaction.* Something about the man and woman triggered him. Did he see the similarities to Doug and Winnie like she and Trent had? Did he *know* it was them? "Cameron, can you tell us who those people are?"

Trent retrieved the picture from the floor and set it on the table again.

"No!" Cameron roared. "Get them out of my face! I *hate* them," he spat with venom.

"Who are they?" she tried again, posing the question in a soft manner, not letting him see that his outburst affected her at all.

"*Them*," he hissed. "And I hate them." When his eyes met hers this time, they were ablaze.

She hated to pressure him anymore as he was clearly suffering. Just looking at their faces seemed to have set him back in time. But she needed him to confirm who they were. "They mean something to you?"

"They hurt me."

"Who are they to you?" The repetition was draining, but she'd stick with it as long as it took. Once Cameron realized she wasn't backing down, he might identify them.

"Mom and Dad." The titles came off his lips with disdain, and when his eyes met hers this time, she saw pain interspersed with anger.

"Doug and Winnie?" She had his statement but wanted to clarify it for the record. Not that she was sure how this interview might ever come up in a legal sense. With the Cofells dead, if they had taken Sadie, there would never be a trial. An earthly one anyhow. As for whether there was another kind, she had no clue.

"Yes, and they hurt me. They probably hurt her. That girl. She was so beautiful."

Was... Amanda picked up on a subtle flavor to his voice beyond the past tense. Had he known she was in the church wall? "You knew her?"

"I think she was my sister."

Tingles laced Amanda's arms. Their suspicions were gaining merit. "You had a sister?"

"Uh-huh. They didn't tell me about her. I didn't even know about her until I found a picture years ago."

"And you're sure she was your sister?" Her heart was picking up speed as her stomach clenched.

"Yes."

Amanda took out a photograph of Sadie from the day she'd been taken, that had been provided by the Jacksons. This picture was in focus.

Cameron looked at it, and the room became still and silent. Though it might as well have been thunder. "So this is her?" she prompted after a few seconds.

Cameron blinked slowly. "I think so, but she looked different in the picture I found."

"In what ways?" Trent asked.

"She was older, and her hair was poofy."

"Like it was teased, or backcombed?" she added.

"Yeah."

Again, a style that predated Sadie, but Winnie could have done that to the girl's hair. "Was there anything else different about her in the picture?"

"I dunno. She was standing and had blue bangles like those." Cameron pointed toward the woman's wrist in the photo.

She looked closer at the photograph, and Trent leaned in too. Sure enough, the blue bangles were on the woman's wrist and Sadie's were bare. Winnie Cofell had not only taken Sadie from her parents but relieved her of her bangles, all within minutes. Amanda imagined her talking soothingly to the girl, complimenting them, and asking if she could wear them. It would ingratiate her with the girl and set her at ease. Sadie would have thought she was making friends. First, the ice cream, then the compliment. The back of Amanda's neck tingled, and a fresh batch of goosebumps shot out from her shoulders and down her arms.

"What made the bangles stand out to you?" Trent asked, his voice low and gentle as if he were tiptoeing across landmines.

"The girl wore them all the time. There were lots of pictures with her wearing them. Is that girl my sister?"

"Her name is Sadie Jackson."

"Jackson?" Cameron's brow pinched.

"That's right. She was taken from an amusement park in Orlando, Florida, when she was just eight years old." Amanda let that sit there, curious if Cameron would fit the pieces together.

"No, no, that's not possible." He was shaking his head.

"Sadie was wearing blue bangles when she was taken." Amanda pointed them out in the Jacksons' photo of Sadie.

"What are you saying?"

She thought her message was clear, but given all Cameron had been through in his life, he had likely slipped into denial. One more thing could be enough to tip him to insanity, even past the point where he had decided to hold the priest hostage. "We believe your mother and father, Doug and Winnie Cofell, kidnapped Sadie Jackson thirty-one years ago. They held her for eight years. We found her in Herald Church after you and Father Linwood were taken away."

"In the church?" Cameron bit down on his bottom lip, his teeth burrowing deeply and puckering the flesh.

"Yes, in the wall of the nave, where your bullet hit," Amanda said.

"I had no idea she was in there." His eyes wet with tears.

Cameron was just a baby when Sadie was killed, but he might have discovered her fate after the fact. She had to find out if he was holding back from them. "Did you know what happened to your sister?"

Cameron shook his head. "I never met her, just saw her pictures."

Suddenly, it clicked. Amanda was quaking as it sank in. She remembered Officer Wyatt's words when they'd first asked about the hostage taker. *Cameron Cofell, twenty-three.* Sadie was killed when she was sixteen years old, twenty-three years ago. Not long after giving birth. The young man across from her was twenty-three. Could it be...?

"She's dead though?" Cameron pushed out. "Did *they* kill her?"

Amanda had less doubt with every passing second. "Did your parents ever talk about her, tell you what happened to her?"

"Long brown hair, blue eyes, face like an angel..." Cameron started rocking back and forth.

Amanda assumed that he must be describing her picture. But what about that had him so upset? It was common to find unfamiliar faces among family albums. "You seem very shaken about this memory, Cameron. Why did the pictures upset you?"

"When I asked about her, they—" He swallowed roughly. "I was punished and told to mind my own business and get out of their things."

Amanda hated that they were forcing Cameron into his past, but there was no way around that. "Where did you find the photos?"

Cameron's eyes took on a distant glaze, and he trembled. "The hidden space."

Nothing ominous about that... "Where is that?"

"In a hole in hell," he said, talking in code.

"Which is where?" she asked.

"Where I grew up."

"The farmhouse?" Trent asked.

Cameron nodded.

"What happened to that house?" Now that they had the Cofells in mind, this was something they could look up in public records, but Cameron might be able to save them the trouble. What they had found out while waiting on Cameron to be brought in for questioning was that the halfway house where he was staying had been court-ordered on his release from prison.

He shrugged. "I wouldn't want it."

Amanda couldn't blame him given all the horrid memories that place would hold for him. But she remembered Vos mentioning one blood relative. Winnie's brother. *Sean Olsen, was it?* She'd have to check their notes. The estate could have passed to him. "Could your uncle have inherited it?"

"Uncle?" Cameron's brow wrinkled like he had a headache. "I don't have an uncle."

Amanda looked at Trent, and he bobbed his head. He'd heard enough for now too.

She got up and said to Cameron, "Thank you for talking to us. You were a big help."

They left Cameron and found Malone next door in the observation room.

"How long have you been here?" she asked him.

"Long enough." Malone's admission came with a sour expression.

"He endured hell, that's for sure," she said.

Malone nodded. "Him and Sadie Jackson, but I can't give too much thought to it. And I guess that's case closed. The Cofells took Sadie Jackson, held her, killed her, but they're dead, so nothing much we can do."

She appreciated the need to skip over the sordid details. "We haven't proved it was them beyond doubt. Leave no stone unturned. Isn't that the way things should be done? We owe it to Sadie and the Jacksons to see this through."

"I'm sure forensics findings will back it all up, but I'm not sure if it's a priority case for you now. The feds might even prefer to take it back off our hands." Malone drilled her with a look, one she was familiar with that was tightly linked to budgetary constraints, but she wasn't going to back down.

"I disagree. We have more to follow through. Like the

photos Cameron found. If we can put them in the Cofells' hands, even better."

"He just identified Doug and Winnie Cofell as the couple leaving that park with Sadie," Malone said firmly. "That does it for me."

"I agree it's compelling, but it's not conclusive." She squared her shoulders. "Cameron is a victim of abuse, and his viewpoint could be prejudiced."

"Then why even talk to him?" Malone volleyed back.

"I'm not saying he's completely unreliable, but we can't just rush to close this case without more. I have no doubt the Cofells took Sadie, but did they kill her? We don't have anything to back that up. What if it wasn't them and her killer is still out there? Would you want another victim on your conscience? Because I don't."

Malone's facial expression softened a micro amount, and she knew she'd finally landed on a point that made impact. "Of course not, but you must admit it's most likely this ends with the Cofells."

She shrugged. "I can't afford to do that. If they didn't kill her, then that person continues to be free to do it again, and again, and a—"

Malone held up a hand. "I get it. Fine. Check out this farmhouse. See who owns it now, or where the Cofells' things might have gone."

"Thank you." She should probably just take the victory and move on, but there was more weighing on her mind. "I thought of something else while speaking with Cameron. It just came to me, and I was surprised it hadn't already. But he's twenty-three, the same number of years that Sadie was in that wall."

Trent nodded at her. "Came to me too."

"Anyone care to enlighten me?" Malone raised his eyebrows.

"Sadie had a baby. If Amanda's thinking what I am, she could be his mother." Trent looked over at her.

"Yep, exactly what I thought. We should get a sample of Cameron's DNA and compare it to Sadie Jackson's and see if they're a match." She looked at Malone, seeking authorization to proceed in that regard.

"Fine. Get it done," Malone said on a sigh.

She smiled at him. "Thanks."

"Uh-huh." With that, Malone left them.

What if right here was as far as they got with this case? There was nothing to say any solid evidence remained.

In the hidden space...

She shook, trying to release the negative energy doing its best to burrow beneath her skin. A series of shivers traveled down her spine. "We'll get Cameron's DNA for that comparison, and in the meantime also look into adoption records and see if we can prove whether he ever was adopted. If none exist, it's more likely he's Sadie's child, off the record."

"Sure, we'll do it all." Trent was nodding.

"I just feel Sadie's his mother in the deepest parts of me. Doug Cofell is probably his biological father." She glanced at her partner, curious how he might be looking at her. Like she'd lost her mind trusting her gut so heavily, or like he respected that she did? The softness in his eyes had her believing the latter.

"I'm not dismissing it," he said. "We also need to confirm who the Cofell estate passed on to. Did it go to the uncle? An uncle Cameron didn't even know about? And what's the situation there anyway? I have the guy's number and can give him a call. It might save us the trouble of looking up what happened to the estate through public records. We probably want to speak with him anyhow."

"Do it."

He pulled his phone and did just that. A few seconds later, he ducked into the hallway, and she followed him. The one-sided dialogue told her he was leaving a message.

Her phone pinged with a text from CSI Blair. *Check your email.*

"I had to leave a voicemail," Trent said from behind her.

"I gathered. I just got a message from Blair, and she told me to check my email." She could do this on her phone but since she was at Central, she decided to return to her desk and read it on her computer instead.

"Sounds mysterious. I'm in." He smiled and bumped his shoulder against hers teasingly as he took up walking next to her.

At her desk, she pulled up Blair's email. Its subject was *Evidence in Jackson case.* Straightforward. Amanda opened it and scanned down the message.

Wood slivers were recovered from the victim's clothing.

Victim's and three additional DNA contributors on her dress. Two male, one female. All unknown.

Epithelium taken from under her nails. DNA contributor matches one male profile from victim's dress.

Victim's and DNA belonging to an unknown female in the shoes. Not a match to the female profile on the dress.

Touch DNA on body. Two profiles, matching the male DNA contributions from her dress.

"Trent," that was all Amanda could say. The list on the screen was small but telling. Lots of DNA, but she was fixated on one tidbit. "Three DNA profiles on her dress. Even if two are a match to Doug and Winnie Cofell, that leaves an unknown male still out there."

EIGHTEEN

The forensic findings just made this case far more urgent. Even if they proved beyond doubt that the Cofells had taken Sadie, held on to her, assaulted her, killed her, and buried her, there was a third party out there. But where were they? Who were they? Were they still alive? What was the extent of their involvement in the murder and disposal of Sadie? Did this person have another victim now, or were they stalking one? Amanda was determined to find the answer to every one of those questions. She sent a thank-you text to Blair.

"It has to be someone close to Doug and Winnie Cofell, a trusted friend or family member," Trent theorized. "Someone from the church. Or the uncle? What's to say he stopped hanging around after her murder? Cameron would have been a baby, and it could explain why he has no knowledge of him."

"It very well could. This uncle could be the mystery man we're looking for, the one the second male DNA contribution belongs to. Let's go chat with Malone, tell him what we just learned, and then get on with things." She led the way to his office.

Malone was behind his desk and quickly swiped a pair of readers from his nose and waved them in. "You guys miss me?"

The glasses were new. His quick abandonment of them told her he wasn't comfortable with them yet. She'd let mention of them pass. For now. "We have some news." She filled him in on Blair's email, putting special emphasis on this second male DNA profile.

"Hmph. Okay, so even if two of those profiles are a match to the Cofells, there's an unknown party."

"That's right. A man. He was likely involved with Sadie's murder and disposal of her body," she said.

"It goes without saying, but finding this person needs to take priority."

"We're going to have a chat with the uncle," Trent began.

"Seems like a solid place to start."

"We'll also need the Cofells' DNA." Amanda had been giving this some thought. It was probably a long shot to get an exhumation for their bodies approved at this point, but she had to bring it up.

"Are you suggesting we exhume their bodies? I can tell you that's not happening at this juncture. Besides, you must suspect this uncle may be involved, likely that second male DNA contribution?"

"We've discussed that possibility," Amanda admitted.

"Get his DNA. That should tell us if he's involved or a relation to another contribution. Which side does he belong to?"

"He's Winnie Cofell's brother," Trent said.

"All right, but until you get us more, a judge won't approve a warrant for his DNA. He'd have to volunteer it, but if you can't get him to, it still may not be the end of the world. We'll be getting Cameron's DNA to confirm paternity, but his could also show a familial match to one of the contributors. A look through the Cofells' things should give you their DNA."

"It's a jumping point anyhow," Trent said.

"Sure. Technically without knowing a contribution one hundred percent came from them, it wouldn't stand up in court. But I think there's the school of logic we can apply here."

"There is some leeway," she agreed.

"I hope you're not fixed on an exhumation though. If you are, I'd let it go. We won't go there unless all other avenues are exhausted."

"I hear you." She turned to leave, Trent with her.

"I suppose that sounded harsh," Malone said, causing her to stop and turn around.

"You're right." As much as she thought of the Cofells as monsters, there was a chance they hadn't killed Sadie. After being kidnapped, she could have run away and found further trouble. Amanda wouldn't want the graves of her family disturbed without resounding evidence to justify doing so. Though, the strong reaction Cameron had when he saw the picture of the couple with Sadie was fresh in her mind.

"Actually, Detective," Malone said, netting her attention. "I realize you've got a lot on your plate, and there is some urgency to this case now. Is there anything I can help with?"

"You could look up Cameron's adoption history, see if you can find the record of it," she said.

"I can squeeze that in. No stone unturned." He smiled at her, and she returned the expression.

"And..."

Malone angled his head. "I'm not doing everything for you."

"Just one more thing. Handle the collection of Cameron Cofell's DNA for testing."

"All right, but that's where I draw the line. Now get out of my office." He waved her off with a subtle grin.

The other detectives under his supervision probably wouldn't have gotten that or the offer to help. He'd give it if asked, but he wouldn't make himself available like he did to her.

Nepotism had its perks. She turned around at the doorway. "By the way, the glasses suit you."

Malone grumbled, and she laughed. She never thought of him as vain, but it seemed the eyewear was a hit to his pride.

In the hall, she joined Trent, who had stopped to wait for her.

"Do we just head over to the uncle's?" he said.

"Yeah. Let's do it. And we'd do good to remember he could have been involved with Sadie's murder," she pointed out.

"You don't need to remind me."

They swooped by their desks to grab their coats, and the phone on her desk was ringing. "Detective Steele," she answered and found that her caller was an officer from the front desk.

"There's a woman here who insists on talking to the investigating detectives on the 'girl-in-the-wall case.' Her words. She says she knows something you'll want to hear."

"Trent and I will be up in a minute." Amanda hung up and narrowed her eyes at Trent. "There's someone at the front wanting to speak with us about the Jackson case. Apparently, this woman has a lead for us and somehow, she knows the victim was a girl."

NINETEEN

A white-haired woman was standing near the front desk, and the officer who had called Amanda nudged her head toward her.

Amanda approached. "Ma'am?" The older woman turned and faced Amanda. "You wanted to speak with the detectives on the case involving the body found at Herald Church?"

"Yes." Her voice was fragile, possibly due to age, but Amanda also sensed nerves. She was juggling an umbrella and the handles of her purse in one hand. "A teenage girl, right? That's what the news is now saying, anyway."

"That's right." Disappointed the explanation of her knowledge was as simple as that. "I'm Detective Amanda Steele, and this is Detective Trent Stenson. Who are you?"

"Audrey Witherspoon."

"Pleased to meet you, Audrey. How about we talk in a more private setting?" Amanda suggested.

"That would be great. Thank you."

Amanda took Audrey to a room that served as an informal interview room. It would seem since Audrey made the effort to come here, she had her mind made up to talk to them, but this would help ease any second thoughts that might arise.

"Oh, this is lovely." She stepped through the doorway into the space that was set up much like a living room. There was a couch and two soft chairs, a few coffee tables, a small credenza with a pod coffee maker and associated paraphernalia including creamer and milk that didn't require refrigeration.

"Would you like a coffee or tea?" Amanda believed there were instant pods there for both.

"No, but thank you for the offer."

"Sit wherever you'd be comfortable," Amanda told her.

Audrey dropped onto the couch and set her umbrella and purse on the cushion beside her.

Amanda and Trent took the chairs.

"I've lived next door to Herald Church for most of my life," Audrey began. "For fifty-one years. It was the first house my husband, Bert, and I bought. And the last. But we were lucky to afford it right after our marriage. We had worked hard to save up though, I tell ya."

"It's lovely when you find a place you can make your home." Amanda was being genuine, but she was anxious as to where this conversation was leading. "And fifty-one years? Wow."

"Yes, well, my Bert's been gone for six years now, but we spent forty-five years together there. I'm probably oversharing. It's just that I want you to understand before I tell you what I must that I've been there for a long time."

There was something in the glint of her eye and mention of *long time* that had Amanda stiffening. She'd have been there when the renovations were done on the church. Had she seen something? "You must have been around when the church did some construction work?"

"You bet I was. That was twenty-some years ago, but I still recall the racket. More than usual too. As much as I loved my house, I was never a fan of Sundays. All that gospel music and the choir singing. It would seep out of that building like the walls were made of gauze." Audrey's gaze fell when she said *walls*, and she fussed with the long skirt she wore. She ran a hand over her lap, smoothing the material over her knees. "I've always been a light sleeper. It used to drive Bert somethin' mad. I was always nudging him awake at some sound or other. He was pretty good about tolerating it, but this one night he had a long day at work and was really tired. He told me to go back to sleep, and I tried, but the tone he took with me made me so angry." She paused there, her gaze taking on a distant look. It captured what Amanda imagined was nostalgia. She bet the woman would take him back even if he aggravated her. "Anyway, I got up, went downstairs, and investigated what I heard. I found two cats fighting in the garden beneath our second-level bedroom. I should have known. The sound was horrendous. Like screeches of the dead. Startled my heart, I tell you. But I let it go. Nothing to worry about, but I wasn't getting back to sleep, so I made myself a cup of tea and took it to the living room. I opened the window for some fresh air. That's when I saw something else."

Amanda hadn't noticed until then that she had edged forward on her chair. The woman's elaborate storytelling had drawn her in. Like any good mystery, it had Amanda longing for the ending. Would the reveal have been worth the investment of her time? Or Trent's? But she dared not interrupt the woman when it sounded like she was just getting around to the good part.

"What did you see?" Trent asked, a slight note of impatience to his voice, possibly not as captivated by the buildup. What Amanda hoped would result in a lead.

"Two men heading toward the church," Audrey said solemnly. "It was around two in the morning at that time. They were carrying a wooden crate, and they seemed to be having a hard time with it. Like it was really heavy."

A wooden crate? Blair had found wood slivers on Sadie's body. Were the two connected, or was all this a coincidence? "How big was it?"

"Large enough for a body, if that's what you're getting at."

That was exactly what Amanda was thinking, but she hadn't expected her to go right there. "It's been a long time, but could you tell us approximately how big it was?"

"At least four feet long, two wide, and a foot or so deep. It took two men to haul it," she reiterated.

Sadie Jackson would have fit in something even smaller than that considering the section of wall she'd been crammed into. "Did you do anything or ask these men what they were doing?"

"You bet I asked what they were doing messing about during the witching hours. I said they should go home, that it was far too late to be doing construction on the church. They told me they were just dropping off some tools and supplies for the next day."

"I get the feeling you didn't believe them," Trent said.

"No, dear, I did not. Not one iota, but what was I to do about it? I certainly never imagined that they would have had the body of a girl in there." Audrey sniffled and reached into her purse. She came out with a used, bunched-up tissue, and dabbed it to her nose. "I wish I had done something more then. If I had..."

"We don't know that they were transporting a body or not, but if they were, you did the right thing. You could have gotten hurt or worse." Her heart was thumping, and her mind getting carried away. Did they actually have an eyewitness related to the disposal of Sadie's body? "It's clear that you weren't satisfied by what they gave you as a reason for being out there. Did you ever mention this to anyone else, report what you saw to the police?"

"And tell them what? That's what Bert said, as well as

telling me to mind my own business. He always said I had an overactive imagination." She crossed her arms and huffed. "I loved that man, but I could have strangled him sometimes."

Amanda stifled a laugh. That sounded like her parents, and she attributed the sibling type of bickering to relationships spanning two decades or more. A theory since she'd never reached such a milestone personally. Back on point, Audrey's story, while interesting, raised a few questions. She asked the first one. "Why do you remember all this so clearly?"

"Dear, I have a memory like a steel trap, even now at eighty-three. It's clear as a bell up here." She smiled and tapped her head. "I'm not likely to be joining my Bert anytime soon, though only the Lord knows when it's our time. My heart could go before I reach my bed tonight."

Amanda wasn't so sure about the whole "Lord knows" thing or predetermined destiny. The uncertainty of life she understood. "Do you remember what these men looked like?"

"One was just very plain and average in every way imaginable. The other man was a bit on the taller side with long, dark sideburns."

Trent pulled out his phone and walked over to Audrey. "Do you recognize the man in this picture?" He held his screen toward the woman.

"Oooh." Audrey shuddered. "Yes, that was the first man. Nothing much noteworthy about him. Why do you have that picture? Was I right to come here? Do you think that they were moving her body into the church that night? That I—" She snapped her mouth shut and looked at Amanda with wide, wet eyes.

Trent flashed the picture toward Amanda so she could see it was Doug Cofell's license photo. She nodded, and Trent tucked his phone away again and returned to his chair.

"Who is that man?" Audrey asked when they didn't touch her other questions.

Trent put his phone away. "His name's Doug Cofell. Does that name sound familiar to you?"

She shook her head. "If he was associated with that church, though, I'd have no reason to know it. Bert and I weren't into organized religion. I am, and he was, spiritual. To us there was always something too mysterious about life and the universe not to have some other beings out there. That might even include an all-powerful *One*. But we didn't believe a person needs to go into a special building and kneel to be approved or saved."

Amanda found it interesting that such a couple had settled next to a church in that case. Same too for the fact that Audrey had expressed her dislike for the music. Clearly other attributes of the house and the property outweighed those negatives. "Thank you for coming to us with this information, Mrs. Witherspoon."

"I just hope it helped you. I couldn't ignore my nudge to report this anymore. I might have been laughed out of any police station as a nosy neighbor lady who read too many Agatha Christie novels, but if I'd come forward... Well...?"

"It might not have made a difference," Amanda told her.

"But it might have?"

Amanda wished she could retract her words. Her intention hadn't been to impress guilt on the woman for taking her late husband's advice to remain quiet. "Honestly, there's no way to know." She wasn't going to dwell on the fact that Sadie Jackson's parents might have received closure twenty-three years ago or that justice might have been leveled on Doug Cofell. No good would come from any of that. There was still the matter of his accomplice. Whoever he was.

TWENTY

Amanda and Trent wrote down Audrey's testimony and she signed off on it. They said nothing about Doug Cofell and his wife, Winnie, kidnapping Sadie Jackson. She'd likely read that in the paper at a future time, but there was no point in burdening her with that now or confirming there was likely a body in that crate she'd seen. For now, Sadie's name wasn't public knowledge.

"All these years later," Trent lamented. "It's such a shame."

"It is, but if you're honest about it, place yourself back in time. Some woman comes into the police department about men carrying a wooden crate into the church. All this during renovations."

"But at two in the morning," Trent countered.

"That's if she found a cop who believed her. Sadly, I think most would have dismissed her, considering her story cockamamie."

"You might be right, but like you said to her, we can't know how things might have turned out."

"Nope, and there's also no turning back the clock." There were times in her life she had desperately wished that was an option. Like how she'd have undone the car accident and brought her family back. But something else was weighing on her mind. "We know Sadie's body was put in that church, so it's clear for us looking back. Two men carrying a heavy wood crate and being shifty about it. Right time period, right place."

"One now ID'd as Doug Cofell. There's no doubt in my mind that Sadie Jackson's body was inside that box."

"Mine either. But where does this leave Winnie Cofell? Was she in on the murder?"

"She was there for the kidnapping, maybe just not the disposal of the body."

"It's time we have that talk with the uncle. He could be the second man Witherspoon saw that night."

According to the system, Sean Olsen was six foot two, tall enough to match Audrey Witherspoon's description, but his license photo didn't show long sideburns. That could have changed from twenty-three years ago though. He was retired and living on the other side of Woodbridge. Since it was after two in the afternoon, Amanda and Trent stopped for a burger on the way. With what was ahead of them, she wasn't sure if she'd be making it home on time for dinner with Zoe again tonight.

Trent pulled into the driveway of a bungalow and said, "Okay, this is it."

"So you didn't just park in front of some random place?" Sarcasm served up with a smirk.

"Smart-ass."

They both got out of the car and rang the doorbell. Twice to get a response.

Heavy-placed footsteps came toward them and cast a shadow in the sidelight. The door swung open. "What?" A man in his mid-sixties, scruffy facial hair, stood there staring at them.

A lit cigarette was perched between his fingers, and he lifted it for a drag.

"Sean Olsen?" Trent raised his badge as he made the inquiry.

"And if I am?" Another pull on his cigarette. This one he took his time with. When he drew it away, he exhaled a plume of smoke out the side of his mouth.

A walking chimney... "We need to talk to you about your sister, Winnie Cofell." Amanda made sure his eyes fell to the badge she was holding up before putting it away.

"Winn's dead. Nothing else to say. Good day." Sean stepped back to close the door.

"Unfortunately, it's not one of those times we're asking," Amanda said firmly. "We can talk here or down at Central."

"Whooo." Sean wriggled the fingers of his left hand as if trembling with fear.

"Fine by me." She reached out to him, and Trent did too. Sean moved out of reach.

"Please. I was just kidding around. Obviously, you're serious about this. Come in." He relented with a sigh and flicked his cigarette butt past them. It landed on the concrete and had flickered out before she turned to go inside.

They sat in a living room full of well-worn furniture.

"I'm not sure why you'd want to talk to me about Winnie. We weren't in contact long before she died. At least three decades."

The Cofells had taken Sadie Jackson thirty-one years ago. Did he know and that's why he pulled out *three decades* or was he telling the truth? Amanda didn't have the luxury of just running on an assumption. "You seem sure it was that long ago."

"Thirty-five precisely since we last spoke. And before you ask, I know that because she'd married that Doug fella, and while she thought he hung the moon, he didn't hold any power over me. We had a falling-out at their wedding, and we haven't spoken since. And now she's dead, that's not going to happen. Well, unless I hire a medium to hold a séance. Not my thing." He mocked shivers. "Even if I could get past my fear of contacting the dead, Winn would be the last person I'd want to summon."

Amanda hadn't looked up when the Cofells were married, but it surprised her that it wasn't too long from then until Sadie's abduction. She had in mind that they were a couple who couldn't have children of their own and had taken Sadie to fill that hole. "Were they together for a while before they got married?"

"About seven years, and they lived together for a bit. They dated off and on in high school too."

"And they never had kids of their own," Trent interjected.

"That's a mighty personal thing is it not, Detective?" Sean raised his eyebrows at Trent and angled his head.

"If you say so," Trent said evenly, clearly not letting this guy affect him. "They adopted a boy."

"And wasn't that a mistake."

"Then you knew about him?" she asked. "Even though you just said you haven't been in touch for thirty-five years?"

"I learned about him and his allegations in the news. The adoption bit you just told me doesn't come as a surprise. Last I knew Winn couldn't have children. A sad thing too since all she had wanted since she was a little girl was a baby."

"Allegations?" she tossed back. "You don't sound like you believe them."

"Rubbish and lies. All of it. My sister would never."

"People we love are capable of things we don't want to think about," Amanda said.

"Not Winn. Like I said, she always wanted to be a mother."

She could tell there was nothing she could say that was going to sway his opinion. There were many reasons people wanted children and not all of them were noble. Some were selfish or misguided. Though even if Winnie hadn't started out intending to be abusive, it seemed that had changed. Cameron identified her as the woman in the kidnapping duo who had snatched Sadie Jackson. But what if that wasn't the entire picture? What was to say Doug hadn't somehow manipulated Winnie into going along with him? It could have been his way of giving her a child. He could have romanticized the crime until she couldn't resist the temptation. But then, how did things switch so drastically? The horror of the broken bones in Sadie's body, rape, being beaten to death... "You've made your dislike for Doug Cofell clear, but did he ever hit your sister or was he abusive in other ways?"

"Pfft. No way she'd let that happen, though I will tell you it was a concern of mine. Doug had a temper and grew up in a very abusive household, but who am I to talk? So did me and Winn. Dad and Mom both used to hit each other. Once Winn got out for college, she never returned home."

The abuse that Doug suffered, and Winnie was exposed to, would have had a bearing on the people they became. And that thinking brought her right back to their original feelings about Winnie Cofell. She was likely just as much a monster as her husband. Amanda considered how best to continue. If she raised the matter of Sadie's kidnapping and murder outright and implicated Winnie, she was certain Sean would shut down out of some misguided loyalty to his dead sibling. If he had inherited the Cofells' things, he would serve as a roadblock. By the time they secured a search warrant, Sean could have even destroyed or tossed everything. Of course, all of this was assuming Sean had access to it anyhow. "It's unfortunate you weren't able to reconnect before she died." She decided to side-step with sympathy. The sentiment had Sean's gaze snapping to her eyes. She'd clearly surprised him with the comment.

"I let the notion of a happy reunion go a long time ago."

If Amanda was right, she sensed a touch of sorrow in him

with this admission. Death, as *natural* as it was, sure didn't feel that way in the aftermath of loss. "Do you know what happened to her and Doug's estate? Did they have a will?"

"It all came to me, and it felt like a real F U."

"Why is that?" Trent asked. "Most people don't mind coming into some money."

Sean laughed. "They had a piece-of-shit farmhouse full of crap. It would cost *me* to unload it by the time I paid people to clear it out and get it ready for sale. That's not even getting into the repairs needed on that deathtrap. Not even touching those and selling it as is, I'd be lucky to walk away with ten bucks. Just not worth my time."

Whether it was that simple or some unconscious connection to his sister, this was good news for the investigation. "Then their farmhouse, with all their things, is just as it was when they left it the day of their car accident?"

"I suspect so. Unless someone's broken in or torched the joint. Haven't gotten a call from the police about it, so I'm assuming it's still standing. I went out there just once and never looked back. The place gave me the willies. All the paintings on the wall were hanging on an angle, and I got goosebumps just stepping through the door."

Amanda could only guess what he took the angled paintings to mean. "You think it's possessed by spirits then?"

"Haunted? No doubts."

She wasn't one for putting faith in such phenomena though she also didn't dismiss the possibility of evil spirits. In her line of work, she'd encountered a lot of darker energy, as she'd put it, and she'd seen it in the eyes of some people she put away. "Would there be any way we could take a look around the house?"

"What for? You still haven't told me why you wanted to discuss Winn."

There would be no more putting off why they were here.

And while they came suspecting Sean Olsen's involvement, of him being the third DNA profile, her instinct was leading her away from that after speaking with him. She believed him when he said he was estranged from his sister. Of course, they'd still get around to requesting his DNA. "You heard about Cameron holding up that priest, but did you also catch the part about the human body pulled from the church's nave?"

"I heard about it." He spoke slowly, clearly cautious about how it involved his sister.

"What the media hasn't yet disclosed is that victim has now been identified as Sadie Jackson. She made national news thirty-one years ago when she was kidnapped at eight years old," Amanda told him.

Silence stretched out for seconds, then a minute, possibly longer. He might not ever put it all together, and they didn't have time to just sit here.

Amanda continued. "We believe your sister was captured on video with Sadie the day she was kidnapped. She was leaving an amusement park in Florida with Doug and the girl."

Sean shoved his back into his chair. "No. I can't believe what I'm hearing. You're telling me my sister— Nope." He shook his head.

"The video wasn't made public. It's grainy but these people have now been identified as your sister and Doug Cofell." Amanda was going by the stills captured from the footage. They hadn't received the videos from Vos's colleague yet.

Sean's face shadowed. "By whom?"

"That's not for me to say," she said.

"It was him," he spat. "Cameron? He seems like he's on some sort of smear campaign to blame other people for his rotten life. So this is why you want a look at their things? You want to build a case against my sister? Well, she's *dead*. She's not even here to defend herself, and you're going to ruin her name."

There was no concern about Doug's reputation. "There's more to it than that. There seems to have been a third person involved in Sadie Jackson's murder."

"Okay— Oh, you think that was me? I think it's time for you to leave."

"I never said it was you," Amanda backpedaled. "Just that someone else is out there. Looking at your sister and brother-in-law's things might be the fastest way for us to find them."

"Nah, you're not getting into their place."

"I'm sorry you feel that way," Amanda said, sliding a look at Trent. "We'll be getting a search warrant to look in their house."

"You do that, because until then, I'm not letting you in." Sean stood. "It's time for you to go."

Amanda and Trent returned to the car.

"He's roadblocking the house, so there's no way he'd hand over his DNA," Trent said.

"Why I didn't bother asking. But..." She looked in the general area where Sean had tossed his cigarette butt. "One minute." She got an evidence bag from the trunk and found her target. She sealed it and got back in the car with Trent.

He was smiling at her. "Within view. No warrant necessary."

"Nope. We'll get this tested and see if he's a match to one of the male DNA profiles. We can have an officer take it to the crime lab and drop it off while we carry on."

"Love it. I can make that call."

"And I'll call Judge Anderson and see if he'll approve a warrant request over the phone that will let us search the Cofell farmhouse."

Trent drove around the corner and pulled over. They both got on their cell phones. She stated their case to the judge and was told the warrant would be expedited and sent over. When Trent finished his call, she said, "We have verbal approval, and the signed authorization is coming ASAP."

"He's a good judge."

"He is and thankfully reasonable. He was somewhat concerned that Audrey Witherspoon's mind could have made fiction of what she saw after all these years."

"I can see that if you weren't talking to her face to face. In person, she struck me as entirely credible."

"I wouldn't have asked that she sign off on her testimony otherwise. Thankfully, Judge Anderson saw reason."

"This does involve a rather high-profile FBI case, so I think that might have played a role too."

"It wouldn't have hurt."

"An officer has been dispatched to this location," Trent informed her, just as a police car pulled up.

"Must have been nearby." Amanda got out and handed the cigarette butt over and thanked the officer. Once back in the car, she texted CSI Blair to let her know she had something coming her way. She received a quick acknowledgment.

Next, Amanda opened her email app. No message from the judge's office yet. She noted that time was moving along though, and once this warrant came through, she'd want to move on it. That meant she could be tied up for hours yet, so there was no way she'd be making it home for dinner with Zoe tonight. "I'm just going to make some arrangements for Zoe," she told Trent before calling her sister Kristen. Libby just took her a couple of days ago, and she didn't want to fling the girl on her again even though she'd rearrange her life to accommodate her. But the point was it wasn't fair to ask or expect that of her. If Libby had been able to take Zoe full-time, she would have as the appointed godmother. But circumstances had changed eliminating that as an option when Zoe's parents were killed.

Kristen answered, and Amanda laid out her request.

"The job interfering again?" Kristen teased. "But give it no thought. I'd love to spend some time with her. I'm sure Ava would like to, as well."

Her niece was a teenager with a budding social life and probably had more important things to do than entertain a nine-year-old. But she did love Zoe. "Thanks."

"Don't mention it. We're family." Her sister ended the call before she could.

"Zoe's all set." She refreshed her email again. Still nothing.

Trent sat back and tapped the steering wheel. Warm air was just starting to flow from the vents. "For what it's worth, I don't think Sean Olsen's involved with any of this."

"I guess we'll see." She looked at her email again, obsessing, just as the message from the judge's office filtered in. "We've got it."

TWENTY-ONE

What Sean Olsen had told them about the old farmhouse wasn't far from Trent's mind. Pulling into the overgrown drive-way, the long grass and weeds were brown from the winter. Getting closer to the house sent chills running down his arms. He wasn't sure about Amanda, but he believed in the existence of evil spirits. It was how he was able to reconcile people doing horrendous things. Not in the sense of "the dog told me to do it" but who could know what influence these beings had on those predisposed?

When he and Amanda had returned to Sean Olsen's door and presented the warrant, he'd cursed but handed over the key without a fight. He did caution them again though. "Don't say I didn't warn you about the place."

Trent was replaying those words as he got out of the car and walked to the back door. It didn't help that the place was derelict and looked like a haunted house. For now, it was just going to be him and Amanda going in. CSIs were requested, but who knew how long it would take for them to get here. If they'd known the search warrant would come through so fast, they could have just passed Olsen's cigarette butt to whoever showed up here.

Amanda stuck the key in the deadbolt and turned it. Something banged. The wind groaned. Both had Trent flinching and looking around.

Amanda laughed. "Someone's jumpy."

"I took Olsen's warning to heart."

"Maybe too much."

"You don't buy into evil spirits." He wasn't asking. Her tone told him that much.

"Evil spirits, I'm not so sure, but I believe in dark energy."

"Same thing. You sense that 'the other' is around."

"Let's leave it as to each their own." She pushed on the door, and a burst of cold air rushed out.

He shivered and shook the chill rolling down his shoulders and back. It was said evil spirits made the air cold. But the place had been shut up for years. No electricity and no heat. That could be the more plausible explanation.

They both brought their flashlights along and stepped inside. It wasn't suffocating, but there was a definite *feeling* to the place.

Another creak had him flinching again.

"If this is too much for you, you can wait in the car." Amanda turned to him, and he caught her grin in the beam of his light.

"I'm fine." He'd lie until he believed it. If he just thought about it a bit more, rationalized it, surely his fears would dissipate. After all, even if evil was at work in this house, what would it want with him? He was safe. *I am safe.* He flipped that around in his mind a few times and found little to no comfort. If they were right about the Cofells, much harm befell occupants of this house. First, Sadie Jackson, then Cameron. *But the Cofells are gone the Cofells are gone...* Another affirmation to prevent him from spinning out.

Amanda said, "I'd suggest we split up to cover more ground, but—"

"I'm fine. Tell me where to go." He smiled, trying to slough off his anxiety with humor.

"I'll go up. You stay down here."

"Sure."

Amanda started up the staircase to the right of the door, and he watched her take a few steps before he moved deeper into the house. He found himself walking down a narrow hallway with a montage of framed photos on the wall. None of them sat straight, just as Sean had said. And not just slightly off level, but haphazard. Still, vibrations in a house could easily shift frames that were balanced on a single nail. *I'm just going to tell myself that...*

Most of the glass covers were coated with dust, and cobwebs dangled from the corners of the frames linking one to the other. He wiped the one closest to him and revealed a picture of a smiling Doug and Winnie on a picnic. Based on their clothing and their ages, it had been some time ago. Trent would guess back in their late twenties, even younger.

He cleared off more frames and those pictures told the same story. That of a happy couple. In fact, all of them were of the Cofells only. No friends or children. Not even one photo of Cameron, which Trent found rather odd for a couple who wanted kids. Then again, he reminded himself the Cofells weren't the typical parents who loved and cherished their "son." In each shot of the couple though, they were smiling and appeared to be genuinely happy.

It takes a certain type of psychopath...

Trent moved along and came to a bathroom on his left. Just a toilet and vanity with a sink. He stepped inside, and gloved up, juggling to keep hold of his flashlight.

A bump from overhead had his heart jackhammering. *It's just Amanda walking around up there... That's all.* But no matter how much he sought to cling to logic, shivers ran through him. He'd welcome a heavy injection of adrenaline to calm him down, but sadly this was it. His system would already be flooded, which meant he was screwed.

He opened the cabinet and bent to look inside. Nothing but a few rolls of toilet paper, a box of facial tissue, and toilet bowl cleaner. He closed the door again, left the room, and carried on toward the back of the house.

The living room was up next on his right. A decent-sized space with a sage-green couch, two mismatched chairs, three pine coffee tables, and a forty-inch flatscreen television. A bookshelf was placed in the corner and full of various translations of the Bible. The display struck him as hypocrisy, given what they had done.

He stepped back then and, for the first time, really took in the paintings on the walls. They were all oil and canvas landscapes showcased in gold-painted sculptured frames. Every single one of them hung crooked.

"I've gotta get outta here," he mumbled to himself and almost tripped over his feet in a hurry to leave the room.

He shook his arms when he reached the hall, but that wasn't enough to fend off the permeating bad juju. It was actually making it worse. Maybe if he shifted his focus from his fears to logic. *The Cofells are gone. They can't hurt you now...*

How he hoped that was true, but he had a respect for the prospect of an afterlife. *What if they are here and I just don't see them?*

He took a steadying breath and continued to the end of the hallway, which led into a typical country kitchen. Red-and-white gingham curtains framed a window over the sink, offering a view of the front yard and the road. It also showed a sky that was only getting darker as evening creeped in.

Upper and lower cabinetry lined more than half the room. In the remaining space, there was a table for four. Oak with spindle-back chairs. The sink had a few dirty dishes in it, and the bottom of the coffeepot was black and dried out. Dishes were on the table with dirty cutlery. Any food scraps that might have remained were long gone, likely scavenged by insects and rodents over the last few years. People moved out, and pests moved in.

The picture here was all so ordinary. The Cofells had expected to return home the day they'd died.

He opened a few cupboards, not sure what damning evidence he expected to find but was just being diligent. There was scurrying and loud squeaking coming from the storage space beneath the sink.

Speaking of rodents... The sound was likely from mice or rats. Gross but not unbearable. He could handle insects and furry things.

When one of the latter scampered across the tip of his boot and ducked behind the fridge, Trent followed it with the beam of his flashlight. The old linoleum floor was scraped from something being repeatedly rolled over it. He crouched and ran his fingers over the grooves. They were the right size and placement for the wheels of the fridge. The markings went out about four feet into the room. How strange. How often did people need to move their fridge?

He stood and noticed the appliance wasn't sitting flush against the wall. The left end was sticking out at least two or three inches farther than the right.

Curious...

Trent shone his flashlight behind the fridge. There was something back there all right, and it sent shivers tearing right through him.

TWENTY-TWO

Amanda explored the second story, already having popped into two bedrooms and a bathroom. One room looked like a guest room slash office, and the other one was nondescript, but the closet had toys typically played with by boys, and suits in various sizes from adolescent to adult hung on hangers. The walls were all papered in wild patterns that would have been popular in the seventies.

As she carried out her tour of this level, she wondered how Trent was doing downstairs. He'd laughed off his fears, but she knew they were genuine. Even she was struggling. A cool breeze danced on the back of her neck, raising goosebumps. It also wasn't lost on her that every portrait she came across was hanging on an angle. She could dismiss this if it were one or two on the same wall, but it was the same throughout the house from what she observed. She wasn't going to leap to the cause being *otherworldly* yet, but she did find it odd. The creaky wide wooden planks of the floor were unforgiving too. Their whines of protest sometimes struck her ears as wails.

She came to the end of the hall and the doorway for the primary bedroom. She had to clear a spider's web from the opening before going in and winced as she did. The gauze was sticky and thick, and she certainly didn't want to meet the spider who had spun it. She was a bit of an arachnophobe, which was likely exacerbated due to her older brother, Kyle, who teased her mercilessly with them when they were kids. He even put a long-legged black number in her bed once.

Inside the room, a queen-size bed with a thick wooden frame sat to the left. Matching nightstands were on each side, but only one had a lamp on it. Cobwebs glistened as her beam danced over the room.

Her thoughts returned to the missing spider from the doorway. It was hidden somewhere, likely watching her with its eight eyes. Possibly with its friends and millions of babies.

Shivers danced over the back of her neck and laced down her arms.

Just be strong, Steele... She coached herself, realigning her focus on the bigger picture. Sadie Jackson.

She blew out a breath and shook her shoulders to loosen the tension pinching her neck. Nothing had turned up so far, and she was running out of rooms in which to find something further incriminating against the Cofells. Same too for any leads on the mystery man. He could be out there right now harming another child, and she wanted to believe the key to stopping him could be discovered within the walls of this house.

She walked over to the nightstand and jumped back when a black, rather juicy long-legged spider scurried across the top. She didn't scream and was impressed by her restraint. If she had, Trent might have crapped his pants. He was already jumpy.

"Damn you, Kyle," she hissed under her breath as she tugged on the handle of the drawer. A Bible, in an otherwise empty space, stared up at her. She shut it again, disgusted by sanctimonious people who, in actuality, were morally bankrupt.

Amanda opened the closet doors. The space was stuffed

with garments. An overhead shelf was filled with several shoe-boxes and totes. She stood on tiptoe to grab one, but her fingers danced over it and caused it to fall. She barely got out of the way in time to avoid it hitting her in the face. It smacked to the floor and splayed open.

"You all right up here?" Trent burst into the room, slightly winded.

"I'm fine."

"Uh-huh. I know what *fine* means. The opposite."

"You have me. There are spiders everywhere, and my skin is crawling."

"You sure it's the spiders?" he tossed back.

"Yes." She bent over to pick up the box and refix the lid. The contents were nothing more than tissue paper and a pair of shoes. But her gaze extended deeper into the closet. "Trent, do you see that?" She pointed at a section in the floor.

He stepped behind her and angled the beam of his flash-light over her head to where she'd indicated. "Not sure exactly what you're seeing..."

"Just keep your light on this spot." She indicated the area in front of her and tucked her flashlight into a pocket of her coat. Then she set about prying her fingers into the edge of the floor-boards. "This section doesn't match the rest of the pattern. Most of the boards are longer. This one here is— Short." The word flew from her mouth as the board came free and exposed an opening.

In the hidden place... That was where Cameron told them he'd found photos of Sadie. Was that here?

"What's in there?" Trent asked, nudging closer, his feet hitting the back of hers. "Sorry. Just don't keep me waiting in suspense here."

She looked over her shoulder at him but pulled out her flashlight again and aimed the beam into the hole.

"So? What is it? What's there?" He battered her with questions.

She leaned forward for a better look, sweeping her beam and flooding the small space with light. Then she sat back on her feet.

"So?" Trent prompted.

"Nothing's there now, but something was at one time. There's a dust outline the size of a shoebox."

"Nothing," Trent repeated, dejected.

"But Cameron said he found the pictures of Sadie in the hidden space. That could describe this location."

"Yeah." Trent backed up to afford her more room to get out of the closet and to her feet. "You said shoebox size. There's more of them up there. It could have been moved." He indicated the few on the top shelf.

"We'll look in every one of them, but if this spot held mementos of Sadie or such things, I doubt Winnie would have moved it from beneath the floor to the top shelf."

"I suppose. Not after Cameron already found it. She'd put it somewhere even better concealed." Trent's tone turned somber, and his expression became dark. Before she could ask why, she heard CSI Blair call out.

"Hello? It's CSIs Blair and Donnelly. Anyone here?"

"We're upstairs," she called out to Emma Blair.

The investigators' footsteps padded up the creaky staircase. Amanda recalled questioning their stability when she'd traversed them. Sean's words about the house needing repairs weren't far from mind.

"This place gives me the heebie-jeebies." Isabelle Donnelly mocked shivers, though Amanda didn't think the show was far from the genuine article. She and Blair were wearing head-lamps, and Donnelly adjusted hers so it didn't shine in their eyes.

"It's something," Trent put in. "But I need us to go to the kitchen."

"After we just hauled ourselves up here?" Blair protested.

"I think it's going to be worth our while," he said, looking at Amanda.

TWENTY-THREE

Amanda followed Trent, who took the stairs down two at a time. He was either afraid of a ghost on his heels or something else was urging him forward. But if his search downstairs had netted a good find, why not say anything right away? Though, knowing him, he wouldn't have wanted to stomp over what she'd found.

"Maybe slow it down for the rest of us," Blair called out from the rear.

"I'll wait for you," Trent said.

"Wise guy," Blair mumbled, and Amanda laughed.

"What is it, Trent?" Not knowing had her anxious and on edge.

"You'll see." He led them down the hall through the center of the house and stopped next to the doorway of the living room. "See where this room ends. Now keep following me." He started walking again until the hall ended in the kitchen. Trent beelined for the fridge. "See how it's against an inside wall? You'd think the one I just pointed out in the living room, but I had a closer look. It doesn't butt right up. There's at least four to six feet between that wall and here."

"Where are you going with this?" Isabelle asked him.

"I think there's a hidden room back here." He looked at Amanda, and her cheeks heated. How she'd gone on about *the hidden space* upstairs when there was *this*. He continued talking. "See how the fridge is angled out more on this side, and there are grooves in the flooring? This appliance has been moved in and out numerous times over the years."

Amanda looked where Trent indicated and saw for herself that there were unmistakable impressions. She was more interested in this suspected hidden room though. She looked behind the fridge and understood why Trent thought one existed. "Holy crap. Is that a—?"

"Padlock?" Trent finished. "It sure looks like one to me."

"Me too," Amanda said. "We need to move this fridge."

"Whoa. Hold up there," Blair wedged in. "Let me take some pictures first. Do everything by the book."

"Right. Of course." Amanda stepped back, reluctant in some ways because her curiosity was overpowering her common sense.

Blair set down her collection case and retrieved her camera and took some shots. She captured the floor, the fridge, the slice of space behind it and the padlock poking out. After a tortuous couple of minutes, Blair gestured toward Trent. "Have at it. Just remember, I need photos every step of the way."

He moved to the front of the fridge, gripped it on both sides, and rolled it forward. Amanda watched the wheels travel the established grooves in the flooring before turning her attention to the widening space.

Donnelly was shining light into the void, and Blair was taking more pictures with the flash on.

"It's definitely a padlock, and there's a door," Blair announced.

"I knew it." Trent was still pulling out the fridge when its wheels seemed to catch on something. The sudden stop caused him to lose his grip, and the fridge door sprung open. A carton of soured milk fell out and spilled on the floor. The stench was immense, but it wasn't holding any of them back from investigating Trent's find closer. He pulled the fridge out some more, and it was clear what had stopped it before. "There's a rip in the linoleum that's sticking up and must have caught in a wheel," he said before giving it one more solid heave, allowing them more room to get back there.

Her focus fixed on the door, the padlock, what all of this meant. It couldn't be anything good.

Blair took a few more pictures and bobbed her head toward Trent, this time gesticulating with her finger at the lock.

He held up his hands. "I'm not sure what you expect me to do with my bare hands."

"Come on. Pry the thing apart," Donnelly teased as she pulled out bolt cutters from her kit.

"You just cart those around with ya?" Blair asked her colleague.

Donnelly shrugged. "You never know when they will come in handy."

"Well, I, for one, am grateful." Trent took them and snapped the padlock off. "Here goes..." He pulled on the latch and opened the door. It groaned on its hinges but when it was fully open, Donnelly shone two flashlights and a headlamp into the opening.

The sight made Amanda ill. It didn't matter that she had her suspicions about what they were going to find behind the door. Seeing it made it real and confirmed their suspicions. The Cofells were evil spirits.

"Dear God," Blair lamented as she took photos.

When the CSI gave Amanda the all-clear, she entered the small room. It was just large enough for the single-size cot it held against the back wall and a waste bucket. Nothing was in it, and it had been cleaned out, and the room had a closed-up smell. The sheets on the bed were tangled but dusty.

"It doesn't look like anyone's been here for a long time," Trent said. "At least that's good news."

She found it hard to accept any silver lining in this. The Cofells were out of reach for the atrocities they committed. But potentially there was an active threat. The mystery man with long, dark sideburns. Was he harming another child as they stood here? The helplessness was overwhelming, and Amanda backed out of the room. She needed space to breathe.

Trent followed and stood next to her. The awful stench of the spilled milk was barely noticeable in the aftermath of their discovery. All Amanda could think about was Sadie Jackson being stuffed into the cubby to live out eight years of her life. A little girl when she went in, a teenager when she emerged.

Flashbacks of the cot attacked Amanda, striking her with a sinister thought that weakened her knees. She squeezed her eyes shut. *If only that will block out the horror…*

She stiffened as Trent's strong and protective arm slipped around her shoulders.

"I'm sorry. I shouldn't have done that." He flinched and started to withdraw.

"No." She opened her eyes, met his straight on. "Please don't."

He stayed put, and she soaked up the moment. Her attraction to him remained despite wishing it away many times, knowing that he was with Kelsey. But right now, it wasn't sexual chemistry having her longing for his touch. It was humanity, warmth, love, affection. The demonstration that good still existed in a world full of so much evil, hatred, and discord.

They stood there in silence until Blair and Donnelly came out, and Blair cleared her throat. Then Amanda and Trent jumped apart.

"Pictures have been taken," Blair said, speaking as if she

hadn't stumbled onto seeing Amanda and Trent pressed together. "Obviously, we'll be processing that room thoroughly for fingerprints and DNA, including the waste bucket that appears clean. I don't have to tell you there's a lot lurking we can't see with the naked eye."

Amanda didn't want to think about that, but nodded. "You two keep working here. Trent and I will check out the rest of the house we haven't hit yet."

Blair let her gaze travel over them, possibly curious if there was more to their venturing off together than just the job. Thankfully, aside from the inquisitive look, she respectfully didn't say anything.

The CSIs got to work, and Amanda turned to Trent. "Did you come across access to the basement?"

"No, but with a house this old, it's more likely a cellar accessed from outside."

"Let's go have a look." She led the way from the house, happy to put some space between her and the hellhole. Forget *hidden space*. Given the rage pulsing through her system, if any evil spirits were around, they should fear her.

She unlocked the back door and turned right. She'd search the foundation clockwise.

Trent stuck close to her side. "What we found makes me speechless."

"What keeps hitting me is the Cofells kept her hidden away from the world in there. She spent eight years of her life…" She couldn't add any more to that because her mind was sinking her back into that abyss. The despair and sinister horrors Sadie would have endured. How terrified she must have been.

They found the cellar door, and there was another padlock securing it. "We'll have to go get—"

Trent pulled the bolt cutters out of a back pocket. "I might not have given them back to Isabelle yet."

"Good thing you didn't." She stepped aside and let him pop

the lock. Once he fed it out of the loop, she swung the door open.

More darkness awaits... But she took the first step without fear, shining the beam from her flashlight over the interior. The space was about eight feet square. There were wood shelves with canning jars and supplies laid out. She found herself breathing a bit easier. "Nothing here."

"Which doesn't come as a surprise to me. It's rather vulnerable out here."

"Yeah, well, we're not done. We have one more room left. The attic." She'd seen the door for it but had chosen the primary bedroom on the opposite side of the hall to explore first.

"Huh, now the attic—"

"Not one more word." Her imagination was already busy conjuring up nightmares that might await them.

TWENTY-FOUR

The attic door was two steps up from the hallway. It wasn't locked. Amanda's hunch they'd find more incriminating evidence against the Cofells might be wrong. Then again, the Cofells were probably careful about who they welcomed into their home. But there was Cameron with his admission of snooping. They hadn't been happy about him discovering the photographs of Sadie. If there was something they kept tucked away in the attic, it was feasible they'd secure the room. But would they need to when they could banish him to that hellhole downstairs?

She was the first to step inside. There was a window at the one side, but with the sun having dipped down the horizon it wasn't offering much light. It was a good thing they had thought to swing by CSIs Blair and Donnelly and see if they had extra headlamps with them. It turned out they had a few more in their van, so both Amanda and Trent were wearing one.

They did little good against the dark corners of the attic that somehow soaked up and deadened the light though. But even in the dull illumination, it was clear to see there was a lot stored here. Boxes and totes, shelving, and garment bags.

"How about you go to that side, and I'll start over here?" Amanda pointed one way and nudged her head in the opposite direction. "We can work toward the middle."

"Fine by me."

She took tentative steps to her starting point. It was a stack of cardboard boxes, and she pulled down the top one. It was blanketed in dust thick enough to leave impressions of her gloved fingertips, as if they'd raked through sand when she opened the flaps.

She angled her headlamp into the box to get a better look. Old purses and belts. She set this box aside, moving on to the next, then the next. Each time she came to a new box, she held her breath, anticipating that she might find some clues to identify the man Audrey Witherspoon had seen helping Doug Cofell that night.

The longer she kept at it without results, the more painstakingly frustrating it became. "I'm not finding anything. You?"

"Nope."

She was considering walking away from this room and leaving it entirely to Blair and Donnelly. She'd seen more spiders in this room alone than she'd seen in her life combined. Some were large enough to be attractions in a zoo. *Shivers...* But the CSIs had their hands full downstairs. A few more minutes wouldn't hurt, so she kept at it.

She pulled down a few more boxes to search through when her eyes landed behind where they had been. "Ah, Trent, come over here, please." She didn't take her gaze from her discovery.

"What is it?"

She answered by pointing.

Trent responded by moving more boxes out of the way, and she pitched in to clear the path. In front of them was a wooden crate of similar dimensions to the one Audrey had seen Doug Cofell and the other man moving.

"Is this...?" Her voice was barely above a whisper, and she left the rest unsaid. Trent would know exactly what she was referring to.

"The chance that it isn't is more unlikely."

She pulled her phone and called Blair, opting for that over yelling for them.

"A little busy here," Blair answered.

"Us, too, but we found something else that's monumental to the case. Please send Isabelle up with the camera."

A brief hesitation, likely reading the tension in Amanda's voice. "She's on her way."

It wasn't long before the investigator's steps pounded up the stairs, down the hall, and into the attic. There was a camera dangling from a strap around her neck.

"You didn't waste any time," Amanda told her.

"I'm efficient. What can I say? So what am I looking at here?"

Amanda indicated the wooden tote, and while Donnelly took photographs, she filled her in on its significance.

Isabelle let the camera rest against her chest. "Do you really think...? Wow."

"The odds of it being the one that our eyewitness saw are good," Trent put in.

"Suppose I'll give you that. It might be a suitable time to mention it's the right color to be a match for those wood slivers we pulled from the victim."

Amanda couldn't wait any longer to look inside. She lifted the edge slowly. Thankfully the way it was stored, the lid opened away from them.

The three of them peered inside. The crate was full of items.

Donnelly snapped a few photographs, and they set out to unload everything.

Girls' clothing was folded neatly on top. On closer inspection, like the suits in the bedroom closet, they ranged in size from child to adult. Amanda became cold when she lifted out a shirt, knowing right where she'd seen it before.

She held it up for Trent. "Look familiar?"

His brow wrinkled in concentration for a few seconds before revelation dawned. "Winnie wore that the day she and Doug kidnapped Sadie."

"Yep." With the admission came the bittersweet realization again that the Cofells would never face prison time for their crimes. But they could still locate the mystery man with the long, dark sideburns. He needed to be stopped, and someone needed to pay for what happened to Sadie.

They kept sifting through the box and found the clothing Sadie was wearing that fateful day too. But as they unloaded the contents for Donnelly to process, it was never far from Amanda's mind that Sadie's body had likely been transported inside this very box. It was probably her imagination, but Amanda could swear she sensed Sadie here, in this room. Not in the form of an angry spirit with a grudge. Rather it was a calming presence that Amanda took as gratitude someone was going to bring her justice.

They reached the bottom, and the last item was a shoebox. Could it be the one that had been stored beneath the floorboards?

Amanda popped the lid, and it was full of photographs and other small mementos. She held up a pink barrette. "Likely the one Sadie was wearing the day she was kidnapped." She shuffled through the photos, holding each up so Trent and Donnelly could see them. Three headlamps reflected moons on the glossy prints making the images impossible to see. They all adjusted the angle of the lamps so the light was more indirect.

There were about ten photos. A few were of Sadie at

different ages. One was of Sadie pregnant. It best matched Cameron's description of his "sister." In this shot, she had long brown hair, blue eyes, a face like an angel, wearing blue bangles and a beaded necklace. But Cameron hadn't mentioned she was pregnant in the photo he'd seen. It was possible she was captured wearing the jewelry more than once around this age. Or had Cameron left the swelled belly out of his recap? Was this what really landed Cameron in trouble with the Cofells? Had he asked questions they didn't want to answer? Did Cameron have some innate suspicion that the teen in the picture was more than his sister? Did it explain his poor choices, his acting out and having brushes with the law? Had it all been some misguided effort to be the voice of justice for his mother? Or was it a combination of that and the abuse he'd suffered at the hands of the Cofells? Though the latter on its own would be enough.

When she got to the last photo, the skin on the back of her neck tightened. The subject was a teenage girl about fourteen years old with long, dark hair like Sadie's. But it wasn't Sadie. Her stomach turned. "This was taken before Sadie," she said. "Look at her clothes and the aging of this photograph."

"Dear Lord, they took another one," Isabelle lamented, placing a hand over her heart.

"And look." Trent pointed at the Mary Janes on her feet, which were identical in appearance to the ones found on Sadie.

"Feet usually stop growing a few years after puberty," Isabelle informed them. "This girl looks younger than sixteen, but still a teenager."

"I was thinking about fourteen," Amanda said.

"If that's the case, from a scientific point of view, the shoes in that picture could be the ones Sadie was wearing. The unknown female DNA in them could belong to her." Isabelle nudged her head at the photo.

"Passed on from one girl to the next." Amanda laid a hand over her stomach as she continued to stare into the photograph. *Who are you, sweetheart, and where are you now?* But Amanda knew in her gut that even if they found out her identity, they were more likely to find her dead than alive.

TWENTY-FIVE

Yesterday had ended at two that morning. Amanda dropped into bed but spent most of the following hours tossing and turning. The hidden room and the stash in the attic haunted her when she closed her eyes, and the images would likely feed her nightmares for a while to come.

Before they left the Cofell property, cadaver dogs were called out to search for the Jane Doe from the photograph. Nothing was found, but it didn't bring Amanda any relief. In her heart she knew that girl was dead. It was a somber, though realistic conclusion, but she wouldn't let it stop her from pursuing justice.

Finding that mystery man was already a priority but took on more urgency. Sadly, nothing in the Cofell home provided them with a clue to his identity. All the pictures they'd found were of the Cofells with the exception of a few that were of Cameron or the two girls, Sadie Jackson and Jane Doe.

The lack of progress had her feeling somewhat of a failure professionally, and this bled into her personal life. As the hours had started ticking off last night, Amanda asked Kristen to keep Zoe overnight and take her to school in the morning. Her sister had to pack Zoe's clothes and haul them and her niece back to her house. Kristen said it wasn't a problem, but it didn't lessen Amanda's guilt about being a bad mother. She could still hear Logan's accusatory voice, "What's your priority anyway? The job or your family?"

All of this replayed in Amanda's head when she woke up that morning, and she had an epiphany. She called Trent. "I thought of a way we might be able to find this guy."

"I'm listening," he said with a smile.

She laughed, getting the reference to an older sitcom about a therapist on a call-in radio talk show. It was rather popular on streaming platforms, and she'd watched every season, even gave the revival a try. "If he helped Doug Cofell dispose of Sadie Jackson, he's likely to be a close friend. Cameron might be able to tell us if he remembers anyone hanging around when he was younger. If we're lucky, he'll be someone who fits Audrey Witherspoon's description."

"Well, we know the church members we've spoken to haven't been too talkative. There's the chance that pattern would just continue. But I'm not sure we'd be cleared to talk to Cameron again. He was in quite a fragile state when we talked to him before."

"True." She'd also heard that he'd been very upset afterward, and a psychologist had been to assess him. That idea combusted to ash but quickly gave way to another one. "We do the next best thing then. We talk to his therapist."

"She'll hide behind patient confidentiality."

She was frustrated at being blocked at every turn. "I want to give it a go, see if she'll reveal something, even if she doesn't intend to."

"Suppose it's worth a shot. I'll meet you at Central and we'll leave from there?"

"You got it."

She got ready and was out of the house in fifteen minutes

and at Central after another ten. Too long for her liking but instant teleportation only existed in science fiction. Unfortunately.

But her delay wasn't Trent's. He lived in Woodbridge, cutting out commute time. She found him waiting for her at the door of the station.

"I have the therapist's info," he began. "But before I get to that, I received the videos from Special Agent Hester, Vos's colleague. There's probably not much point to us watching them at this stage, but I wanted you to know I have them."

"All right. Good to know, and I'm with you. No need to watch them at this juncture."

"So moving on then, Vos gave us the therapist's name. Beverly Campbell. I started with the halfway house where Cameron lives, knowing they often have therapists and counselors on staff at those places. Well, Campbell does work out of there, but she also runs her own practice part-time. And she's there today. Her office is in town and set to open in twenty minutes."

"Let's go."

Trent got them on the road, and it wasn't long before they were parked and waiting for the office to open. With ten minutes on the clock, a silver BMW sedan pulled into the lot.

Trent quickly keyed the plate into the onboard computer. "That's her."

"We'll hang back, let her get in and settled for a minute first." Her voice returned to her own ears as belonging to a calm and relaxed individual, a front. This woman could provide them something to break the case.

Campbell slipped a long leg out of the car, exposing the hem of a short pencil skirt beneath an unbuttoned full-length coat. The tip of her high heel touched the pavement, and she turned her body and put out the second leg. Her movements were like a graceful gazelle, and once she was standing, she straightened her jacket and grabbed a huge purse from the back-seat. She threw a cursory glance their way as she walked past. Otherwise she didn't really pay them any attention.

"She doesn't exactly strike me as the friendly type. I'm not so sure if she's going to talk to us," Trent said.

"It could be a persona she puts on. She must have a soft spot for people if she's a therapist." She was digging to find a gem of optimism.

They waited for a few minutes after Beverly had slipped inside before getting out of the car and following. The office was quiet except for soft music coming through wall-mounted speakers at a low volume. It made Amanda think of being in a spa, and that was probably the intention. The more relaxed the patient, the more talkative they were.

Rustling drew their notice. It was coming down a short hallway, and they both headed that way.

Beverly was putting her coat and purse into a wardrobe, her back to the doorway.

"Excuse us. Bev—"

Beverly let out a startled cry and turned around, a hand clamped over her chest. "Dear heaven." Her face transformed from shock to pure irritation. "I don't know who you are, but you can't be in here."

Amanda and Trent held up their badges and made their introductions.

"Yes, well, you might as well see yourselves out. If you're here to talk to me, it must be about one of my clients, and I can't disclose anything they've confided in me. Doctor-patient confidentiality." She walked to her desk, lowered herself in the chair, and flipped a laptop open. She looked up at them when they hadn't moved. "You did hear what I said?" With her chin lifted, her gaze traveled down the slope of her nose.

"Oh, we heard you, but it's not entirely true," Amanda said. "You're exempt from that confidentiality if a client tells you about a crime they've committed or if you believe them to be a danger to themselves or others."

"Yes, well, I have no intention of breaking their trust in me under any circumstances, so if you would kindly…" Beverly flicked a manicured finger toward the door.

"We'll leave shortly." Amanda peacocked her stature, and it had Beverly sighing and slumping back in her chair. It was the first inelegant move the woman had made.

Beverly perched her elbows on the arms of her chair and clasped her hands in front of herself. "I'd love to accommodate the Prince William County PD but, unfortunately, I have a very tight schedule today. If you book an appointment with—"

There was some thumping in the front office, and a sly smile lifted Beverly's lips. "Ah, and by the sound of it, Tanya's here. She's my assistant, and she'll put something in the books."

Amanda remained where she stood, holding her ground. "Five minutes. That's all we're asking for."

Beverly locked her jaw and crossed her arms. "Fine," she seethed. "Five minutes." She slinked across the room, shut the door, then sat in an egg-shaped chair and gestured toward the couch across from it.

Amanda sat down next to Trent. Discomfort and flashbacks to her time in a therapist's chair rushed in. All the conversations about losing her family. But this visit wasn't about her. She cleared her throat. "We're here about your client Cameron Cofell."

She gave them a tight smile, and her eyes darkened. "And as I said, I can't be disclosing what a client shares in any of his or her sessions."

"Except I'm going to guess you know that this client made the news," Trent put in.

Beverly shrugged. "It changes nothing."

"Cameron Cofell suffered extreme abuse at the hands of his *adopted* parents." Amanda wouldn't typically stress that point as she knew firsthand there wasn't a distinction between adopted children and those of the same flesh and blood. She was curious if Beverly knew that Cameron wasn't a Cofell by birth.

"Again, I can't comment."

Amanda would wager she knew but was giving nothing away. "We went to the Cofell farm and found the hidden room off the kitchen."

Beverly crossed her arms and nudged into the side of the chair.

She was still on the defensive and locked down. Amanda continued. "I'm going to guess that Cameron told you about it, but I understand you can't say anything." This was her being kind because she *didn't* understand. Not when something the therapist knew could help someone else. "That room has been processed, and we have reason to believe that we'll find forensic evidence Cameron wasn't the only one hurt in that room."

Beverly's eyes met Amanda's. In them, compassion and sorrow despite the wall that remained in place.

"We also found some other things in the home that were disturbing," Amanda said. "There was evidence the Cofells had other children in the house. Two girls."

"Two—" Beverly snapped her mouth shut.

"No, please, what were you going to say?" Amanda asked her.

The therapist shook her head. "Go on."

"You might have heard that the body of a teenage girl was discovered in Herald Church?" Amanda imagined the doctor took pride in being in the know, but this time there was a strong link to her client. She would have likely been glued to anything being said about the church and the standoff.

Beverly nodded. "She was identified as Sadie Jackson, but I'm not sure what any of this has to do with Cameron."

So her name has hit the news now...

"Did he ever tell you about a girl with long brown hair, blue eyes, a face like an angel, wearing blue bangles and a beaded necklace?" Trent asked.

The therapist repositioned on her chair. "Possibly."

"The girl that we found, Sadie Jackson, was wearing that jewelry. She's one of the girls we believe the Cofells kept at their home." Amanda watched as the revelation landed.

The therapist's shoulders lowered. "That can't be. I mean, I had no reason to think that she was real. Not the way he spoke about her. It was always in a chant as he stared blankly across the room." There were a few beats, then Beverly added, "Did Cameron do this to her? Actually, never mind. Sadie was taken over thirty years ago, wasn't she?" Wrinkles burrowed in her brow. "What is the connection?"

The therapist's walls had fallen. "Well, we found a photograph of Sadie in the Cofell farmhouse. In the shot, she was pregnant and about sixteen years old." Amanda paused, giving Beverly a chance to cut in, but she didn't. "That was twenty-three years ago."

"Okay, I'm not sure what you're trying to say— Oh."

Trent nodded. "We suspect Sadie Jackson is Cameron's mother."

"Mother," Beverly parroted.

Amanda and Trent remained silent, giving the therapist time to assimilate the information.

There was a knock on the door, and it was cracked open. A twenty-something woman tucked her head into the room. "Dr. Campbell?"

"Not now, Tanya," Beverly rushed out, her tone harsh.

The younger woman reversed course and didn't say another word. Whatever she thought warranted the interruption must not be worth a confrontation.

"Cameron's parents kidnapped Sadie as a young girl, kept her, and then..." Her mouth gaped open, then slowly closed.

"Tests will be done to confirm if Sadie is Cameron's biological mother, but the math works," Amanda pointed out.

"And this other girl? You mentioned the Cofells had two. Did they"—she rubbed her throat—"take her too?"

Trent sat up straighter and leaned slightly forward. "That's part of why we're here hoping you can help us. There was a photo of another girl, and some clothing. Did Cameron ever mention anyone else living at the farm?"

"No."

Trent moved his finger around the screen of his tablet. Amanda watched as he brought up the photo they had found. He stood and took it over to the therapist. "Does she look like anyone Cameron might have described?"

Beverly studied the picture, then shook her head. "As I said, he only mentioned the one girl."

"Sadie." A name that hadn't been said near as often as it should have been in the last thirty-one years. Saying it now somehow breathed life back into the girl, resurrecting the fact that she had existed, that she did matter.

Trent returned to the couch.

"But what can be done about any of this now?" the therapist asked. "The Cofells are dead. This was something I tried to help Cameron to process. Sadly it seemed his anger transferred from them to someone he saw as equally accountable. But how do you expect to get any justice here?"

"The Cofells are obviously out of reach," Amanda said. "But there's evidence that at least one other person may have been involved, and that means another girl might be in danger while we speak." Most pedophiles didn't change their ways. Amanda thought this drastic approach might jar the therapist into speaking.

"The other reason you're here. You think I know something about that?"

Amanda shook her head. "Not exactly, but we'd like to

know if Cameron ever alleged someone else was involved in his abuse. Did he talk about a family friend who hung around?"

Beverly shook her head. "I don't know about that latter part, but Cameron and I have done rather intensive work to recall his trauma, including hypnotism. If he'd had another abuser, it likely would have surfaced."

Likely... Amanda didn't take that as a definitive answer any more than she viewed hypnotism as hard science. "Then he's never mentioned any other people to you? By name? Description?"

Beverly shook her head.

"Any men with long, dark sideburns?" It was a shot in the dark but worth pulling the trigger if it stood any chance of hitting the bull's-eye.

"The only other person he mentioned was that one girl... Sadie, as it turns out. Otherwise, you must realize that Cameron grew up very sheltered."

"They did what they could to isolate him, make him feel helpless," Trent said.

"That's right." Beverly leveled her gaze at Trent, a seeming understanding traversing between them.

"He spent most of his time in *the hole*. That hidden room you found," Beverly said. "Whenever I tried to get him to elaborate about it, he'd shut down, become catatonic. I got the sense it was where his abuse took place or where he was sent for punishment. He was home-schooled. Aside from Sunday school, church functions, and some arranged playdates, he never spent time with other children. But these dates were never at his home. Even as he grew older, his parents didn't afford him any liberties like most teens are given."

"Do you know who these playdates were with?" There could be a clue in that answer. From the sound of it the Cofells did what they could to guard their dark secrets. That would mean limiting their friendships and acquaintances as well.

"I don't, and I'm only going to say one more thing. Cameron has much more work ahead of him before he'll properly heal. His issues go much deeper than we've had time to get into. But look at the extreme lengths Cameron took trying to expose his truth. Look *where* he went." She let that sit for a few seconds before standing. "I believe I gave you more than five minutes." She glanced at the clock on the wall.

"We appreciate your time and insights, Dr. Campbell." Amanda held out her hand to the therapist. "Thank you."

Beverly nodded and shook Amanda's hand. They saw themselves out, and Amanda rolled the doctor's words over in her head all the way to the car. *Look* where *he went.* The more she thought about them, the puzzle seemed to unravel.

She did up her belt in the passenger seat. "Campbell specifically flagged *where* Cameron had gone to 'expose his truth.' That brings us all the way back to the accusations he made against Father Linwood. That the priest knew about the abuse he suffered."

"She could have been referring to the Church as an institution, or someone else Cameron encountered there," Trent suggested.

"Maybe, and I appreciate you looking at all the angles, but if it was a reference to another member or a group of people, why didn't Cameron go after anyone else? Why just the priest?" She'd talked herself in a circle.

"Don't have an answer for you. I *can* say that Cameron clearly held Father Linwood responsible. Whether it was for more than keeping quiet, it's hard to say. He could have had long, dark sideburns twenty-three years ago, but I would think Audrey would have recognized him. She lived next door and would know he was the priest there, even if she didn't attend mass."

"We need to talk with Audrey Witherspoon again to see if

the crate we found looks familiar to her. When we're there, we'll also ask how well she knows Father Linwood."

"Sounds like a plan." Trent got them on the road in the direction of Audrey's house.

As Trent drove, Amanda considered the priest as a suspect again. There was a possibility, albeit slim, that Witherspoon didn't know the priest by sight. What if Father Linwood had been the person who helped move Sadie's body into the church? What if his DNA was one of the profiles found on her body?

TWENTY-SIX

Amanda had just told Trent she was going to call Malone and update him on their visit to Cameron's therapist when her phone rang and his name flashed on the screen. "His ears must be burning," she said to Trent before she answered on speaker.

"I got news on the adoption front," Malone said, wasting no time.

He wasn't the type to delay news, but for him to rush ahead like this, he had something good. She kept quiet and patiently waited.

"There's no adoption record for Cameron Cofell, but there is a birth record. Winnie Cofell is listed as his mother. It was a home birth."

At this stage in her career, nothing should shock her. This did. Even though it shouldn't come as a surprise. Cameron had to legally exist somewhere, or he couldn't have gotten medical coverage, a driving license, or held a job... She imagined the Cofells thought it all through and put on a grand performance for the doctors. "Sure it was," she said, drenched with sarcasm. "Meanwhile, she told other people Cameron was adopted, and Winnie's brother told us she couldn't have children."

"There you go then. As if we didn't already know it. This case is twisted and dark as all heck."

"It is that. We just left the therapist's office, and she turned out to be more helpful than we could have imagined." Amanda filled him in on their visit and what they were on their way to do now.

"Keep me posted." Malone ended the call, and Trent turned down the street for Audrey Witherspoon. Herald Church loomed next door. Linwood could be there now if he'd been discharged from hospital.

It was midmorning, but the curtains were still closed in Audrey's front window, which Amanda noted and found somewhat strange. From talking with Audrey, she imagined her always rising before the sun and greeting a new day by drawing the curtains back.

Trent knocked a few times, and there was no answer. "Her car's in the driveway," he said. "Presumably she's here. Though she could have gone out with someone in their vehicle, or gone for a walk."

"Well, it's too cool to be sitting out back with a coffee or tea." She walked along the deck to the front window. The curtains were closed, but the edge of one fluttered, presumably catching a breeze from a floor vent, and cleared an opening. She peered inside. "Witherspoon's lying on the couch." Amanda rapped on the glass, and the woman didn't stir. Amanda became more persistent. Still no movement from the older lady. *Let's hope she's a deep sleeper!* "We need to call her phone number."

"I'll go get it." Trent rushed back to the department car to bring up Audrey's record. They had collected her number when they took her eyewitness statement.

Amanda continued to tap on the glass, trying to rouse the woman. No reaction.

Then, a dampened ringtone sounded from inside. Trent was back with his phone to his ear and shaking his head.

"She's not moving at all, Trent. We've got to call this in."

Trent pocketed his phone. "I hope there's an innocent explanation for this. Like she drank a bit too much and is just sleeping like the dead."

"You and me both." Though even as she said this, she couldn't imagine the eighty-three-year-old Audrey drinking like a sorority sister. The curtain blew back again, and Amanda knew what they had to do, and they technically had probable cause. "Tell me you know how to pick a lock."

"Would this help?" He pulled a lock-picking kit from his back pocket.

"Since when do you carry one of those around?" She recalled thinking the tool would come in handy in a previous investigation.

He shrugged. "For a while now."

She could get into why she never knew this before, but now wasn't the time. "You need to get us inside now."

"But she could be alive, and then we'd have a lot of explaining to do."

"Even more reason to get in there. She could be in need of medical attention."

"Yeah, okay, you're right." He jogged to the front door and tried the handle first. "It's unlocked." He tucked his kit back into his pocket, then opened the door. Amanda wasted no time running inside.

"Prince William County PD!" she called out as she hurried to Audrey Witherspoon. Trent's steps pounded behind her, but they both came to a standstill in front of the couch.

The older woman was deathly pale and a tinge blue. Her airway might be blocked, but any hope of helping her was wiped out when Amanda took her wrist to check for a pulse. "She's cold and stiff."

"Rigor..."

Amanda nodded. "She's gone."

"I guess we call it in." Trent took out his phone.

"You ever feel like we're cursed? Why does this keep happening to us?" It wasn't far from her mind that Malone had raised this same point not long ago on a previous investigation. This wasn't the first time they'd stumbled onto another body while already trying to solve a murder. In fact, it was quickly becoming a regular thing.

"You'd have to ask someone with more authority." Trent pointed upward to denote God.

Given her fractured relationship with the Big Guy, that wasn't happening. "Guess we just have all the luck," she said, dismissing his suggestion.

Trent called for a medical examiner and Crime Scene, and she called Malone. She landed in his voicemail and left a message. That decision might come back to bite her in the ass, but at least she had time to prepare for his arrival.

While Trent finished up his call, she studied the scene. Until manner of death was confirmed, they'd take precautions just as they would when it was evident there had been a murder. Both took booties out from their pockets and put them over their shoes. They would have already left prints in the home, but they could prevent more contamination. They also gloved up and stepped back from the body.

Nothing appeared to have been upset. Audrey looked like she'd just laid down for a nap and had fallen asleep. Sometimes the features of the dead were locked in emotion, whereas Audrey showcased none. Neither peace, anguish, nor confusion. If anything, Amanda would describe her resting face as accepting. Her passing had likely been graceful.

Balls of yarn and knitting needles were in a tote next to the couch in front of a coffee table. On its top was a teacup on a saucer, a pill case with compartments for a week, and a cell phone. None of the lids were open, and there was still some liquid in the cup, which had skinned over. These observations didn't necessarily gel with the rest of the scene.

"So it looks like she made herself tea and came in here to sit. But to do what? There's nothing to read, and no television in here to watch. She wasn't knitting. The curtains are closed, so no people-watching. Something's not right here." She'd like to dismiss it as nothing more than her imagination creating a mystery where none existed, but her instinct wouldn't allow that concession.

"All right, well, we'll figure it out." Trent set off to look around the house, and she branched off too. They wouldn't touch or move anything in the immediate area in case Audrey was murdered and it did end up factoring into evidence. The possibility was there that Audrey had succumbed due to age. She had been eighty-three, and the pill case suggested she had several prescriptions that she needed to keep straight.

In the kitchen, Amanda found an electric kettle on the countertop with a box of English Breakfast tea. There was a stirring spoon resting on a saucer. A dirty frypan sat on the stove with food remnants clinging to its edges that looked like butter, rice, and green onions. The air smelled slightly of fried chicken too. All this was probably residual of last night's dinner. If Audrey died after her meal, that might explain the closed curtains, but it didn't explain what would motivate her to go into the living room with a tea to stare at a blank wall. Then again, she could have worked on her knitting for a bit, became tired, and laid down on the couch.

"Amanda," Trent called out, and she followed the direction of his voice down a hall and into a small guest room.

There was a double bed in there and a desk with a computer and a chair. Trent gestured toward the monitor displaying a text document. She walked over and leaned forward to read what was there.

"'I just can't take it anymore. The burden of seeing what I

did and doing nothing all these years... To think that a young girl had been killed and I had done nothing to help.'" Amanda straightened up and asked Trent, "Did you touch that keyboard?"

"Nope. The screen was on when I came in."

"Huh, so no screensaver. Whoever wrote this wanted us to find it."

"*Whoever?* You don't think it was Audrey Witherspoon?"

"I'm not making any bold statements yet, but..."

"I hear you. It seems rather coincidental that an eyewitness suddenly dies. She seemed in fine health to me. Her mind was certainly sharp."

"I know, but as I said, no bold statement. But she certainly didn't strike me as suicidal."

"Though she clearly regretted not saying something about what she saw much sooner."

"I got that too, but coming to us and telling her story must have cleared her conscience some."

"The note points out not doing anything for years." Trent shrugged. "She came to us and essentially had her worst fears validated. Maybe she took the murder itself onto her shoulders. She could have become so consumed by guilt that she killed herself over it."

"Yeah, I don't know. Speaking out might have led to Sadie being found sooner, but it wouldn't have stopped her murder."

"Hello? Prince William County PD!" a woman's voice called out.

Amanda was the first to leave the room, and Officer Traci Cochran was peeking through the front door.

"I got here as fast as I could. Guess I was the first available unit," Traci said as they approached her. "I didn't want to step inside if it wasn't necessary. I hear there's been a death."

"You heard right. The resident," Amanda told her.

"I just wanted to let you know I'm here, and I'll stay posted by the door. I'm assuming the others are on their way?"

"They are, and thank you." Amanda smiled at Traci, having respect for the uniformed officer. She was good at her job and sympathetic toward victims.

Officer Cochran stepped outside, and Amanda returned to the sitting room.

She stood at a distance but studied Audrey. Tea, a pill case, no clear sign as to cause or manner of death. And there was the suicide note. Typed though... "I really don't think Audrey killed herself."

"I didn't think you were making any bold statements?"

"I changed my mind."

"Okay, but let's think about where that would take us."

"I know exactly where it takes us. The mystery man who was involved with Sadie Jackson's murder. He's still out there. He knew that she saw him that night moving the crate into the church."

"Which made her an immediate threat, so why not kill her back then? Why wait all these years?"

She shrugged. "He could have figured if nothing came of her seeing him, he'd let her go on with her life. Now that Sadie's body was found, that's changed."

"The older woman became a liability, a loose end to tie up."

"He'd have to assume she remembered what she saw that night. Even still, why turn up and risk everything by staging a suicide?"

"Which we're assuming was staged," he corrected. "But if our suspicion is right and Audrey Witherspoon was killed, this guy must be spiraling. What he didn't think about was another body comes with more clues. I tell you, I'm grateful for narcissistic murderers. They make our jobs easier."

Amanda wasn't so sure she'd go that far, and there was a contradiction in his words. If there weren't murders in the first place, there would be no job. "The thing is, though, she hadn't said anything about what she saw for twenty-three years. Running with our theory, was it just the discovery of Sadie's body that had him spooked? Or did he see Witherspoon go to the station? Has he been keeping tabs on her all these years?" As that last question tumbled out, her eyes widened. "Huh. There's an interesting thought."

"What is it?"

"Much easier to keep an eye on someone if you..."

"Live nearby," they said together.

"The church is next door," she said. "Father Linwood could have returned home from the hospital by the time Audrey came to us."

"Could have. Though we ruled him out as the man with the long, dark sideburns because we said that Audrey would recognize him."

"No. We assumed that. We didn't exactly get a chance to ask her."

"Shit. You're right," Trent said. "Then the priest isn't exactly in the clear."

There was a knock on the door, then it opened. Amanda popped forward to see who had entered the house.

Malone was standing there. "Steele. I'd like a word."

He pulled out the surname *and* phrased his request in two sentences. "Sure." She gave a pressed-lip smile to Trent and walked over to Malone.

"Voicemail? Why didn't you have me tracked down for something like this?"

"I didn't think it was worth interrupting you." *Not entirely the truth.* She didn't want to hear what was likely coming now.

"Meanwhile, my detectives entered a civilian's house without proper clearance."

"A woman is dead."

"Which you know *after* trespassing."

"Trent and I let ourselves inside. I'm not going to deny that, but there were also exigent circumstances. Audrey Wither- spoon was nonresponsive. We tried knocking several times and calling. I caught a glimpse of her through the front window and saw her lying on the couch, appearing to be unconscious. We thought she might need medical attention."

Malone held up a hand. "Did you know she was deceased when you entered the home? And be honest with me, Steele."

"Absolutely not. There was no way for me to know that from looking through the window. Her welfare was foremost in my mind."

Malone scanned her eyes, as if she were under a microscope.

"I swear to you," she added when he didn't say anything.

Eventually, he nodded. "Well, it seems we're down a familiar road. What happened?"

He didn't need to say it in so many words. His tone said it all. They turned up to question someone and found a body. "There's no clear signs of cause or manner of death," she said evenly.

"Though I sense a *but* coming."

Trent stepped up next to her, clearly picking up on the fact her reprimand was over. Malone barely passed him a glance.

"There's what appears to be a typed suicide note on the home computer," she began.

Malone huffed at the word *appears*. "And what's your initial assessment of the scene?"

This question had her penned into a corner, because based solely on face value, without getting into the pill case, testing her tea, the contents of Audrey's stomach… "It looks like she made herself a cup of tea and took it to her sitting room. I'm going to guess this was last night after her dinner based on the remnants of food in the frying pan. When I was going to check for a pulse, I found her hand and arm were in rigor."

"Food poisoning then? Old age?"

Was he goading her into committing to a manner of death? The one she'd give him wouldn't be one he wanted to hear. She didn't understand why he was pressuring her. "I'm not a medical examiner, but I'd say at some point during her tea, she didn't feel well."

"But she wrote the note before sitting down?"

"If she killed herself, yes." She could only withstand so much pressure.

"Huh."

The front door opened again, and they stepped back to make room for CSIs Blair and Donnelly to come inside.

"I'm going to leave," Malone said, wedging past the investigators, "but I want to be kept informed of everything you find here. Don't leave it in a message."

Trent, Blair, and Donnelly leveled looks at Amanda. None of them said anything verbally but their eyes said everything. *What's his problem?* Amanda wasn't sure why Malone was giving her such a hard time and didn't care for it. The last time he treated her this way, a cancerous tumor was pressing on his brain and affecting his character.

"She's in the front sitting room," Amanda said, all business, cutting through the awkward tension. "But there's also what resembles a suicide note on her computer. Please make sure the keyboard is dusted for prints."

"You think this might be murder?" Donnelly asked.

"Too soon to know," Amanda responded.

"Before I get to work," Blair said, "I'd thought you'd want to know the DNA on that cigarette butt you sent in wasn't a match to either male DNA found with Sadie Jackson. It was, however, a familial match to the female profile."

"Makes sense," Amanda replied. "The butt belonged to Sean Olsen, Winnie Cofell's brother, so now her involvement is confirmed."

"We didn't get the feeling Olsen was involved," Trent said.

"At least it's backed by science now," Amanda replied.

Blair set off with her colleague at her heels.

Trent turned to her. "What was that all about with Malone?"

"Please, not another word. I don't know, and I'm not sure I want to know. Besides, figuring out Malone isn't my priority." It pained her to say this, to shove his treatment of her aside. It was so unlike him and the association with his health scare was doing little to settle her nerves. Had another tumor grown? She swallowed roughly, needing to put him out of her mind. "We'll need to wait for the scene to be processed, obviously, but I can't shake the wording of that suicide note. She refers to carrying the burden of seeing what she had and doing nothing. But if she was so distraught, why not leave us more than that? A name, a more detailed description? Why not elaborate for anyone finding the note?"

"She made a written testimony. She honestly could have told us everything she remembered, but that doesn't mean that afterward she didn't start to suffer immense guilt, as we discussed. The fact she found out that Sadie Jackson was hidden in the walls of the church for twenty-three years, her family without closure all that time and the girl without justice, could have weighed on her and got to be too much."

"As you said, 'she made a written testimony.' How does that reconcile with the note and 'I had done *nothing* to help'?"

"I don't know, Amanda. I'm just keeping open to all the possibilities until we learn more."

She nodded. He was right, of course. Any time a detective pigeon-holed an investigation, it was doomed. With that in mind, was the suicide note legit? Had Audrey Witherspoon been the victim of her own guilt? Or was it as Amanda feared and her death was the result of something far more sinister?

TWENTY-SEVEN

Time never stopped. It was a fact of life just like the reality everyone had an expiry date. Amanda was dwelling on that a lot as the CSIs processed the sitting room. Her gaze often returned to Audrey Witherspoon. Regardless of how she died, it was sad that a woman with such a sharp mind was gone.

Blair was taking photographs and gestured for Donnelly to collect the pill case. The investigator lifted it and said, "Huh."

One little utterance, and it had the hairs rising on the back of Amanda's neck. "What is it?"

"It feels rather light." Donnelly shook it, and there was a rather subdued ticking of pills against the plastic. She snapped the compartment lid for Friday, then Saturday. "Okay, this is strange."

Donnelly's reaction to each new discovery was testing Amanda's patience.

"For heaven's sake, Isabelle. Could you be any more dramatic?" Emma Blair shook her head and set her camera back in her collection case.

"I could try." Isabelle smiled at her colleague. "It's just there's only one pill in each of the remaining compartments."

"What's strange about that?" Trent asked.

"Well, normally people get these things because they take lots of medication, and they want to remember to take them. But she only has one pill," Donnelly repeated.

"She still could have wanted to make sure she took it," Blair put in.

Remember... make sure... "No. Something's not right here," Amanda said, dread washing through her. Everyone looked at her. She made eye contact with Trent. "She told us she had an incredible memory even at eighty-three."

"Unless she was exaggerating that," he countered.

"No, she was clear-minded when she spoke to us. You even said that yourself a few moments ago," she pointed out.

"Fair enough."

"Right, so why would a woman with a strong memory need a pill case at all? Even more so, why for *one* pill a day? If she had to sort out a few, I could understand the purpose. They'd just all be ready in one place."

"What are you saying, Amanda?" Blair asked her.

"I'm saying that..." She paused there, realizing that what she was entertaining may be crazy, but to hell with it. "I wonder if that's even her pill case."

"Who else would it belong to?" Donnelly's voice was soft like she was tiptoeing in a minefield.

"Whoever staged this to look like a suicide," Amanda pushed out. She'd shared her suspicion about murder with the CSIs when they first showed up by asking them to process the keyboard. "Trent, you and I will need to track down Audrey's next of kin and closest friends and ask them about her mental and emotional state."

"Suicidal people often present a front to the world. They might not have even known," Blair said.

"That might be the case, but obviously they need to know that Audrey's dead regardless of how. You happen to look in the bathroom, Trent?" She remembered passing it on the way to the home office slash guest room.

"I saw it but didn't go in."

"Do you remember seeing a medicine cabinet?"

He nodded. "Behind the mirror."

She took off, wondering if it would help them out at all. She opened the door, and there were the usual things. Toothpaste, toothbrush, floss, deodorant, a box of Band-Aids, a tube of cream for treating bug bites, and one prescription bottle. She lifted it and confirmed Audrey's name was on the label. "It's oxycodone. Directions say 'take as needed.'" She unscrewed the lid, and there were quite a few inside.

"That's a no-nonsense pain pill," Trent said.

"Lethal if one isn't careful."

"Maybe that's why Audrey set aside a pill a day then. She was just taking a precaution."

"Could be." She might be making more out of all this than was there, but she didn't care for coincidence. Witherspoon came to them, and the next thing, she's dead. It was hard to set that timing aside. "I'd like to confirm the remaining pills in the organizer were oxycodone." She took the prescription bottle with her to the sitting room. "Are the pills in the case these ones?" She handed the bottle to Donnelly, who came over.

She looked at them and nodded. "They have the same stamp."

"Then I need you to bag that bottle as evidence, please. And I might be erring on the side of an abundance of caution, but check the bottle for prints. Clearly, I'm not interested in ones belonging to Audrey Witherspoon. Same too for the organizer."

"We can do that," Blair said, speaking up. "You really don't think this was suicide, do you?"

"Not in the least." Amanda was owning her truth now, as she should have before. Any other time she never had any issue standing her ground. It must have been Malone's treatment of her earlier that had thrown her off.

"Well, that's good enough for me." Blair smiled at her, and Amanda was grateful for the CSI's confidence.

"You know how I feel about it," Trent said. "I'm with you in that this scene isn't all adding up. But let's say Witherspoon was murdered. How did her killer gain access to her house? How did they even kill her?"

"I might be able to help with one of those things," Rideout said from the entry.

The man was stealthy, as Amanda hadn't heard him come in. It didn't seem the others had either. The screen door smacked shut, and Liam poked his head into the room and waved.

"That's if you're ready for me," Rideout added as he entered the room. His comment was directed to the CSIs.

"It's all yours," Blair told him and suggested to Donnelly that the two of them search the house for any signs of forced entry.

Amanda mouthed, "Thanks," and the investigator nodded.

The ME got to work with his assistant recording any observations Rideout made.

"Deceased female in her late sixties, early seventies," he said.

"Technically, she was eighty-three," Amanda cut in with Audrey's factual age.

"Wow. I'd say she looks good for a woman her age but..." Rideout touched Audrey's hands, feet, and face. "She's in full rigor." Next, he pierced the body with a thermometer. It beeped a moment later, and Rideout withdrew the instrument and looked over his shoulder at Liam, who had shot off into the house and returned a little winded.

"The house is set at seventy-two degrees," he told Rideout.

Rideout examined the reading and said, "Death occurred between eighteen to twenty hours ago."

Amanda checked the time on her phone and did the quick math in her head. Rideout's estimation put TOD between four and seven thirty last night. Not long after Audrey gave her statement.

The medical examiner straightened and addressed Amanda and Trent. "Until I have her back to the morgue, there's nothing more I can tell you. Cause of death isn't apparent, and neither is manner of death."

"We have reason to suspect that she might have been killed," Amanda said.

"Why doesn't that surprise me?" Rideout smiled at her, and taken at face value, it was rather odd considering the context of their conversation. They were talking about murder, standing in front of the body, *and* he was smiling. But that was nothing new for Rideout. In fact, she was rather used to it and found his easy manner lessened the tension at a death scene. "There's nothing immediately standing out to me. Liam, help me lift her to get a look at her backside. More precisely the rear of her body. What I can see anyway."

Liam set down the tablet he'd been making his notes on and helped Rideout lift Audrey up.

"No signs of any injuries on the back of her head, neck, or arms. The rest of her is covered. Okay, let's bag her up." Rideout snapped the clasps on his medical bag while Liam scurried out the front door. A moment later, he came back with a wheeled gurney. Officer Cochran must have held the screen door back for him.

Amanda and Trent watched Rideout and Liam bag the hands, seal up the body, and load it.

"What time for the autopsy?" Amanda asked Liam, who kept the ME's schedule.

Liam consulted his tablet and said, "Tomorrow at nine."

"Thanks." She and Trent were always welcome to observe the postmortems Rideout conducted, but it wasn't always necessary or the best use of their time. Not when they could get the highlights of the findings and carry on following leads in the case.

Rideout and Liam left, and Trent said, "Guess that's that."

"Except we're not much further ahead. No clear sign of murder, just our cop instinct and some anomalies." Usually Rideout had far more to offer when he popped in for a body. But often there were more clear indications of what had taken place and how the deceased had died. She should be happy they at least knew Audrey Witherspoon had died last evening. Amanda put herself back in the scene. "The front door was unlocked. Was she expecting company? Had she let her killer into her home?"

"No sign of an altercation, so it must have started off peacefully. That's if she was killed," Trent added with a smile.

It was good having a partner who balanced her out. She also could count on him to have her back. Normally the same could be said about Malone too. What was all the earlier skepticism about anyway? Thinking of Malone, she'd better give him a call and update him on everything.

TWENTY-EIGHT

Audrey Witherspoon's next of kin turned out to be her granddaughter, Brenda Witherspoon. Brenda's mother had died when she was young. Amanda called Malone on the way to Brenda's place. As Amanda listened to the line ring, she was crossing her fingers that he wouldn't answer, not sure she really wanted to hear his voice. When she thought back to how he'd treated her earlier, rage had her breathing heavier. She'd proven herself at this job repeatedly and for someone who was supposed to be a family friend—

"What have you got, Steele?"

His abrupt answer threw her off. It might be worth taking the time to swing by Central and have a conversation in person. It would be easier to request the reason for his attitude toward her. With Trent in the driver's seat beside her that was rather tough to do. She told Malone about their findings and their leaning toward her death being suspicious.

"Yet, there's no sign of forced entry," Malone countered.

"That doesn't necessarily mean anything. She could have let her killer in."

"Okay, and if she was killed, any inkling as to who might have done it?"

"No one specifically, just that her murder's connected to Sadie Jackson." That's all she was saying given the contentious mood he was in. If she said she suspected the man with the long, dark sideburns from twenty-three years ago, he'd ask why Audrey would let him into her home. And she didn't have the answer to that, so why get into it?

"More to the point, her eyewitness account of what she saw outside the church?"

He'd seen through her. "We believe so."

"It's plausible, but we need facts before we make any moves."

She wasn't sure why he was talking to her like she'd just received her detective badge. "I understand that."

"And don't move in on any suspects until you run it past me."

She cringed at being micromanaged. "Is there something else we should be discussing, Sarge?" Her body trembled as she set the question out there. He might be a family friend, but he also held her career in his hands.

A few beats of silence then, "Now's not the time." With that he hung up.

She tried to slough it off, pretend that his curtness didn't hurt her, that he hadn't ended the call without saying *goodbye*.

"Do you know what's going on with Malone?" Trent asked her.

She should have known he'd pick up on her unsettled energy. "No clue, but I hope he tells me soon." Her initial fear about another tumor returned. Was it to blame for his altered behavior?

"Me too. He was all over you at the Witherspoon scene."

"Tell me something I didn't notice." The words spilled out. "Sorry, I'm just..."

"Pissed, confused? Yeah, I get it. Me too. He never talks to you like that."

"Something bigger must be going on." *Need facts before we make any moves... Don't move in on any suspects until you run it past me...* As she tossed Malone's words around in her head, she landed back on one repeated word. *Move.* Had she done something that let him down? If she had, she couldn't think of what. But her mind was rather preoccupied with the Jackson case and now the Witherspoon one. "Enough about Malone. We need to focus on what's about to happen." *How we're going to break someone's heart...*

"We better focus fast." Trent gestured toward an apartment building. "We're here."

They took the elevator up to the fourth floor.

Amanda knocked on the door for Brenda's unit, wishing she had more answers for her.

"I'm coming," a woman said at the same time as the deadbolt was unlocked and the door was opened.

Amanda and Trent held up their badges and introduced themselves, leaving out the name of their unit at the PWCPD. "Are you Brenda Witherspoon?" Amanda asked her.

"Yeah."

"Could we come in for a moment?" Amanda tagged on a subtle smile.

"Ah, sure." Brenda stepped away, clearing a path for them to enter.

The apartment was rather open concept from the doorway. A kitchen straight ahead with a hallway branching to the left, a coat closet to the immediate left, the living room to the right, a dining table to the rear of that.

"We can sit in here." Brenda gestured toward the living room and sat on a rocker recliner. "Please, wherever you're comfortable."

There was a candle burning on the long coffee table, and the subtle hint of vanilla blanketed the room.

"Thank you," Amanda said, taking a spot on one end of the couch and Trent the other.

Brenda was looking at them, a puzzled expression on her face.

"Unfortunately, we've come with bad news," Amanda began. "Your grandmother, Audrey Witherspoon, was found dead in her home this morning."

"What? No, that can't... No." Brenda's eyes filled with tears, and she shook her head. She palmed her cheeks even though tears had yet to fall.

"We're sorry for your loss, Ms. Witherspoon," Amanda said.

"Please just call me Brenda." She sniffled. "How did this happen?"

"She passed last evening, but we're not entirely sure what caused her death. But there are some things that we'd like to ask you about."

"Ah, sure." Brenda's hands were trembling.

Trent took out his tablet, which Brenda didn't miss. She did a doubletake.

"Why are you taking notes?" She pointed at the device.

"It's just procedure," Trent told her.

Amanda wasn't sure how clear that would be for Brenda, but for them, notifications were much more. They involved questioning and could be a fount of information to help the investigation.

"Procedure?" Brenda said this as if chewing on the word. "Then you're investigating her death. You think someone did this to my grandmother? That someone killed her?"

"At this time, all I can confirm is her death is being investigated." Amanda would toe that line as closely as she could. Without the autopsy to confirm cause of death, manner was left in the air. That is unless they learned something from Brenda that would tip things. "She was found lying on the couch in her sitting room with a tea and her pill case on the table next to her."

"Her *pill case?*" Brenda's forehead scrunched up.

"Are you surprised she had one?" Amanda asked, tingles lacing down her arms.

"First, just to make sure I'm on the same page, you're talking about those plastic containers that divvy up pills? So people remember to take them?"

"That's right, and it helps organize them," Amanda responded.

"Here's the thing. Grandma had only one prescription, if you can believe it. She was eighty-three, mind clear as a bell with a memory like an elephant."

"What was the prescription?" Amanda asked, just for the record.

"Oxy. She hated taking them and rarely did, even when her arthritis flared up."

If what Brenda was telling them was true, it only made the existence of a pill case even more suspicious. "Is it possible that she was starting to take the pills more regularly? That she bought the case to ensure she didn't take more than one a day?"

"I guess it's possible, but I really don't see it."

Amanda nodded. "There was also a letter found on her computer, which reads like a suicide note."

"What? No. My grandmother would never..." Brenda gripped her sweater tight to herself.

"Was your grandmother depressed at all?" Trent asked.

"No way. She loves life. *Loved.*" Tears fell down Brenda's cheeks at her self-correction. "Besides, Grandma might not have been religious, but she viewed suicide as a sin."

Her adamant stand only confirmed for Amanda things

weren't what they appeared to be at the Witherspoon home. It also led in nicely with questions that she and Trent needed to ask. "Well, if she didn't do this to herself, do you know who might have had reason to kill her?"

"Oh my God, kill her. So we are back to that. It's hard to even fathom."

"When we found your grandmother, Brenda, she also had the curtains closed," Amanda said. "There didn't seem to be anything in the room to entertain her—"

"Closed?"

The pitch of Brenda's voice had the hairs on Amanda's arms standing up. "That's right."

"No, Grandma never closes the curtains. And I mean *never*. Grandma Audrey raised me. I lived with her from the time I was twelve until I got a place with a roommate at nineteen. And I'm telling you she never closed the curtains."

"That could have changed after you moved out," Trent said.

"No. It didn't. We got into this just last week when we had tea in that room after dinner. It was a rainy day and already dark at six. Grandma loves to eat between five and six. Anyway, I hate sitting in a room with the curtains open at night. I might as well be on stage with anybody and everybody able to look in."

Amanda found the paranoia somewhat interesting as it wasn't a busy street, but to each their own. "Was it customary to retreat to that room for tea?"

"Every night after dinner. Often, she'd knit in there. You might have noticed there isn't a TV. None in the entire house. I hated that growing up, and I might be making up for lost time." She pointed at the huge flatscreen mounted to the wall. It had to be over seventy inches.

Watching it from this distance would give Amanda a headache, especially with the way most shows tended to zoom in on the actors. Their faces sometimes took up the entire screen. "Do you know of anyone who might have had some-thing against your grandmother?"

"It's hard to imagine. I mean she was an older woman who mostly stuck to her own business."

"Mostly?" Amanda clung on to that.

"Well, she wasn't a fan of the church next door."

"Why's that?" Amanda asked.

"She thought they were a bunch of zealots, but she's also convinced that she saw something years ago. I never heard anything about it until that girl was found in the church this week. She hasn't talked about much else since. Maybe she was losing her mind."

If Audrey was obsessed about it, who else might she have told or confronted in the last few days? Could one be the man she'd seen twenty-three years ago? "For what it's worth, I think your grandmother's mind was sound."

"Then she went to you? To the police?" When Amanda and Trent nodded, Brenda shook her head. "I told her not to bother you, but I guess you know firsthand then that she was obsessed about what she thought she saw."

"You don't think she saw anything?" Trent countered.

"Who knows?"

"And what did she see, from your knowledge?" Amanda asked.

"Two men carrying a wooden crate into the church during the *witching hours*." Brenda put finger quotes around the latter words. "Grandma made a point of emphasizing that and said nothing good happens at that time."

Amanda wasn't getting caught up in that. "Do you know if your grandmother was expecting company last night?"

Brenda's eyes glazed over.

"Brenda?" Amanda prompted.

"Not that I know of." It was an absentminded response.

"Her doors were unlocked. We thought she may have let someone in," Amanda said.

"Unlocked doors don't mean anything. I could never get her to lock them."

Brenda continued to respond, but wasn't entirely present. Her gaze was blank and her words robotic. "What is it, Brenda?"

"Grandma said she was tired of sitting around. She even said the police had enough to keep them busy."

Was Amanda's earlier thought more a bull's-eye than she gave it credit? Had Audrey taken things further than just speaking with her and Trent? "Did she do something besides report what she saw?"

"I don't know. I didn't even know she went to the police." Brenda started crying into her hands.

Amanda let a few minutes pass and glanced over at Trent. He'd made some notes in his tablet.

Once Brenda composed herself some, Amanda broke the silence. "We're very sorry for your loss, Brenda. Here's my card if you think of something after we leave." Amanda handed one over and stood.

Back in the car, Amanda and Trent discussed what they'd just gathered.

"Audrey was tired of doing nothing," Trent said. "That smacks close to the note on the computer, though we already rebutted that because she did do something by coming to us and giving a statement."

"Yeah, but was that all? Also her doors are always unlocked. Did the killer somehow know this and take advantage? Or did Audrey unwittingly let them in?"

"The killer? I take it we're settled on that now?"

"Too many things aren't adding up, not to mention the potential motive someone would have for wanting her dead."

"Namely, one person."

"And Brenda had no idea her grandmother had a pill case. Did the one next to her even belong to her?" Her phone rang, and she hesitated to answer as Malone's name showed on the screen. She took a deep breath and picked up. "Detective Steele."

"A lead came in from one of the canvassing officers. It got routed to me for some reason, but a neighbor saw Father Linwood go into Audrey's house last evening."

"We'll have him brought in." She looked over at Trent, but he'd be in the dark as to who or why. She hadn't answered on speaker given Malone's recent attitude toward her.

"No need. That's already in the works. You headed back?"

"We are. We just finished speaking with Audrey's grand-daughter and found out a few things. I can bring you up to speed when we get to Central."

"Just tell me now."

It was like he was putting off the inevitable conversation they needed to have to clear the air.

"Steele?" he prompted.

My surname again! She gathered her courage and dismissed her rising insecurities. Then she filled him in on the pill case and unlocked doors, and Audrey's sudden obsession with not having done enough.

"Hmph. I'll watch you conduct the interview with Father Linwood. Just text me once you get here. I'll make sure room two is reserved for you."

"Thank—"

He hung up on her, cutting her off.

Her cheeks flamed. "I don't know what the hell his problem is, but he better tell me before I strangle him," she vented.

"Did I hear that we're headed back to Central?"

"I appreciate you getting right to the point."

"Are we in trouble over something?"

"I don't know, but it sure feels like it. Enough about Malone, though. We'll have someone else to talk to when we get back to the station. Father Linwood," she said before he could ask. Then she told him about the neighbor's account.

"Huh. So did Father Linwood kill Witherspoon? Was he the man with the long, dark sideburns?"

"I guess we're going to find out."

TWENTY-NINE

It was getting close to four o'clock when Amanda texted Malone that she and Trent were headed for the interview room. It bothered her that he asked for her to communicate that way, especially after his scolding about leaving voicemail.

One thing pushing her through was the thought of getting home in time to rescue the night with Zoe. She'd resolved to do that even if the priest looked guilty. Laying charges and moving forward could wait until morning. After all, it was Valentine's Day, and she had made restaurant reservations for her and Zoe last month.

She passed the observation room that looked in on Interview Room Two, and it was empty.

Huh... No response to her text. Shame on him. She refused to let his behavior continue to unnerve her. She couldn't afford to. Not when she was about to face Father Linwood. She got the door for herself and Trent.

At the sight of them, Father Linwood crossed himself, pressed his palms together, and gazed upward. "I pray that both of your souls will be saved."

"I'd save your prayers. It might be yours that needs saving,"

Amanda pushed back as she sat across from him. She didn't much care for the priest assuming things about her and trying to paint himself her savior.

"Excuse me, young lady, but—"

"Audrey Witherspoon died under suspicious circumstances last night." She sat back, crossed her arms, stared him down. She usually employed a little more finesse with her interrogations, but they had the priest at the victim's home.

"She's..." The priest signed the cross again.

He may have been sincere, but it irked her regardless. "Were you at her house last evening?"

"If that's what you call four thirty. I consider that to be the afternoon."

Four, four thirty, both fit with the estimated TOD. "Why were you there?"

Father Linwood smiled. "She was a troubled woman."

Amanda bit back from asking if he was there praying for her soul too. She heard how she sounded in her own head right now and didn't like it. Blame it on transference. Her irritation with Malone spilling over onto Linwood despite her best intentions to push it aside. "Can you be more specific, or tell us what prompted the visit? From what we understand the two of you weren't friends."

"I held no ill will toward the woman, though I did sense hostility coming from her."

"Over what?" Trent asked, stealing the priest's attention.

"She was convinced we were hiding something, more specifically, covering up wrongdoing."

She resisted the urge to voice her agreement. After all, in a way, the priest was guilty of doing just that. He would have heard the Cofells' confessions, possibly those admitting to kidnapping and assault as well as abuse, yet he kept quiet. In her mind, that was equivalent to Witherspoon's accusation. The sanctity of the confessional booth aside. "And how would you know this?"

"She made that perfectly clear when she stormed into the church yesterday afternoon. Several of the congregation can testify to this."

Audrey Witherspoon had taken the matter into her own hands, but what was she thinking by going into the church? "What time was this?"

"That would have been around four."

Not long after she'd left Central and signed off on her testimony. She must have gone straight to the church. "You said several of the congregation were there?" She was thinking in terms of collecting names. Was one among them the man who had the long, dark sideburns twenty-three years ago? Or were she and Trent currently sitting across from that man? The collar did little to quiet her suspicions. There were people in all sorts of respectable positions who didn't deserve to be.

"Five, excluding myself."

"We'll need their names," she volleyed back.

Father Linwood narrowed his eyes. "For what reason?"

"Audrey Witherspoon died under suspicious circumstances not long after your meeting. That puts all of you in the frame," she said matter-of-factly.

"Even me?" Father Linwood touched his collar.

"You were seen going to her house. Something you just admitted to doing."

"If you're implying that I was upset by her accusations, I'll admit to that, but I would never kill a person. That is a sin against God."

People acted in contrast to their beliefs all the time. The priest's words didn't sway her. "I'm sure you can appreciate we need more than your word."

Father Linwood opened his mouth, closed it, opened it again, as if deciding how to respond. "I believe the burden of proving guilt rests on your shoulders, Detective. But I will say that all of us were rather shaken by her showing up like that."

This wasn't the first time he'd phrased it like Audrey had interrupted something special. "Why was everyone there?"

"The church was just released. We needed to discuss repairs to the wall. We also talked about organizing a memorial for the girl, a formal occasion to pray over her departed soul. It was on the tail end of that when she came in and accused us of being a bunch of killers."

That had Amanda falling silent.

"How did everyone react to that?" Trent asked.

"Everyone was shaken."

"Yet, you decided to pay her a visit shortly afterward?" Amanda would bet it was prompted by more than going to save her soul.

"To make peace, but she wasn't open to listening to a word out of my mouth. She kept going on about a man with long, dark sideburns. I had no idea who or what she was talking about, but I told her I used to have long ones, but I was dirty blond."

Which could appear dark in the wee hours of the morning... "How close were you to the Cofells?"

"Just as close as I am with all my flock. They are precious children of God, and I'm here to protect them in a dangerous world."

"You didn't do much for Cameron," Trent accused. "I should say that I respect the confessional booth. I never grew up baptized into any religion, but I respect that people have their own beliefs and ways of thinking. But any vow of confidentiality crosses a moral line when it protects criminals, whether it be religious or medical. As a priest, you must know the Bible speaks of respecting the authorities that God has put in place, that being the government. If people confess to breaking laws, then where should your allegiance lie?"

Father Linwood bit his bottom lip and said nothing. Amanda was moved by what Trent said, and she respected his viewpoint and agreed with it.

"Did you know they were hurting that boy?" Trent asked.

"I'm not comfortable responding to that question."

"But they're gone now, Father Linwood," Trent said. "You are holding on to the secrets of the dead. Not only that but they were criminals."

"All sins are forgiven upon death. It's the debt all men pay…"

Amanda was quite sure he was quoting scripture with that last part, but she remained silent. Trent seemed to be making some headway.

"And I don't see what good it would do to say anything now," Linwood said. "It will accomplish nothing."

"Not entirely true," Trent said.

"I don't see it any other way."

"We have reason to believe that the Cofells took that girl we found in the walls of your church." Trent was laying everything out so smoothly, Amanda just sat back.

Father Linwood wet his lips. "I'd know nothing about that."

"Then they never confessed this to you?" Amanda wedged in, unable to help herself.

"No."

"Did they ever mention kidnapping anyone?" Her mind was now on that picture of Jane Doe.

"No. Was there someone else?"

Trent glanced at her before speaking again, and she nudged her head for him to go ahead. She'd circle back to Jane Doe. "The Cofells must have been close to other members of the church."

"We're all close."

Trent angled his head. "We're interested in who might have

been close friends with them. The type of friends who are confidantes, people who have each other's backs."

"I can't say."

"Can't or won't?" Trent countered.

"Both."

Amanda looked at Trent, and he appeared as confused by that statement as she was. "I don't understand," she told the priest.

"Me either," Trent said.

"That was a long time ago. Twenty-some years."

"Twenty-three," she provided him.

Father Linwood nodded. "A long time, as I said. I couldn't tell you who members of my church regularly associated with after all these years. Even if I thought I could, I give you a name and I'm wrong... What then?"

"We'll talk to this person, see what they have to say. No one innocent is going away." A bold claim since many innocent people were living behind bars. Just not due to her. That she knew about anyway. "Detective Stenson, can you bring up the photo of Jane Doe?"

"Sure." Trent already had his tablet out, and he swiped his finger around until the image was on the screen. He angled it toward the priest.

"Do you recognize her?" They didn't even know when the Cofells had taken her, but it seemed apparent they had. After looking at the hellhole, they were beyond all benefit of the doubt.

Father Linwood studied the photo and shook his head. "Who is she?"

"For now, she's just Jane Doe." Amanda made sure to meet his eye when she said this.

"As in she's dead too?"

"It's most likely. We found her picture among the Cofells' things," she told him.

"I'm sorry, but I can't help you."

His apology meant nothing. He hadn't earned her trust. Not by a long shot. "What we haven't told you yet, Father, is there were three DNA profiles on Sadie Jackson's clothing. We're sure that two will tie back to the Cofells, but that third one is unknown." As she spoke, she was leaning forward, and the priest was moving back. "Are you sure you have no idea who the Cofells hung out with back then?"

Something dark flitted across his eyes. He might have had a suspicion, but he wasn't talking.

"Here's the thing. While you think you're protecting your flock from false allegations, Detective Stenson and I are tasked with finding a killer who murdered Sadie Jackson, Audrey Witherspoon, and possibly another girl. The Cofells are undoubtedly responsible for Sadie, but another male is also caught up in that. There still may be a chance to bring him to justice. Since you have nothing to hide, let us test your DNA and rule you out."

"I'm not sure I'm comfortable with that." He swallowed roughly. "I think it's time I get a lawyer."

"As you wish." Amanda stood and led the way from the room. Once Trent joined her, she said, "We've got him. We'll get that warrant for his DNA, and it will soon be over."

She headed toward the observation room, but it was empty.

"I thought Malone was going to watch," Trent said.

"Far as I knew he was." Her phone rang, but it wasn't Malone. It was CSI Blair. Amanda answered on speaker.

"You're not sounding quite like yourself," Blair said, and that took Amanda back. The investigator was more business than most of them.

"I'm fine. You have something?"

"More like *big* somethings. Plural. You already know Winnie Cofell's DNA was tied to Sadie Jackson's dress, aided along by that familial hit to her brother's. Now, I can tell you

Doug's DNA was present too. He's not a match to the DNA under her nails though. Doug is, however, Cameron's father. Sadie is his mother."

The CSIs had access to a plethora of DNA at the Cofell farmhouse. Amanda wasn't sure what to react to first. She decided to go with the truth. "I can't say any of this surprises me."

"Me either, but I wanted to let you know right away."

"Which I appreciate. Are you still at the Witherspoon scene?"

"Oh, we are. I just received a notification with the results."

"I don't know how you do it all."

"Well, you don't think Isabelle and I are the only ones working in the lab, do you? But if that belief keeps the illusion alive and makes us appear magical, keep it." Blair laughed.

"Thanks again."

"You bet."

They said their goodbyes.

"There's further confirmation Doug Cofell was a sick prick," Trent said.

"But don't leave Winnie out. She wasn't some saint and victim of Doug's charms."

"Guess we might never know the answer to that."

Her phone pinged with a message. It was from Malone.

Had to leave

"Unbelievable." She held her phone for Trent to see.

"He didn't even ask for an update."

"Nope. Well, I don't have time for this. Let's start things rolling to get Father Linwood's DNA, but then I'm running out the door. You should get going too."

"Why?"

"You're joking, right? It's Valentine's Day. I'm sure you have some big plans with Kelsey." She cursed in her head. Prepared herself to hear all about their couple bliss. Instead, panic flooded his features. "You don't?"

He slowly shook his head. "I tried, but the Jackson case, then today…"

"*Today?* It's too late to make plans on the day. Any restaurant worth taking her to will have been booked up weeks ago."

"Try months ago, but I get it. I screwed up."

"Yeah, you did, but I understand." As panicked as he looked, she could relate. It likely closely resembled the same face she made when defending herself to Logan when they were together. She'd pick up a case, and it would ruin plans they had made. Disappointment and disapproval would coat his features, and she'd end up on the defensive. She hated letting him down, but what she resented more was being made to feel like her job wasn't important. The next person she was with would understand her dedication to the badge or she'd send him packing. And much faster than she had Logan. Though their breakup could be seen as a mutual decision and her job was only one fault point.

"I hope Kelsey understands," Trent said.

"So do I." She was familiar with what the outcome would be if she didn't. But a selfish part of her wondered what the future might be like if she and Trent were free to see each other. She took a few steps away from him but stopped and turned around. "You know what? Why don't you take my reservation? Treat Kelsey to a nice dinner out."

"Really?"

"Yeah." *Why am I doing this?* After all, it was best Trent find out sooner than later if Kelsey was accepting of his job. It would save further investment and a larger heartbreak in the future.

"I can't do that. You and Zoe..."

"You're not doing anything. Consider it a gift. Besides, it's not anyplace fancy."

"Still, I'll owe you. Where is it?"

"Dimitri's."

"Not fancy? You're kidding, right?"

She shrugged. Dimitri's was an Italian restaurant with white tablecloths, candles, and servers in tuxedos.

"You had plans to wine and dine your nine-year-old?"

She shoved his shoulder. "No wine, though they probably have a renowned wine list. The way I see it, it doesn't hurt for her to have a nice meal out sometimes. Be exposed to how some people live."

"Now I feel bad. She's probably been looking forward to this. The last thing I want to do is let her down."

Amanda shook her head. "She has no idea. With this job, I rarely make promises. There's less chance of breaking them that way. I especially don't like to tell Zoe about my plans. That way if they don't work out, she's not hurt."

"You're a good mom."

She'd like to just roll with the compliment, but it was tough when she could list a number of times she didn't follow through on her intentions. Zoe might not know, but Amanda did. "All right, go. It's for six thirty, so you don't want to be late."

"Okay, thanks again. I'll owe you." He started off down the hall.

"Oh, Trent."

He looked over his shoulder and stopped walking.

"I'll change the reservation to your name."

"Great thinking." He tapped his head and turned to start walking again.

"Also be sure to pick her up some roses on the way home too."

He gave her a thumbs-up and kept moving.

As she watched him disappear, she was left to come up with something else to do with Zoe and where to take her. It wouldn't be anything approaching Dimitri's, but she knew her girl loved Petey's Patties. It just might be burgers for two in a faux-leather booth.

THIRTY

Before leaving last night, Amanda had a warrant rushed through for Father Linwood's DNA. Otherwise, she didn't waste any time shooting out of the station. Amanda always thought Valentine's Day was overrated, embraced and promoted by commercialism. It was about the bottom line and what these companies were raking in with all their gimmicks. To her the day was one to remember romance, and she never let the job interfere. Though she liked to keep things simple. When she was married, her husband would buy her some roses and take her out for a nice dinner. Logan liked making grand gestures, leaving her lost on how to respond. Looking back, she wondered if he was overcompensating, trying to compel deeper feelings for her than he had. She had no way of knowing, but she'd fallen in love more with the idea of him than the man himself. A hard thing to admit, but if it wasn't the truth, she'd be having a harder time with their breakup. Not to say that she wasn't saddened by it for a while, but it didn't devastate her. The biggest upheaval was going back to being a single parent.

And that was a gift she planned on treasuring for a while yet. It was hard work but rewarding. Getting into another relationship too soon would just be irresponsible. Even if she met a guy she liked, she'd be taking it slow. She and Zoe had it good on their own.

They had ended up at Petey's Patties for dinner. Zoe wasn't contesting the restaurant choice because she loved the place, and as Amanda watched her stick fries into her mouth, the girl probably had a better time there than she would have had at Dimitri's dressed up and formal. But one day, Amanda would expose her to that side of things. If for nothing more than to give Zoe the experience.

Amanda came into Central the next morning armed with an extra-large coffee from Hannah's Diner and found a list of names provided by Father Linwood on her desk. He must have changed his mind after a few hours in a holding cell and decided to hand them over to an officer. Now she'd just need to compare them with the congregation list. But she set that aside and took care of something else first.

When she returned to her desk, her coffee was cold but still delicious. She sipped it as she scanned the list, recording the names to memory. Then she took out the congregation list, a little tattered and creased from its travels. She glanced at the circled names, not liking what she ascertained.

"Good morning." Trent swept into her cubicle and set a coffee from Hannah's Diner on her desk. "For you— Oh, you have one." He pointed at the cup she held.

"Almost finished." She took the last gulp and tossed the empty into her garbage can. "But even if I wasn't, I'm always prepared to double-fist it." She raised the new coffee in a toast gesture and said, "Thank you," before taking a tentative sip.

"No, thank *you*. You saved my ass last night. I went home, and Kelsey was all dressed up, looking amazing, smelling amazing. She had faith that I'd come through for her. I didn't have the heart to mention that I'd dropped the ball, but you stepped in to save the day. As far as she knows I set it all up." He winced.

She laughed, even as a bolt of heartache and jealousy zapped her. "Good. That's how I wanted it to work out for you."

"Well, I won't forget this, Mandy."

She managed to smile at him, as she did her best to ignore the warmth that always filled her when he called her *Mandy*.

"So what did I interrupt?" He pointed at the papers on the desk in front of her. "Is that a list of those five names?"

"It is. As it turns out, Father Linwood had a change of heart last night."

"Now we just need to see if any are a match to—" He stopped talking when she shook her head.

"I did that already. None of them were members twenty-three years ago."

"Huh, so much for the theory that one of them might have been the mystery man. And thinking about this more, if Audrey saw the man with long, dark sideburns at the meeting, she surely would have pointed him right out, even called us."

"Sure, but we're talking about a description that applied twenty-three years ago. This man's looks could have changed a lot since then."

"Very true, but that leaves us nowhere."

"There's Father Linwood still."

"Yeah, and we'll get his DNA this morning. I don't see any problem getting that warrant rolling."

"Everything's done."

"Not sure what you mean..."

"I got the warrant last night and have already forwarded his DNA to the lab to process." That was what had delayed her comparing the list to the names the priest had provided.

"When did you get in? It *is* Saturday."

"Six AM."

"Six? Wow. I'm impressed by your dedication."

"Or obsession."

"Whatever the case, impressive." He smiled at her.

His genuine compliment only improved her mood some. She might be a great detective, but she wasn't sure sometimes how she rated as a mother. Sure, last night had been fun. Dinner, then she took Zoe to the movies, but she'd also made the decision that she was going to make an early start today. She'd tried to bury the fact she wasn't going to be around on Saturday by distracting Zoe with a "surprise" last-minute sleepover. Amanda's teenage niece, Ava, had recently called off things with a boy she had been seeing for a couple of months. As a result of that, she'd completely sworn off guys for the time being. She had no qualms about sacrificing her evening to sit with Zoe and be with her today. Amanda would throw some money her way, but Ava was a real lifesaver.

"Have you thought about what we'll do if Father Linwood isn't a match?" Trent asked her, then took a sip of his coffee. "Though I suppose we still have other church members to talk with."

"We do. Fifteen in the right age range." *Still, that doesn't feel daunting at all...* "But I also made a call to the jail to follow up on Cameron Cofell's status. I was thinking if he was better today, we could talk to him and ask about any family friends he might remember hanging around. Unfortunately, he's still not doing good. But we have another avenue to follow up. We have permission to enter his room at the halfway house where he was staying."

"Someone's been busy this morning."

"I'm just grateful that Judge Anderson was on call."

"You and me both. Okay, where do we get the key?"

"The people there will have a copy and let us in once we present the warrant."

"Which you have?"

"Which I have." She smiled. She just hoped they found

something among Cameron's things that would help. It was spurred on by this niggling in the back of her mind, likely planted there from talking with Cameron's therapist. Did Cameron have a list of people he blamed, only his plans to go after them were thwarted after his attempt with the priest was unsuccessful?

THIRTY-ONE

Desperation seeped off the halfway house as Trent pulled into the parking lot. He appreciated that energy conflicted with its purpose of being a place of hope and a launching pad to help integrate criminals back into society. This one was a two-story house, a century or more old, made of redbrick and in good condition for its age. It had fifteen rooms, but sometimes people bunked together, allowing the occupancy numbers to stretch beyond that.

Amanda's phone rang on their way inside. She pulled it from her pocket and stopped walking. "It's the lab," she told him before answering.

He waited next to her. The downward angle to her lips told him it was unexpected news.

"Thanks." She shoved her phone back into her pocket and shook her head. "Guess we have to cut the good father loose. Rapid DNA typing tells us he isn't a match."

"Leaving us with a mystery man to still find."

"Yep, but that's not all. The CSI who called also processed the wooden crate collected from the Cofells' house as a favor to

Blair. First, the wood slivers recovered from Sadie's clothing were a match. Secondly, her DNA was in there."

"Then her body was likely transported in there."

Amanda angled her head. "*Likely?*"

"I'm not saying it wasn't used for that, but they might have put her in there for punishment or for some other reason too." He wished he hadn't tried to play Devil's advocate given the frown on Amanda's face. "Though they had the hellhole for that."

"Yeah," she punched out. "We also have science to back us up. Prints belonging to three people were lifted from the crate, including where you'd hold it to lift it. I'd wager one of the prints belong to our mystery man."

"Which means what Audrey Witherspoon saw that night was unmistakably Doug Cofell and a buddy moving her dead body."

"As we thought."

She made confirmation sound like a bad thing. It was certainly ugly, but it was a fact, and they could work with those.

The clerk in the administration office of the halfway house directed them to speak with Clark Levy. He was the house manager and responsible for all staff from administrative to counselors. They were told to take a seat and he'd be out shortly.

Amanda remained standing, while Trent sat down. While he tried to corral his thoughts strictly to the case, it kept drifting to last night. Kelsey was an amazing woman, and they got along so well. But equally important was she trusted him and had confidence that he'd always do the right thing. There was a lot of pressure in that, and it made him feel like a fraud. Their delicious dinner and impeccable service at Dimitri's had nothing to do with him and everything to do with Amanda's sacrifice. As he'd given his name to the host last night, the deception poked his conscience, even as Kelsey smiled at him and linked her arm through his.

"Detectives?" A heavy-set man in his mid-to-late forties came over to them. He had a round face and a chin dimple, and his mouth was set in a thin line.

Trent stood as Amanda introduced them and stated the purpose for their visit.

"Cameron Cofell, yes, well... He's got himself into a bit of trouble, hasn't he? I assure you that as manager of this house, it's not representative of what we're setting out to accomplish here."

The man was clearly concerned about the house's image. For good reason. Most were financially backed by the government, and if they weren't effective, funding would be routed elsewhere. The fact Cameron had gotten out after curfew alone would have landed the manager in a heap of trouble with the board.

"How about we move this conversation to my office?" He led the way down a hall and through a doorway with a stained-glass transom overhead. Large windows let the sun in despite heavy grilles and trim work. "Please, make yourselves comfortable."

There were two cushy chairs across from a stately desk, and Trent was the first to sit. Amanda eventually followed his lead.

"I heard about your visit to Beverly Campbell," Levy began. "You showed up at her private practice. Surely you didn't think that she'd disclose anything Cameron might have told her."

The therapist must have reported their visit to cover herself. "Cameron Cofell is closely connected to two murder investigations that we're working on."

"Murders? I thought he just held that priest at gunpoint."

"Connected, not responsible," Trent clarified. "But we'd like to take a look at his room and his things."

"We have a warrant." Amanda set the hard-copy version on his desk. "Are we going to have a problem?"

Levy picked up the paper and read it. The further along he got, the brighter his puffy red cheeks became. Eventually, he huffed and set the page back down. "No problem, and I am more than happy to cooperate with the police. After all, we're trying to prepare our residents to integrate back into society after prison. We provide training and education in practical life skills and household management. But with that said, some people here are in a rather delicate state. They are recovering from drug and alcohol abuse. Some struggle with mental health issues. It could be very upsetting to them having you going through the home—"

"Just Cameron's things," Trent pointed out.

"Yes, well, the warrant appears to cover his room as well. The thing is, after Cameron's arrest, we released his room. We don't really have much choice in the matter. Rooms here are in high demand, and it's clear that Cameron is unlikely to be returning any time soon. But Cameron had a roommate. He's one of those people I just described. In a delicate state. We try to match our residents up with those who have similar struggles whether that be mental issues, abuse, criminal backgrounds, and/or those who have the same addictions. Jasper, Cameron's roommate, shared a lot of the same experiences as Cameron. With Cameron being a little further along in his journey, he seemed to be helping Jasper. He's extremely upset now that Cameron's gone."

"His things then?" Trent asked.

"They are in storage here until next of kin come to collect them."

Though Trent didn't imagine Cameron's estranged uncle would be turning up any time soon.

"But obviously you're entitled to take a look through everything." Levy gestured toward the warrant.

"Could we talk with Jasper?" Trent thought he'd ask,

though he suspected the house manager would reiterate the man's delicate state.

"Technically, the rules of this house allow me to answer on his behalf, and I can't see how talking with you would be beneficial for him. It might even set him back. I'm sorry I can't do more."

Amanda shifted in her chair, and Trent sensed her temper. He could understand why, but in all fairness, Levy didn't know how valuable talking to Jasper could prove to be, the difference it might make for the investigation.

"The cases we're working on are connected to Cameron, as I said earlier," Trent began. "What neither of us has yet said is that our investigations have led us to discover that Cameron's past is darker than he even necessarily knows."

Levy leaned forward, putting his arms on his desk and clasping his hands.

"You heard about the teenage girl who was found in the walls of Herald Church?" Trent asked him.

"Of course. Sadie Jackson."

"Well, evidence is coming to light to suggest the Cofells were the ones who took her." Trent was sharing something that wasn't public knowledge yet. It probably wouldn't be until everything was wrapped up. All that had been said in the news was that Sadie Jackson was finally found after missing for thirty-one years. Trent watched Levy's mind work. His eyes shadowed, and then his mouth twitched. The earlier color left his cheeks.

"Cameron's parents? But even if they did what you're saying they did, they are dead."

"We have reason to believe they weren't working alone," he said.

"Cameron? No, he wouldn't have been born yet. What am I missing?"

"Forensic evidence tells us a third person was involved with

Sadie Jackson's murder. We believe it was a friend of the family." Trent was watching what he was saying because he didn't want to give away too much. Telling him about the picture they found of Jane Doe might instill more urgency but at what cost to the investigation?

"So someone is still out there?"

"Yes, and we think that Cameron might know who that person is," Amanda interjected. "It's possible this person was around during Cameron's childhood. This person might have even taken part in abusing Cameron."

"Dear Lord." Levy cupped his chin.

Silence stretched for a few seconds.

"It's possible that Cameron and Jasper talked about all this, if they were as close as you say," Amanda said.

"I can see if Jasper feels up to talking to you," Clark eventually offered.

"That's all we ask," Amanda said.

Trent was trying to contain his excitement. If Jasper valued Cameron's companionship as much as Levy suggested, it might be about more than just sharing similar experiences. Bonds were tightened when people spoke openly with each other. Had Cameron confided something in Jasper that might lead Trent and Amanda to this mystery man?

THIRTY-TWO

Amanda made the call to Central to release Father Linwood. There was no sense having him hanging around when he wasn't the man they were after. The finding in that regard had been frustrating as it set them back to square one. They didn't have a prime suspect. All they had were potential leads that might pay off. As macabre as it was having the crate confirmed as being what transported Sadie's body, it advanced the investigation. It added even more credit to the theory someone involved back then had killed Audrey Witherspoon. It was just the haunting question of why this man had waited so long to silence her. What had suddenly made her a threat?

As she put her phone away, she realized she had no missed calls or text messages. She thought for sure she'd have heard from Malone seeking updates. It was approaching ten in the morning now.

She and Trent were shown to a storage room by Clark's assistant while the manager was going to ask Jasper if he was willing to talk to them. He'd promised to put it in such a way that they were there to help Cameron, which was the truth.

"There's only the two boxes," the assistant told them as she reached up to grab one off a higher shelf.

"Let me help." Trent moved in there and took the box down.

"Thank you. I should know better than to try. I've tweaked my back before from pulling something down from over my head."

"No problem." Trent set the box on a table in the room and turned to the assistant again. "The other one...?"

"I've got it, but thanks again." She smiled and grabbed another box from a middle shelf and put it next to the other one.

"I'll leave you two alone, but let me know if you need anything. Either of you want coffee, tea, or water?"

"I'd love some coffee," Amanda told her with a smile.

The woman leveled her gaze at Trent.

"Same," he told her.

"I'll be right back. Oh, sugar or cream?"

"Black," Amanda and Trent said in unison.

"Right then." She left the room with a glance at Amanda. If she thought she was eyeing her competition, she was far off the mark. Professional only. No lines crossed.

Except for those two times...

Amanda wished to forget they'd even happened. Better yet, if there was a way to reverse and undo those slips. But it didn't stop the romantic feelings she had for her partner, and she could only be held accountable if she acted on them again. She'd resolved that wouldn't happen as long as Trent was with Kelsey. Even then, he'd need to be the one to make the first move.

"Okay, so should we dig in?" Trent didn't wait for her response but opened the flaps on one of the boxes.

Her answer was to dig into the other one, which was disappointing at first glance. It was just a pile of folded clothes. Jeans,

T-shirts, sweaters. She stacked each garment next to articles of clothing Trent had put out.

Don't tell me it's all *clothes...* She thought this just as her fingers ran over something else at the bottom of the box.

"You getting anywhere over there? I have nothing." He lifted his box upside down as if for emphasis.

"I might be." She dug out the rest of the clothing and reached the bottom. "Toiletries." She pulled out the clear bag, her shoulders slumping. Nothing stood out but she unzipped it and moved everything inside around anyhow.

"Sorry, that took longer than I would have thought." The assistant returned with two steaming mugs. The aroma of coffee teased Amanda's nose and lifted her spirits, if only slightly.

"Thank you." She wasted no time claiming a cup and took a cautious sip to gauge temperature and taste. Both came up perfection. "This is good."

"It's just some no-name pod, but I'm glad you like it. I will confess that I sprinkled a dash of salt in there though. I find it cuts the bitter edge."

"Well, it's delicious," Amanda told her. She'd heard that tip before but never employed it. She would in future. Just not with Hannah's Diner coffee because it didn't need any help.

"Thanks." Trent got in there and took his coffee.

"Don't mention it. Oh, I was told to pass along that Jasper is willing to talk with you when you're ready."

"Great news," Amanda said.

The assistant left the room, leaving Amanda and Trent staring at a pile of nothing. At least nothing as far as the investigation was concerned.

"I guess looking at his things was a huge waste of time," she said, taking another sip of the heavenly coffee.

"Coming here might not have been though. Cameron's roommate is willing to talk to us."

"We can only hope he knows something."

They drank their coffee as they put the items back into the boxes.

"Why do things never go back in the same way?" Trent struggled to lay the flaps down flat.

"Let me." She got in there and made his match hers.

"Magic."

She laughed and set out of the room. They caught up with the assistant and told her they were finished with Cameron's things and ready to talk with Jasper. Hopefully he'd have something to offer the investigation that would get them closer to the mystery man.

THIRTY-THREE

Amanda had expected Jasper to be younger than Cameron after the house manager told them Cameron was ahead of Jasper in his recovery. But he was thirty-five. His last name was Quinn, and she and Trent were filled in on his colorful past. His criminal record started at eighteen when he was arrested and imprisoned for drug possession with intent to distribute. Clark told them that wasn't the only time Jasper had seen the inside of a prison cell. The house manager didn't detail all his crimes but stuck to the overview. Same too for his time at the house. Apparently, he was just coming around after being weaned off meth and alcohol over the last several months. He'd been a resident of the home on and off for ten years. According to Clark, when he wasn't here, he was behind bars or living rough on the streets.

Amanda and Trent entered the meeting room where they were directed. It was much the same as the soft interview room at Central. Comfortable, decorated with a neutral, warm palette. She and Trent had decided she'd do all the talking so as not to overwhelm Jasper.

Jasper swept his hair back and smacked his lips. His eyes roved over them like he was a small animal deciding whether to attack or make a run for it. At only thirty-five, he was losing his hair. What remained lay in thin greasy strands across his scalp. His eyes were sunken and shadowed. His physical appearance was no doubt affected by the way he'd treated his body over the years. He'd had a hard life, and it showed.

She walked slowly toward a chair and sat down. No fast movements, and she thought it best to approach with a kind and unassuming manner. "Jasper, I'm Amanda Steele, and this is Trent Stenson. He's just going to sit with me, if that's okay."

"How do you know my name?" he muttered.

It was sad to see the impact drugs had on a person. He was far less coherent than Audrey had been at eighty-three. "We were told you would talk with us. We were wanting to ask you a few questions about a mutual friend of ours." She was painting the relationship with broad strokes, but she held no ill will toward Cameron. What he had done was wrong and a crime. He'd have to pay for that, but he was also a victim who had endured so much, it's amazing that he hadn't done much worse.

He sniffled and wiped his hand under his nose. "Cameron."

"Uh-huh. He's suffered an awful lot, and we want to make those responsible pay." All of that was the truth. It was just bittersweet to acknowledge that two were out of reach. It was unknown whether the mystery man was around to torture Cameron.

"It was his parents. They screwed him up." Jasper slumped farther into his chair, then slinked back up, back down. He was either uncomfortable talking about his friend or the subject matter struck personal for him. Clark had said that roommates were matched based on similar backgrounds and experiences. He started to gnaw on the nail of his left index finger.

"They did," she said with authority.

"But they're dead. What can you do about that?"

"Well, we think other people hurt Cameron too. People besides his parents. Maybe friends of theirs..."

Jasper was going to town on that nail. She wouldn't be surprised to see blood soon.

"Did he tell you if anyone else hurt him?" she asked, treading gently.

Jasper shook his head with the side of his finger hanging out of his mouth.

"You're sure?"

He nodded.

It sank in her gut that it was possible the mystery man was long gone before Cameron was old enough to remember him. She'd try another tack. "He ever tell you about any friends that would come over to the farm?"

He finally relinquished the finger. "He had a couple of pictures, but he never let me see them. He'd tell me to mind my own business."

They'd just looked through Cameron's things and hadn't found any photos, so where were they now? "So you never looked at them? Not even a peek when Cameron was out?"

Jasper rubbed his cheek to his shoulder.

"I know when I'm told not to do something, it makes me want to do it more." She smiled, hoping to hook him.

"Cam's going away, right? Prison for a long time?"

"Probably, yes."

"Then, fine, I'll tell you. Not that I like the police, but I love Cam. He's like a brother to me. If someone else hurt him who's still out there, they should pay. Like that priest."

The last statement dug into her like a burr. She'd released Father Linwood based on the evidence, but he still wasn't absolved in her mind. Not in her moral court. "Then you looked?" She circled back to the main point of what Jasper had said.

"I tried, but the photos weren't where I always saw him tuck them away."

"They were gone?"

"Yep. But Cam was real obsessed with those pictures. He'd stare at them for hours. All intent like, ya know?"

Amanda nodded. She was chilled by her thoughts, but she also had a feeling she knew where to find the photos. "Thanks for talking to us, Jasper. You've helped a lot."

"Now you help Cam. Get him out of jail. He's a good guy with a bad deal."

Not going to disagree with you on that... She kept the thought to herself, knowing that was for the best, and left the room with Trent.

Once they were back in the car, she turned to him. "Cameron had photos he valued, wanted to keep to himself, but they weren't in his boxes of things."

"Nope. I bet they're with his personal effects that were taken from him when he was arrested."

She smiled at Trent. "Great minds." It wasn't the first time they thought alike, and it was unlikely to be the last. "But did you pick up on something else? It sounds like Cameron was obsessed with the photos, staring at them for hours."

"Clearly something had his attention. We might understand once we get a look at them."

She nodded as he started to drive, holding back her earlier thought about a hit list. Was it too much to hope those photos would give them the lead necessary to break the case wide open?

THIRTY-FOUR

The processing officer at the jail was an unfamiliar face to Amanda, but he was friendly and professional when they asked for items that Cameron Cofell was seized with. They had to fill out a release form, but it wasn't long before she and Trent were looking at a tray of Cameron's property. There wasn't much. A wallet, a keyring with two keys, and two photos folded into numerous squares.

She reached for these and unfurled them. Time slowed as she did so. Trent stood looking over her shoulder, his warm breath cascading down the side of her neck. But at this moment, she barely noticed.

Two photos, three-by-five inches in size. The one on top was of Sadie.

"It must have been taken around the same time as another we found at the farmhouse," Trent said.

Amanda nodded. In this picture, Sadie was that image Cameron had described when they spoke with him. Along the lines of long brown hair, blue eyes, face like an angel, but in this picture she wasn't wearing bangles or the necklace. She also wasn't pregnant, or showing anyhow.

"What's the other one of?" Trent prompted her, brushing his thumb over hers.

To get me to move faster, or as an excuse to touch me? A frivolous thought at a time like this. She shuffled the second photo to the front.

It was taken on a sunny summer day, given away by the assortment of shorts and T-shirts. There was also a baseball diamond in the background, and some of the kids held on to bats and gloves. It was a group shot of about fifty people with one man off to the left. He stood slightly separate from the rest, and his face had been scrawled out by blue ink. But she could make out the white collar around his neck. "Is that Father Linwood?"

"I'd say that's a good guess. Jasper said he was obsessing over these photos, yet Cameron never told us he had them. Why? Even that picture of Sadie that he did mention, he made it sound like he was made to put it back."

"I don't have an answer for you. He could have gone back for them at some later point. Even after the Cofells' deaths. He does have two keys." She lifted the key ring, and the keys jingled as they hit each other. "One is probably for his room at the halfway house. The other might be for the farmhouse."

"Even though he told us he wanted nothing to do with the place? Still, what's so important about these two photos that he chose them?"

Some things were inexplicable. Feelings surfaced, sensations, nothing rooted in science. "Okay, this might sound crazy, but it's possible that Cameron felt a connection to Sadie and didn't know why."

"He told us he thought she was a sister that died."

"Could just be that, or he might have had a deeper, unexplained draw to her. I mean, we know she was his mother. Maybe as he got older, even more recently, he started to wonder if she was."

"Possible, I suppose. That could explain the one of Sadie, but why the group shot?"

"It's clearly a church outing, a picnic and ballgame. He may have taken it as a reminder of his childhood. A normal day, the chance to be a kid for a moment, anyhow. May also be one of the rare days he got to socialize. Based on what Cameron's therapist told us, he wasn't allowed much of that." She took a closer look at the photo. Doug Cofell was standing beside Cameron with a possessive hand on his shoulder. Nothing about his body language was warm and fuzzy. But next to Cameron, there was a boy about Cameron's age, who looked to be about eight, and they were facing each other. In the row in front of them, there was a couple with another boy with blond hair like the one next to Cameron. Presumably their father was standing next to the priest, but a few strokes of the blue ink covered his right cheek as he was turned toward the middle of the group. Maybe checking on his boys. His wife had her head turned that way too.

"I think there's more to it." He pointed to the priest's scratched-out face. "This might have been the only photo he had of Father Linwood. He looked at it, obsessing over it as he built up the courage to confront the man. He was clearly angry when he took the pen to Linwood's face. The scratch marks cut into the photo paper. Ask me, and he did this just before he decided to act."

Which would suggest one purpose the photo served for Cameron. To know if it meant more, they'd need to talk to him. "You could be right, but there are more people in this photograph than just the priest." Her earlier speculation was back. Did Cameron have plans to go after someone else? The man with the long, dark sideburns? Though there was nothing to say he was around as Cameron grew up. And no one matched that description that she could discern from this compact photograph.

"You've got something in mind. What is it?"

"I've been wondering if Cameron held other people accountable in his head, others besides Linwood."

"Then what? You see this as a sort of hitlist?"

"It was just a thought."

"Okay, but no one else is marked or scratched out."

"Maybe not, but look..." She pointed out the man who was presumably next to his wife and facing the two boys. "Cameron and the younger boy are with each other in the row behind and looking at each other. They could have been friends."

"Okay..."

"But that kid clearly belongs to this man and woman. Were they close to the Cofells?"

"What you really want to know is whether there's a long, dark sideburn hiding beneath the pen strokes on that man's right cheek."

"You know me well."

"We need to find out. This is the strongest lead we've gotten yet in finding a friend of the Cofells. We could see if Cameron is feeling better now, or head over to Father Linwood."

"Won't he be happy to see us?" she jibed. "But we're here, so let's see if something's changed for Cameron since earlier today. He wasn't well enough to receive visitors then."

"We'll give it a try. As you said, we're here."

"Yep. We've got nothing to lose."

THIRTY-FIVE

As it turned out, Cameron Cofell was willing to talk with Amanda and Trent. When Amanda laid eyes on him in the interview room, she was filled with compassion. He was only twenty-three but had endured hell in his short lifetime. The Cofells, in a way, had made him take the action he had, yet they would shoulder no blame. It was unfair. Though it was no different for many abusers who pushed their victims to the brink and walked free, while those they tortured battled addictions, sometimes worse. There were those who passed on the same treatment they received to others.

"Thank you for agreeing to talk to us, Cameron," Amanda said, easing herself into a chair across from him. "Are you feeling better?"

"A bit. It's just hard to get sleep in here." Cameron's eyes were bloodshot, and he rubbed his face.

"We won't be long, but we found this." She gestured to Trent, and he pulled his tablet out for Cameron to see. They had taken photos of Cameron's pictures with it. The one up was the group photo.

"That's mine. You have no right to—"

She calmly held up her hand. "We're trying to help you, Cameron."

"Bullshit. People only help themselves."

Jaded. Understandably. "Not me, not my partner," she assured him. "We told you before that we believed you. We still do. It looks like you were good friends with this boy." She pointed out the one standing next to him in the photo. "Do you remember his name?"

"No."

"You look about eight or so," she said.

"I don't remember him," he hissed.

She tried to think back on the childhood friends that she had. Most weren't in her life anymore, and many of their faces were blurry after all this time. But if that boy's father was the man with the long sideburns and had partaken in abusing Cameron, surely, he would have remembered him. She'd come right out and ask but by doing so she'd risk him shutting down. She decided to build up to it. "Where did you get these pictures?"

"From the farmhouse, not long after I first found all the pictures. I hid these ones away from Doug and Winnie and took them when I left."

She noted the disassociation, how Cameron never referred to the place as *home*. How the Cofells weren't Mom and Dad now but referenced by given names. All understandable. The worn frayed edges on the photos supported his timeline. "But why take them?" She was curious, considering he'd told them Winnie was angry that he'd seen the photos. She didn't want to stress this point for fear of making him go quiet.

"One's of my sister. Winnie and Doug told me she's dead, but I carry her around because I feel a connection to her. I don't know why." Sadness rolled over his face.

On some level he knows... "Why did you keep the other

picture?" She wasn't going to ask why he'd scratched out Linwood's face. The answer to that seemed straightforward.

"I wanted to remember…"

"Remember what?" Trent eased in.

He shrugged.

"To remind you of a happy time?" Amanda guessed.

Cameron's eyes set ablaze. "The night after that game, Doug beat me. He blamed me for our team losing. It was just supposed to be for fun." His chin quivered, and Amanda's heart ached for him.

"Then why the reminder?" she asked.

"I'm an idiot? I don't know, but the more I looked at it, I hated everyone more and more. They're all guilty!"

There was no way an entire congregation could have been physically involved in the abuse, but they could have known and kept quiet.

"But him!" Cameron jabbed a pointed finger over Linwood's head and spit on the floor. "That man is the devil. Doug and Winnie made their confessions. They always forced me to, but I never bared my soul."

"But no one else in this picture ever hurt you? Touched you?"

"They didn't have to touch me to hurt me. But they had to know. At least some of them. They had to know." Cameron rocked back and forth.

Amanda glanced at Trent. She didn't want to keep Cameron any longer. Every time they spoke to him, they made him relive everything. She wanted to leave him now, but how could she without telling him about Sadie being his mother? But that news could shatter him. Then again, he might appreciate the knowledge because it would explain the connection he felt with her picture. She opened her mouth to tell Cameron when he spoke.

"There's more you don't know, and I think I'm ready to tell

you." He trembled but shook his arms as if by doing so he were releasing the last of his demons. "I told you before, but I'm quite sure that Doug and Winnie Cofell killed my sister. I, ah, heard them talking about it after I found the picture the first time. Doug was upset, and I heard Winnie telling him that bad girls get what they have coming to them and there's no going back. Winnie said it was a long time ago and to stop whining about it. Can you believe that?" His eyes were blank and unfocused.

There had been a time when they considered Winnie Cofell might have been a victim forced to submit to her abusive husband. Given what Cameron just said, Winnie was a monster herself. She may have had less of a conscience than Doug. There was also the fact Winnie had said *bad girls* get what they deserve. Plural. Did that discussion extend beyond Sadie Jackson and include Jane Doe? "When you were looking at photos, did you find any of—"

"Another girl? Yes."

"Why didn't you take her picture with you?" Amanda asked.

"I don't know."

"Did you ever ask Doug and Winnie who she was?" Yet another question, as if Cameron were being interrogated. She hated doing this to him.

"I didn't dare."

She steadied herself, detaching. "Did they ever talk about her?"

"No." Cameron yawned, and Amanda took that as their cue.

"We'll be off. We're so sorry that we had to ask so many things but appreciate that you spoke with us. More than you can realize. Thank you."

Cameron nodded slowly, and Amanda and Trent left the room and let the officer outside the door know they could take him back to his cell.

"What do you make of all that?" Trent asked her as they headed toward the exit.

"It breaks my heart, all that he's been through. I realize I should probably view him differently. He did hold a man at gunpoint."

"And fired."

"Though thankfully he missed," she added with a sardonic smile. While she might not be a fan of Father Linwood's, if Cameron hadn't fired the gun, how much longer would Sadie Jackson have remained in that wall?

"I get what you're saying, but we need to find out who that family is."

"Which means another conversation with Linwood."

"I think he'd be the best place to start."

"Then again, we're assuming that the father of those boys was involved with the murder of Sadie Jackson. In that case, he stuck around for eight years afterward." She based this on Cameron's age in the photo.

"I'm not sure I'm sold on that. Cameron doesn't remember the man. If he'd been abusive, some part of his psyche would."

"Unless it's buried too deep."

"Possible, but it's also feasible that man isn't guilty of any wrongdoing. I still think he's a good lead though. The kids were friends, so presumably the couples would be, or at least friendly. And if that man isn't the one we're after, he or his partner might know who else was close with the Cofells at an earlier time."

"Which could still get us what we want. Another shit behind bars."

"And that would make for a good day."

"That it would." She wasn't thrilled about talking to Father Linwood again, but she had a feeling this time it would pay off.

THIRTY-SIX

Amanda pointed out the van from Gray's Building Projects when Trent pulled into the church parking lot. It was there along with a few other cars. Knowing they were repairing the wall was bittersweet. Like a bandage on a fractured arm. That section of the church would always be where Sadie Jackson had been entombed for twenty-three years.

They got out of the car and walked toward the church. The whine of a drill could be heard from the front steps. Trent held the door, and they went inside. Five people turned to them, including Father Linwood and his assistant, Chet Solomon, and Robert Gray. The other two faces belonged to strangers.

Robert, who had been screwing in a sheet of drywall, stopped working, his power tool in hand.

Father Linwood leaned in toward Chet, whispering something into his ear, and the assistant then scurried over to them.

"Detectives, is something wrong?" Chet asked them.

A rather loaded question to ask homicide detectives investigating two open murder cases. "We need to speak to Father Linwood."

The priest's sigh could be heard from across the room. He

slowly walked toward them, dragging his heels as if approaching his execution. "From my understanding, you let me go."

"You're no longer under suspicion, but we must ask you something." She slid her gaze to the others in the room, trying to spare the priest any more scrutiny. "Possibly somewhere private."

"If we must. Chet, please come along. He can accompany us?"

"No problem at all. You didn't waste any time getting to work," Trent said to the priest as they walked toward his office.

Father Linwood slowed his pace and looked over his shoulder. "Nothing can stop the Lord's work." The unstated implication was clearly a dig at his temporary arrest. "I do believe I mentioned we were discussing the repair and a memorial for Sadie Jackson?"

"You did," Trent said.

"A date and time has been set. Next Tuesday at seven PM. We chose that day to coincide with the day she was discovered one week prior. We also have the lofty goal of getting this place tidied up enough to hold mass tomorrow. We mustn't let the sins of men derail our service to the Almighty."

It was admirable that he wanted to honor Sadie's memory, and Amanda wanted to believe the memorial wasn't a move made for the sake of appearances. She took in their progress as she walked past. A few more screws were needed to secure the drywall. They might be able to get the drywall taped and a coat of mud on there, maybe even get it sanded in time. She'd think primer and paint would need to wait until after the service unless they worked all night.

Chet closed the office door behind them once they were all inside.

"So what is it I can help you with now?" Father Linwood asked.

Amanda gestured to Trent, who was already on his tablet. "We have a picture we need to show you."

Trent moved his finger around the screen. A few seconds later, he flipped it over to Father Linwood. Chet was looking too, but Amanda didn't expect him to know anything about the people shown. He hadn't been around at the time it was taken.

Father Linwood looked at the image, squinted, then huffed and pulled out a pair of reading glasses from his desk drawer. The move reminded Amanda that Malone was wearing a new pair the other day, and worry moved in again. Had another tumor formed on his brain, affecting not just his personality but his vision? She still hadn't heard from him, which was unusual.

"I could have zoomed in if you'd asked," Trent said. "I still can."

Linwood dismissed him with a curt wave. "All good." With the frames perched on his nose, he took another look, but he pulled back a moment later and removed his glasses. "Dear me. That's... My face has been scratched through. Where did you get this photo?"

"It was on Cameron's person when he was arrested."

"And why in heaven's sake would he have this? Did he say?"

It was probably best not to answer that question. "He's not saying a lot." Truth and avoidance wrapped in one package.

"I suppose he crossed out my picture because he holds me responsible for his childhood." Father Linwood swallowed roughly.

Amanda wasn't touching that comment, and it didn't seem like Trent was in any hurry to do so either. "We'd like to know what you can tell us about this photo. When was it taken?" she asked.

The priest put the glasses back on his nose and looked again. "This picture looks familiar, but it's from a while back. A decade or more. A photographer would have taken the group photo and then congregation members could order copies for themselves. The proceeds from the sales went to the church. That's probably how the Cofells got this one."

"Do you know these people?" She bobbed her head toward Trent, and he nodded.

"Let me zoom in," he said, and focused on the family next to the Cofells.

"Hmm, if I remember right, they left the church many years ago."

That answer wasn't surprising. Especially if they had anything to do with the Cofells and their dark secrets. But then this picture showed they'd hung around for about eight years after Sadie's murder. "They move out of town?"

"Not sure about that, but they lost their way from the path of God."

"How long ago was this?" Trent took his tablet back.

"Hmm, it would have to be the better part of twenty years ago now. In fact, I don't think it was long after this photo."

"Do you remember their names?" She'd figured that might be one of the first things he'd offered, but one never knew with him.

"I would tell you if I did, but we might not be without resources. We had a little baseball team back then. We called it the Herald Criers. Nothing serious, just some games here and there against other churches in the area."

"Not even serious enough for uniforms?" she asked.

Linwood shook his head. "Oh, we did, but this day was just about having some fun. There was also a picnic that day."

"You seem to remember those details all right." She could barely hide her skepticism that he recalled all this but not the names of that family.

Father Linwood gave her a knowing smile. "I know because we used to hold them monthly during the summer. The kids have bats and gloves and no uniformed shirts. I also caught a corner of a plastic tablecloth to the far right of the shot."

Amanda moved in to take a look. *I'll be...* "Okay, well you had this baseball team and uniforms, surely you had a list of the players' names."

Linwood smiled. "We did at one point. We also had more formal shots of the team taken with me and their coach." He turned to Chet. "The names were listed beneath in order left to right and by row."

She'd reserve her excitement for a minute longer. "And those boys with the blond hair were on the team?"

"Yes, and Cameron Cofell."

Now she was getting excited. If they could get the names of the boys and track them and the family down, they might be able to tell them more about the Cofells' friends. That's if the husband wasn't the man they were after. "Can we look at that right now? It could be a tremendous help."

Everyone was looking at the priest, including Chet.

Father Linwood dipped his head at his assistant. "They are framed and kept in the back of the storage room."

"Come with me. Let's see if we can find them." Chet had already opened the office door and was standing just outside it.

"Thank you," Amanda told the priest. Up until now he hadn't made the greatest impression on her, but her viewpoint could be skewed by her personal issue with God. From another perspective, Father Linwood could be seen as a loyal protector of his congregation, doing what he thought was right.

"You are very welcome. Don't think for one second my heart does not ache for the downtrodden and abused."

She held eye contact for a bit, creeped out by the fact he seemed to have read her thoughts. She left the office with Trent, and they followed Chet to the rear of the church and down a tight staircase to the basement.

He flicked a light on, but it didn't do much to chase the shadows away. The darkness transported her back to the energy of the Cofell farmhouse, and goosebumps rose on her arms.

"I haven't had much need to come down here, but I'm quite sure I know where Father Linwood meant." Chet continued going through a low arched doorway. "Just watch your heads."

It was unfinished down here, with exposed stone walls and a dirt floor. No musty smell or dampness, which was surprising for the age of the structure. Dust particles floating through the air winked when the light caught them.

Chet stopped at the back wall of the church. There was shelving here and a crate made of plywood. It was crudely constructed and held together with thin strips of wood. She could see from where she stood a few feet back that it held several picture frames.

"So we just have to go through these, and see if we can spot those boys with the blond hair." Chet smiled at them, an uneasy expression that graced his lips for a flash and disappeared.

She'd love to get right on shuffling through them, but it was rather dark in this part of the basement. A fluorescent lighting fixture had been installed to the raw beams overhead but only one side of it was giving off light. "Is there another bulb we could put in?"

"Unfortunately, I haven't seen any of them kicking around," Chet said. "But there is a flashlight around here somewhere." He left the room and returned a moment later. In that time, she and Trent had moved in on the crate.

She'd use her phone for additional light if it came down to it. Her patience was running out. So close, yet so far...

"Here we go." Chet flicked a flashlight on, and its beam flooded the room. "If you guys want to go through them, I'll hold the light over the area."

"Thank you," she told him, as she reached into the crate.

Trent helped her lift the first frame out. None of the faces in the photo were the ones they were after.

They kept going and came across a few team shots of the Herald Criers. None with the boys they were looking for.

When they reached the second to last one, they hit the jackpot. The older boy with blond hair was in the back row, and the younger one up front. The picture had been professionally framed, and there was a list of names at the bottom just as Father Linwood said there would be.

She quickly scanned the text. *Back row (in order)...* She tapped her finger on the name. "Peyton Hamamy is the older boy." Next, she turned to the front row and easily pulled out his brother. "And his younger brother is Jarvis Hamamy." *Hamamy...* The surname sounded familiar from the congregation list. It must have been one of the ones no longer active, based on what Father Linwood had told them.

"We've got their names. Now, we just need their parents'."

"I can look it up for you in my system," Chet offered. "It would save you the time of looking at the printout I gave you."

"That would be helpful, Chet. Thank you." Amanda began to set the photo back when she caught sight of the one behind it. *Don't tell me...* "Trent..." She exchanged the one they had out with the last one in the crate. As it emerged and they laid it flat, her heart kicked up speed. No names were noted on this one, but it was an enlarged version of the picnic photo. Only in this one, Father Linwood's face wasn't scratched out and neither was the other man's right cheek. Plain to see was a long, dark sideburn.

THIRTY-SEVEN

Amanda and Trent confirmed the parents' names were Bruce and Linda Hamamy before leaving Herald Church. Back in the car, they did a search on the onboard computer and netted an address. It was five o'clock by this point, and Amanda's phone rang, and the screen flashed Ava's name. Amanda answered, "I'm so sorry. I didn't expect to be at this all day, but—"

Ava was laughing. "Don't worry about it at all. Me and Zoe are having fun."

As if to prove the point, Zoe broke out in a rash of laughter in the background. "Hi, Mandy!" she yelled.

"Hello, Zoe!" Amanda smiled and looked over at Trent.

"Eek," Ava said. "Next time you do that, warn me so I can hold the phone away from my ear."

"Sorry." She laughed, and Trent smiled at her.

"Like I said, don't worry about us. I just wanted to know if I should make something for dinner for all of us."

"There should be some cash in an envelope. You know where to find it?" She kept some tucked away in a kitchen drawer for paying for deliveries. She preferred cash because it was easier to keep a hold on than charging a credit card.

"I do. You sure though? I don't mind cooking something simple."

"It's fine. Order some pizza, load it up."

"All right. Sounds delicious to me."

"What does?" Zoe said to Ava.

"We're ordering in pizza for dinner."

Zoe squealed. "Pizza. Pizza."

Amanda was pleased Zoe was happy, but it still did little to take the sting out of not being home. "Okay, well you two continue to have fun. I'm not sure exactly when I'll be home tonight." She felt they were on the brink of closing this investigation, but she'd been wrong before.

"Don't worry at all. I can sleep over again too."

"Yeah!" Zoe called out.

"Okay. Behave though."

"Always."

Amanda detected the mischievous grin and smiled. Ava was growing up to be an amazing young lady. "Love you both. Bye."

"We love you. Good—" Ava was gone.

Amanda laughed. "Just like her mother."

"In what way?" Trent looked over at her.

"Kristen barely hangs on long enough to finish saying the word *goodbye*. Ava's the same."

"Ambitious, on the move. That sounds a lot like her aunt too."

"I suppose you're right, and I'll accept the compliment."

"Only meant it as such. Okay, so I couldn't help but hear you talking about pizza, and now I'm hungry. Since we don't know how much longer we're going to be at this, do you want to stop for some before heading over to the Hamamy residence?"

As much as she wanted to get over there and speak to them, all the talk about pizza had made her hungry. Lunch was a long time ago. "Sure."

"Luigi's?"

"Couldn't stop me now, but should you call Kelsey and give her a heads up you'll be home later?"

"Nah, she'll be fine. She's rather independent. Sometimes I find it intimidating."

She angled her head. "Come on."

"No, I mean it. Anyway, Luigi's here we come." He smiled at her and made a turn to set them in the right direction for the restaurant.

Luigi's Pizzeria served the best pizza in the area and boasted fresh homemade sauce. Something she and Trent knew to be true. They'd seen the huge cauldron simmering away when they questioned the owner in a previous case. Just the memory conjured up the glorious aroma. Her stomach growled.

Trent glanced over. "Sounds like we're getting food just in time."

"Think so."

They got a table and ordered a medium to share. When discussing toppings, she broached the heated debate. "To pineapple or not pineapple?" she joked.

"To pineapple, of course."

She smiled at him, pleased to find they had one more thing in common. But even as she made that observation, she judged herself for why that mattered. She just had to get along with him as a coworker and friend. They didn't need to share a list of commonalities.

When they ordered, they told their server they were in a rush and if she could just bring the check with the food, that would be great. Forty minutes later, they were leaving the restaurant with full bellies.

"That took the edge off. I wouldn't have made it," Trent said, slipping behind the wheel.

"Me either."

They hadn't talked about the case much while they ate, but her mind never left it. Their next stop could be their last. Bruce

Hamamy had long, dark sideburns. Sure that photo was eight years after Audrey had seen a man of that description, but he could have kept that look. They could very well be making an arrest before heading home tonight. She pulled out her phone and checked her messages. Still nothing from Malone, but surely, he'd be curious about their progress. She texted him, *Have lots of updates. Should I call?*

"You all right over there? You've gone quiet."

"I just texted Malone, asked if he wants some updates."

"You haven't talked to him at all since yesterday?"

"No."

"Wow. That's not like him."

"No, it's not." She pushed off concerns about his health again and decided to distract herself by checking her email. "Another person I haven't heard from is Rideout. He was scheduled to start the autopsy on Audrey Witherspoon this morning. Oh, I spoke too soon. There is an email with his findings." She read down and shared the highlights with Trent. She started with the most crucial conclusion. "We can rule out suicide. Rideout found lorazepam in her stomach along with oxycodone. Lorazepam is an anxiety medication and a controlled substance."

"All right, but Audrey wasn't prescribed any."

"Per her granddaughter. We haven't confirmed that through her medical records, but Rideout said that no doctor would prescribe both to one person, and would certainly never recommend they be taken together. Rideout said the combination is lethal. Audrey's heart would have slowed down, along with her breathing, and she would have fallen into a coma then death."

"Not to downplay what happened, but one mercy is it doesn't sound like she suffered. But where did she get the lorazepam? How did the killer get into her house and get her to take it?"

"Obviously, Rideout can't help us there," she said drily.

"I'm just sayin'."

"I know. Now, Rideout did pass along that the lab still has to test the tea. That could have been the delivery method. What we can take away from this is the person we're after must know that Audrey was prescribed oxycodone."

"That and that the combo was lethal."

"Right, and then they set up the scene to make it look like Audrey had just fallen asleep on the couch. They placed the pill case out for us and wrote the suicide note. Probably all of this was after she died."

"Shooting her would have been far easier."

"But potentially more traceable, and this killer might not have access to a gun."

"All right, but they would need access to lorazepam."

She nodded but her thoughts were taking her to a dark place. "The granddaughter knew about her grandmother's prescription. She'd have access to her house, be able to slip the drugs into her tea. Could she have…?"

"What would be her motive? We feel Audrey's murder must be connected to what she saw twenty-three years ago."

"Unless there's something we're missing." Her phone chimed with a text from Malone, and she read the message as it popped up on the screen.

Any arrests?

She responded, *Could be close to one.*
His bubble indicated he was typing.

Call me if it happens. Otherwise update first thing Monday morning.

"Huh." She lowered her phone. Ticked off, hurt, and confused.

"What?" Trent parked in front of a modest bungalow and looked over at her.

She shook her head. Anger became the forefront emotion. "He wants an update Monday morning."

"Monday?"

"I even told him we could be close to making an arrest."

"Really?"

"Yep. He said if that happens call before. Otherwise..."

"He's really acting strangely. I hate to say it but the last time he was like this..."

"If you're going to say he had a tumor, I know. Trust me." She pointed at the house. "We're here." Clearly it wasn't in question, and she got out of the vehicle. She didn't want to sit around discussing Malone's odd behavior when they could be slapping cuffs on someone or in the least getting a strong lead. That's *if* Bruce wasn't the man with long, dark sideburns they were after.

Linda Hamamy answered the door after Trent rang the doorbell. She had an oval face with a dusting of freckles on the bridge of her narrow nose. At fifty-eight, she was a beautiful woman.

Amanda held up her badge, and so did Trent. "Detectives Steele, and Stenson," she told the woman. "Are you Linda Hamamy?" The question a formality, as the driver's license photo matched the woman in front of them.

"I am."

"Would your husband, Bruce, be home as well?"

"Pfft. That cheating scumbag, good for nothing piece of shit." Linda crossed her arms and snorted. Her nostrils were flaring.

"Mrs. Hamamy," Amanda said.

"No, please. No missus. Let's stick with Linda or better still, nothing. You have business with Bruce, not me, correct?"

Bruce was the man with the notable sideburns, but this

woman was a link to getting to him. "We'd like to speak with you. Shouldn't be for long. Just a few minutes."

"Whatever, but if he's done something you'd be best to talk to one of his whores." Linda stepped back into the house, allowing them room to enter.

They were seen to the living room. On the way, Amanda noted the pictures on the wall of the two boys at different ages. It looked like the eldest, Peyton, went on to play baseball for a local team outside of the church. There was a picture of him wearing a cap and gown on graduation day from university but nothing past that. Since he looked about fifteen years old in that picnic photo, he'd be early thirties current day. The younger brother would be around twenty-three, same as Cameron. There were pictures of Jarvis too. It looked like he leaned toward hockey instead of baseball.

Once everyone sat down, Amanda got started right away. She didn't want to waste any time when Bruce could be their killer. "We have come to understand that you and your husband were friends with Doug and Winnie Cofell."

"Ah, many years ago, but it was more Bruce and Doug that were close. Bruce seemed to cling to that man for some reason. I just recently found out that Doug and Winnie died in a car accident a few years back. We fell out of touch with each other, which was fine by me."

Amanda would poke that more, but if Bruce was who they were after, his *clinging* to Doug could be due to them sharing a dark, horrid secret.

Linda added, "I was around too, of course. Though I'd have rather been anywhere else, but Bruce convinced me that would have been rude. Thing is, they always wanted to come over to our place. They never opened up their home."

Having been to the Cofell farmhouse and knowing what they were hiding there, Amanda could understand the reason. "Did they ever say why?"

"Never asked. It seemed a taboo subject. I told Bruce several times I was going to bring it up, and he begged me not to. But it turns out them coming here was for the best anyhow."

"Why's that?" Trent asked. He had his tablet out and was making notes.

"I popped by once when the family missed Sunday mass. The word going around was Cameron was ill, and Doug and Winnie were tending to him. I remember because it was the day after a church picnic. The beginning of the end for me and that church, *those people*."

Father Linwood recalled the Hamamy family leaving the church not long after the picnic in the photo they showed him. Cameron told her and Trent that Doug had beaten him after the game. He likely wasn't ill, but black and blue. "What happened?" Amanda imagined it must have been something severe for her to stress the words she had.

"I thought it would be nice to turn up with a batch of home-made chicken noodle soup, so that's what I did. Winnie stood in the doorway, didn't even invite me in. She had the audacity to look down her nose at my offering and ask me what I was doing there *really*. I had no idea what she was talking about. I told her I heard Cameron was sick, that's all. Thought I'd do something nice. She didn't care. Didn't say another word, but she took the soup and slammed the door." Linda shook her head. "Some people, but it was probably a blessing she didn't invite me inside."

"Why is that?" Amanda asked.

"The place gave me the creeps from the doorway. A cold breeze was coming out of the home." She shivered and shook her shoulders. "Bad spirits. I'd had my doubts about the Cofells before that, but then I knew without a doubt something dark was going on in that home. Cameron had always struck me as a shy kid, socially awkward. But that was on the parents. They didn't let him out much and even homeschooled him. Like they wanted to control him. And I swear that I heard him crying when I was talking with Winnie at the door."

"And this was around the time you left the church?" Amanda asked, picking up on Linda's earlier comment to that effect.

Linda nodded. "That's right. I told Bruce how Winnie treated me, and he paled and asked what I thought I was doing, 'just showing up unannounced?' I thought he was joking around but then I realized he was serious. I wasn't really into the church anyhow, so I told him I was leaving it and him. He was cheating on me. I'd known for a while by that point but ignored it because he was the sole provider at the time. I did end up leaving him for a bit years ago, but like a fool I let him talk me into giving him another chance. Then another and another until"—she flailed an arm—"I just finally got tired of it and kicked him out this past Wednesday. Hearing about Cameron in the news gave me the courage. I heard what he accused Father Linwood of doing, and the Cofells. I wish I'd said something, but it was just a hunch something was off. I didn't have proof."

Amanda nodded, saddened because that was how abuse was left unchecked. People downgraded their instinct to paranoia or imagination.

"It didn't help that Bruce was so close to them either," she added. "He seemed to worship Doug. If Cofell asked him to jump, Bruce would ask how high. He'd get up and go whenever Doug called and needed anything."

Amanda and Trent looked at each other, likely both thinking the same thing. Had Bruce jumped when Doug had killed Sadie, or had he asked for help doing that? Did it go deeper than that? "Did he go to their house without you?"

"I guess he did."

"You said that you heard about the incident at Herald Church," Amanda began.

"Oh, yeah. I reached out to my boys about it too. They're out of the house, all grown up, but they used to play with Cameron sometimes. I asked them, but they didn't know anything about abuse going on in the home. And with all this coming up, I wondered if Bruce..." She shook her head. "I don't want to believe it of him."

"Believe what?" Amanda tiptoed here.

"Was he somehow involved with what was going on in that home? Did he ever touch Cameron? I asked him, you know, when I was kicking him out. He adamantly denied even knowing about Cameron's abuse. He swore if it was going on, he didn't play a part."

Amanda imagined how horrible it would be in her shoes. But none of what she'd just told them eliminated Bruce from Amanda's suspect list. "You seem up on the news. Did you hear it was a girl pulled from the walls?"

"Yes. Sadie Jackson, kidnapped from Florida, right?"

"That's right. Did you ever know the Cofells' daughter?" Amanda put that out there, curious if Linda would link her questioning.

"Their daughter? I never knew they had one."

"How long were you friends?" Trent asked.

"For longer than I would have liked," she said coolly. "A year or two before our youngest, Jarvis, was born."

Sadie would have been around. "So no daughter, that you're aware of?"

Linda slowly shook her head. "Never saw them with one. They never spoke of one."

The answer was sickening. That cubby behind the kitchen wall had been her entire world. Probably Jane Doe's before her.

"Wait. Are you telling me that..." She laid a hand on her chest. "Did the Cofells kidnap Sadie Jackson?"

"We have reason to believe they did," Amanda said. "And another girl before that."

"Oh my God." Linda breathed heavily for a few moments. "I really wish I reported them then, even if was just baseless suspicions."

"Never baseless when it comes to our intuition." Soothing Linda's conscience wasn't Amanda's job.

"What about Cameron? Did they kidnap him too?" Her brows were corkscrewed.

"Not exactly. DNA has come back confirming he was the offspring of Doug Cofell and Sadie Jackson." Amanda let that sit out there, watching the shock play on Linda's face.

Her mouth opened and shut. Tears streamed down her face. "Are you here looking for Bruce because you think that he... that he was somehow involved with any of this?"

Amanda glanced at Trent, and he got up and showed Linda the group photo. This was the picture showing Bruce's entire face. "That is your husband?" he asked her.

"Yes. Those blasted sideburns. He had them when we met and didn't let go of the look for years. At least he finally saw sense and got rid of them."

"We need to find Bruce, Linda," Amanda told her.

"You do think he's mixed up in all this."

"We have an eyewitness testimony that places a man of your husband's description transporting a wooden crate into Herald Church," Amanda laid out. "We have reason to believe that Sadie's body was inside."

Linda gasped. "My God, I know Bruce is no good, but to do something like this?"

Possibly even worse... Amanda let the thought roll through and saw no sense pointing it out to Linda.

"But you said eyewitness? Where have they been all these years, and who is this person?"

"Typically, we wouldn't disclose that, but the woman lived next door to the church, and she was murdered two nights ago."

Linda sat in silence. More tears fell. Her chin quivered as

she met Amanda's gaze. "If Bruce is in on this, it could explain his behavior."

Amanda inched forward. "Which was?"

"Not long before... actually, I guess around the time of Jarvis's birth, he went off the rails. He started drinking a lot and lost a job he had for a long time. Since then he's lost a lot of them. All because of his drinking."

That sounded like a man with a guilty conscience. Jarvis and Cameron were the same age. The timing would align with when Sadie was killed and put in the wall. Did that absolve him of abuse before that? Amanda wasn't so gracious. Murder might have just been what pushed him over the edge. "As I said, we need to find Bruce. Do you have any way of reaching him?"

She shook her head. "He worked at Luke's, a hardware store in town, when I kicked him out a few days ago. Who knows if he's messed that up since. I don't have his recent number."

Amanda found that strange, but Trent spoke before she could probe any further.

"What about the latest woman you think he's seeing? Do you know how to reach her?" Trent asked.

"I don't know. I didn't care to know. I'm sorry."

"Then you have no idea who she is or what she looks like?" Amanda couldn't just let this slip. If Linda didn't know then they'd try the Hamamy boys. Assuming they were in contact with their father.

"No. But I do remember when I first suspected Bruce was cheating on me. It was back around the time of that photo, actually. I found him holed up in the walk-in closet on the cordless phone. He told someone he called Bren not to call him at home."

Bren? That could be short for Brenda, Audrey's granddaughter. She was a little too close to the investigation to ignore the coincidence. She was also the one person they were aware of who knew about her grandmother's prescription for oxycodone. Had she murdered her own grandmother to protect Bruce? Had her grief been an act? Were the two of them still in contact? "That was a while ago, though. You hear him say her name more recently?"

"No."

"What about checking for numbers on your phone bills?" Amanda asked, desperation rising inside of her.

"We got rid of the landline and got cell phones, but when Bruce didn't pay the bill, we lost the service to those. That was years ago. I opened a new account with my credit and set up my phone. He used prepaid ones and kept changing his number. That's why I couldn't tell you his latest one."

"We'll take the last one you know about," Trent told her, and as she rattled it off, he tapped it into his tablet.

"The signs were there. I was stupid to ignore them. He'd always lock up his phone and password-protect his laptop. Whatever he could do to keep me out. At least I finally saw sense and had enough. I was sick of his drinking and his secrecy. And I suppose with all this coming out about Cameron's accusations, a part of me did wonder about my husband's time at the Cofell farm."

Amanda couldn't blame her for any of this. It would get any sane person asking questions. She stood and thanked Linda for her time. "Call me if you hear from Bruce or he turns up here." She handed Linda her card.

"You bet I will."

"Just be safe yourself, Linda. Don't threaten him," Amanda cautioned. "We don't know what he might be capable of." Though Amanda was quite sure she did.

"I'll be smart."

Linda saw them out, and in the car, Amanda and Trent looked at each other.

"That poor woman. She's going to be beating herself up now." Amanda felt for the woman, but there with a fire burning in her belly for another reason. "Let's try that number she gave us."

Trent took out his tablet and gave her Bruce's latest number. Amanda made the call. Within a second, she was listening to an automated voice telling her it was out of service. She shook her head.

"That avenue's gone, but she said that she overheard Bruce say the name Bren. Short for Brenda? We know of one, and she is also rather close to one of our murders."

"I don't know. It's hard to see it. Audrey took her in and raised her. She seemed genuinely upset."

"Sure, but you can think of it two ways. One, Brenda is involved with the murder of her grandmother, or she is in danger. She knew what her grandmother saw. If she is the Bren that Bruce was on the phone with, the timeline adds up for him having long, dark sideburns."

"Okay, still following..."

"Brenda might want to protect Bruce, to protect them."

"You think they're still together?"

"They could be. And if they are, what's to say Brenda didn't vent to Bruce about her grandmother going on about what she'd seen? If they were ever in a relationship, Bruce could know Audrey was prescribed oxy."

"Which he could have used to kill her, and now he might feel pressed against the wall and want to silence the one other person who could point a finger at him. Assuming Brenda's not involved with her grandmother's murder."

"Which could mean, Brenda is in danger, as I said."

"We still don't even know if she or Bruce have access to lorazepam. If he's an alcoholic, I can't see a doctor writing a prescription for it."

"People lie about how much they drink all the time. Let me settle this right now." She got out of the car and went back to Linda's door. She answered with a glass of red wine in her hand. "Does Bruce have a prescription for lorazepam?" Amanda asked her.

"No, but I had one. I'm pretty sure I still have some pills kicking around. I take them to settle my nerves whenever I fly."

Bruce had been in this house until Wednesday when Linda told them she'd kicked him out. What was to stop him from taking Linda's drugs? That's assuming he knew about Audrey's oxy medication because of a relationship with Brenda. Past or present. "Could you check to make sure that you still have them?"

"Why? Where would they have gone? Never mind. Step in if you like. I'll be right back." Linda set her wineglass on the table near the door and stomped through the house. She returned after a few seconds, red-faced and nostrils flaring. "The bottle and the pills are gone. Are you telling me Bruce took them?"

"I don't know yet."

"That son of a bitch."

"How many pills were there?"

"Six or seven."

Amanda turned and left, and Linda slammed the door behind her. She wouldn't take that personally as she was quite certain the rage behind it was directed at Bruce.

"I heard that door from here," Trent said when she got back into the car.

"It's not good. I just confirmed that Linda had a prescription for lorazepam, but all the pills she had left were gone. She had six or seven."

"Far more than enough."

"Rideout made it sound like it wouldn't take much combined with oxy."

"Even still, it doesn't tell us if Brenda is an accomplice or in trouble. We don't even know for sure if she was the mistress then or now. It could have been another Brenda. Or Brenna? Or—"

She held up a hand. "I get it. But I don't think it's farfetched that Brenda and Bruce at least met. She grew up in the house next to the church. It's entirely plausible she attended mass, met Bruce, and they hit it off. During their relationship, whether years ago or if it's still going on, he could have found out about Audrey's prescription."

"Which leads me to another thought I had while you were talking to Linda. Even if Bruce knew about the oxy, how would he know mixing it with lorazepam was lethal? There's nothing to indicate a medical education in Bruce's background, or Brenda's, for that matter."

It didn't take long for Amanda to hatch a theory. "The internet. I mean, why not? If Bruce wanted Audrey gone badly enough, finding a murder method is a click away."

"Nothing unsettling about that."

"It's the truth though. And I think most people know oxy is a powerful medication. If he knew Audrey was taking it, he could have started his search with what to avoid when taking it."

"Good point. Now while you were gone, I called the Hamamy boys. They have the same number for Bruce as Linda gave us. Both say they don't know where their father is, and I believe them. I also looked up Luke's Hardware, and they're closed until Monday."

"Then we track the owner down at home. They could have Bruce's current address and a number we don't have."

Trent shook his head. "Already tried. No luck."

"Someone was busy. I didn't think I was gone that long."

"Just long enough."

"Okay, well, we only have one immediate move."

"You don't need to say it. I'll get us over to Brenda's house." Trent pulled away at speed, and for Amanda he still wasn't driving fast enough.

THIRTY-EIGHT

Amanda knocked on Brenda's apartment for a third time. She was getting flashbacks of finding Audrey. "What if we're too late?"

"Let's just think positively," Trent said. "She could be out. Her phone might be off."

Amanda would go through the pain of trying to secure a warrant to track Brenda's number, but they didn't have enough to justify violating her privacy. They were just assuming Brenda Witherspoon was who Bruce Hamamy had an affair with. But there was another way of looking at this. Regardless of whether Bruce was the killer or someone else, could they take the chance Audrey didn't talk to her granddaughter in more detail about what she saw? The killer could have found out and seen her as a liability.

She had her hand poised to knock again when the peephole lifted. "It's Detectives Steele and Stenson," Amanda said.

The cover fell back into place, and the chain slid across. Brenda opened the door for them to come inside, all without a word.

"We tried calling you and knocked a few times. Are you all

right?" Amanda took in her haggard appearance. Her hair was mussed, and her mascara was smudged under her eyes.

"Sorry, I was napping when my phone rang, and I was too tired to answer. I wasn't out of bed long after and noticed it was an unknown number. And just now I was in the bathroom. Got here as quick as I could. Should we sit?" She added that latter bit as if embarrassed by admitting to a natural bodily function.

Amanda nodded. "It would be a good idea."

They all sat in the living room like the last time. The vanilla candle was unlit but had been burned almost all the way down.

"Losing Grandma's been tough. A lot tougher than I would have thought. She had a good life, and a fairly long one. But it's not like she went out on her own terms. I don't buy that for one second anyhow. Someone killed her."

"We think so too," Amanda told her, and Brenda's shoulders relaxed. "You told us she had a prescription for oxy for when her arthritis flared up."

"She did." Brenda stiffened again.

Amanda held up her hand. "You're not on trial here, Brenda. Might you have told someone else about that?"

"It's not exactly something I'd have reason to talk about with other people."

She tried another tack. "All right. Anyone else who might have known about it?"

"Her friends."

She studied Brenda, who had started to fidget a bit more in her chair, and Amanda turned to Trent.

He had his tablet out. "Does this man look familiar to you?"

Amanda caught the screen when Trent got up. The picnic photo, zoomed in on Bruce Hamamy.

Brenda worried her bottom lip. "Yeah. I knew him."

"His name?" Amanda prompted.

"Bruce Hamamy." More chewing of her lip.

"How well do you know him?" Trent asked as he returned to the couch.

"I said I *knew* him."

"Were you in a relationship with him?" Amanda asked.

Brenda nodded.

"How did you and Bruce meet?" Amanda held back all judgment at her choice to sleep with a married man.

"I attended Herald Church for a while. Grandma never knew, though. I'd moved out of home by that time. Bruce really listened to me, and he liked the same music I did. He was easy to talk to. The sex just happened, and kept happening. I knew his wife too, but she was just an aloof person. I'm probably in that picture you just showed me. Let me see it again."

Trent walked over with the tablet again.

Brenda looked at the screen. "That's me right there." She pointed and Trent came back to the couch to show Amanda.

There's no way they could have ever made the connection. The Brenda from fifteen years ago looked a lot different. Brown hair pulled back and she was super thin. Present-day Brenda's form had filled out and she was a bottle blond.

"I would have been in my late twenties then. Bruce and I were sleeping together for years by that point. We started when I was twenty."

There was one inconsistency Amanda wanted to probe. "You became a part of the church then?" Brenda's name wasn't on the congregation list they'd been given.

"No, I was never baptized. I mostly went to be close to Bruce. Even if his wife and kids were usually with him. Why are you so interested in Bruce?"

"Before I get to that, did you ever have reason to mention your grandmother's medications to him?" Amanda was easing in, but she could tell the question did nothing in that regard.

"What are you asking me?" Brenda's face paled, and she waved a hand over her chest.

"Please, just answer Detective Steele's question," Trent said.

"Uh, I don't think so. I don't see what reason I'd have. But when she'd get in a lot of pain, Grandma would call and ask me to go over and help with things. I'd often tell her to take one of her pills, and I'd get there when I could. It's possible I said this when Bruce was around, even mentioned oxy."

"She's had a prescription for them a long time then?" Amanda asked.

"Long as I can remember. Tell me, how did she die? Just don't tell me that..." Brenda's chin quivered.

"I'm sorry, Brenda, but the medical examiner found that she had oxy and lorazepam in her system. The combination is lethal." This was feeling like a second notification, with more details. Not that it lessened the blow.

"But who would do such a thing? Oh... You think *he* did this?"

"Your grandmother described seeing two men—"

"Moving a crate into the church. We covered that. She was seeing things."

"We don't think she was. She described two men. One had long, dark sideburns." Amanda served that matter-of-factly and slowly.

"And you think that's Bruce? For all the times she told me what she saw, I never thought it was him. Why would he be out there in the middle of the night?"

"Sadie Jackson's body was in that crate," Amanda told her. "They were taking her into the church."

"No. I can't believe that. You think that he... that he killed that girl, and then my grandmother?" Her voice took on a high pitch.

"The evidence is leading us in that direction. Do you have any idea where we can find him? What his number might be?"

"I couldn't tell you where he is or how to reach him. We

were on-again, off-again for years, but I swear I haven't been in contact with him for years now. I just can't believe he'd do this. Why he'd do it. The man I knew was mostly kind. It's hard to imagine him killing anyone, let alone a teenage girl or an older woman."

"*Mostly* kind?" Amanda kicked back.

"He was an adulterer, and he could be moody."

"We were told that he was close friends with Doug Cofell," she said. "Is that how you know it?"

"You're kidding, right? Whoever told you that is delusional. Bruce hated the guy."

The skin tightened on the back of Amanda's neck. That contradicted what Bruce's wife had told them, but what reason could she have to misdirect them? Then again, it wouldn't be the first time a cheating husband presented two fronts, one to his wife and another to his mistress. "Do you know why?"

"Bruce would never tell me, but I got the feeling it had something to do with me and our affair."

"Do yourself a favor, Brenda, and be careful, okay?" Amanda stood.

"You think Bruce would hurt me?"

"He knew you and your grandmother were close. He'd expect you to know all about what she saw that night," Amanda said.

"I still can't believe he'd kill a soul. Do you have hard evidence he killed my grandmother?"

"No, but she saw him move that crate, and we're quite sure forensic evidence will tie him to Sadie Jackson."

Brenda's eyes watered, and her mouth opened. Then she shook her head. "No, there has to be an innocent explanation."

"Please, just watch your back. You have any issues, call me. You have my card?" Amanda was sure she gave it to her the other day.

"I don't know where it is now."

Amanda pressed a fresh one into her palm. "Call me any time, day or night."

With that, Amanda ended the interview and left the apartment with Trent.

"Someone was in a hurry to get out of there," Trent said as he rushed to catch up with her.

They loaded onto the elevator. She hit the button for the ground floor and said, "The timing of the affair between Brenda and Bruce puts us back to around the time Sadie Jackson was murdered. If Bruce is *mostly good* as Brenda told us, did Doug know about the affair and use it to manipulate him into helping him move Sadie's body?"

"If he had, that could explain why Bruce hated the guy. But if that was what happened, why keep quiet all these years?"

"Well, who would believe him? But it could explain why he's turned to the bottle and can't hold a job. His mind is wracked with guilt."

"Though he can't be that broken up about it. After all, it sure looks like he killed Audrey Witherspoon."

"Then there's that."

The elevator beeped on the ground floor, and they got out.

She resumed their conversation in the car. "We need to find him. As of right now, Bruce Hamamy is our prime suspect."

THIRTY-NINE

After leaving Brenda, Amanda and Trent issued an APB on Bruce Hamamy, but beyond that there was nothing else they could do. They agreed to leave things for the rest of the week-end. That let her spend yesterday with Zoe and make it over to her parents for the ritual Sunday-night roast dinner with the entire family.

Amanda was in early at Central on Monday, though, in the hopes of catching Malone before Trent arrived at work. It was eight o'clock, and she found Malone in his office.

He looked up when she cleared the doorway. He was wearing the reading glasses again, and her fear resurfaced about another tumor.

"Someone's been busy this weekend. I heard about the APB. On a Bruce Hamamy, was it?"

"That's right." She bit back the urge to say that he would have known all about it if he'd just picked up his phone. She closed the door, and Malone removed his glasses. "There's a lot I need to catch you up on."

"I figured as much." He gestured to the chairs across from his desk, and she sat on one. Given the recent way he'd been treating her, standing before him was turning her legs to jelly. Not from fear as much as uncertainty and a bit of anger toward him.

Amanda filled him in on everything from Friday night to Saturday night.

"I understand the APB now."

"Trent and I know Hamamy's last place of employment. They open at nine, and we'll be there to pick him up. That's if he's still employed there."

"Anything else?" Malone picked up his glasses but didn't put them on.

"Yeah, there is actually."

Malone stiffened, and so did she.

"Are you okay? You've been acting a little... unlike yourself." She thought that was the most delicate way of putting it.

"I haven't felt much like myself." Malone pressed his lips into a firm line and leaned back.

Her insides were fluttering with nerves. "Your health?"

Malone popped forward. "No, nothing like that, and I'm sorry you were worried about that."

"It's just you've been short with me, rude, actually, and I don't know what I've done to deserve it. When you had the tumor you—"

"I was the same way. It's not that."

"Then I don't understand." Her heart was hurting. She thought of Malone as a second father having grown up with him always around.

"I was hoping to keep this from you, but clearly it's not going to happen with that nosy nature of yours."

"I like to think of myself as inquisitive."

"Nosy, inquisitive... Both fit."

"Are you going to tell me what's going on?" she blurted out. "If there's something I've done, please let me know."

Malone tensed again and clasped his hands across his front.

"There is something actually. Several somethings, and it's caught the attention of Chief Buchanan."

"I still don't follow." She and Trent had an impeccable record for closing cases. Was this like a marriage proposal, where it seemed a breakup was on the horizon, only to have the man pop the question? Or in this case instead of a reprimand, praise and a suggestion she take the sergeant's exam?

Malone took a deep sigh. "Back in December, you remember how the Glover case played out?"

"Yes."

"How you went ahead before backup arrived?"

"Am I in trouble?"

"You could be if you don't start watching your steps."

"Why not just warn me of that? Why treat me—"

"Amanda, we may be friends but I'm also your sergeant. As your friend, I've been trying to decide how best to tell you all of this. The Glover case wasn't the first time you put yourself in danger. In fact, we might have even had this conversation before, the one about your tendency to rush ahead. Well, these things make it to the record. They must or I'm not doing my job."

She was shaking. "I get that."

"Unfortunately, these instances have caught the chief's attention. You've worked a lot of high-profile cases recently. First the Glover case, now the Jackson case. But these investigations bring a lot of public scrutiny along with them. He's concerned about your ability to do your job properly, to follow procedure."

"I—" She snapped her mouth shut, unable to find a suitable defense considering what he'd just told her. She was guilty of the accusations against her. "What do I do now?"

"Don't make any more false steps or I might not be able to help you."

"He wants my badge?"

"I never said anything so drastic as that, but he can ruin all your chances for future advancement. I know you were thinking police chief for yourself one day. You have ranks to work through before that, but Buchanan could hold you back from all those opportunities."

"He would do that over a few..." She didn't know what word to use that wouldn't make things sound worse than they were. *Indiscretions* or *errors in judgment* certainly didn't fit. Every time she moved ahead without backup, the situation was urgent and failure to act would result in people getting injured or worse.

"I'm sorry to say that he would, and it's his job to think of the interests of this department. As I said, high-profile cases bring attention to the department. He wants to make sure that we come out in a favorable light."

"Someone has lofty ambitions," she quipped. "The media will never have our backs."

"Steele."

"I'm sorry, Sarge, but they will always find fault with the police department."

"They might, but it's up to us to make sure any accusations won't stand up."

She processed what he'd told her, trying to reconcile it with how he'd been treating her and drew one conclusion. "You've been shielding me from him."

"In part, I suppose, but I might be guilty of passing his treatment of me on to you. He's been coming down hard on me. After all, you're in my charge and if I can't manage my department then... well..." Malone sneered and avoided eye contact.

Now it was sinking in. Not only had he been concerned with her future, but his own. He'd been trying to protect them both. "I'll do better."

"All I can ask."

"Thank you for telling me all this." She got up and touched the back of his hand.

"You know it, Mandy Monkey." Malone winked at her, and she shook her head. His calling her by her family's nickname for her showed they'd made a successful truce.

Still, she had a lot to think about. As she walked back to her desk, she was grateful for his loyalty even if it manifested poorly. She could even understand his and the chief's position from a procedural black-and-white viewpoint, but her actions were always in the best interests of other people. Was she supposed to stop weighing the cost to human lives? Surely, they wouldn't want that. There had to be a balance she could strike, but until she figured out what that was, she had something else to distract her. She was determined to put Sadie Jackson and Audrey Witherspoon's killer behind bars. Today.

FORTY

Amanda's meeting with Malone had lasted a long twenty minutes. When she got back to her desk, Trent wasn't in yet, so she checked her email. There was a message from CSI Blair sent at eight that morning. The subject was *Cofell and Witherspoon Investigations*. Amanda clicked on it, and Blair started off by recapping that some items were processed by a colleague over the weekend.

She began her message by confirming Audrey Witherspoon's tea was contaminated with lorazepam and oxy. Just as Rideout had found in her system.

The rest wasn't much like Christmas either. Blair only had two things listed in bullet form.

- Hidden room in Cofell farmhouse showed two female contributors and one male. One DNA profile was a match to Sadie Jackson, the other a match to the unknown DNA in the Mary Janes that Jackson was found in. Male DNA a match to Cameron Cofell.

Amanda let herself absorb this first point. Cameron being in that hellhole was no surprise. But *two* girls... Again, it shouldn't shock her. Not after finding that photo of Jane Doe. Clearly the Cofells' depravity knew no bounds. And these findings confirmed the Mary Janes were passed along from Jane Doe to Sadie. At least Sadie's body had been found. Amanda wished she could bring the same dignity to Jane Doe, provide her family some closure, and allow for a proper burial. She wasn't under any illusions Jane Doe was alive.

She read the second point.

- Pills don't provide enough surface for prints, but prints were lifted from the keyboard at the Witherspoon house, the prescription bottle, and the teacup. All belong to the victim. No prints on the pill organizer.

"Good morning." Trent came in and had two coffees from Hannah's Diner again. He handed one to her.

"You don't have to keep doing this." She took the cup appreciatively anyhow.

"I know I don't have to, but this case has been hard on you and so has..." He motioned in the direction of Malone's office.

"We had a talk. Everything's fine now." She'd gained some clarity anyway. Even if she didn't know what she'd do differently in future.

"And I take it you don't want to talk about it?"

"Nope."

He nodded, and she appreciated he didn't pry. "Did you also fill him in on everything?"

"I looped him in. I was just reading an email from Blair. She confirmed Audrey's tea was contaminated with a mix of oxy and lorazepam."

"Not a surprise, but it's curious how Bruce was able to get that close. With her memory so sharp, she might have recognized him even without the sideburns. She'd be more likely to call us than let him into her home."

She could think of one possibility. "Unless he put on a pretense. He might have told her he was full of regret and planning to turn himself in."

"I suppose it's possible."

Amanda told him there were no unknown fingerprints left at Witherspoon's house.

"So he dumped the pills into her cup, but never touched it," Trent said.

"Or he prepared it and wore gloves while he was with Audrey. Though, I'm sure she would have noticed and asked about them. How would he explain that away?"

"Well, Luke's Hardware should be open. Let's go bring him in and ask him."

"You couldn't stop me."

An hour later, Amanda and Trent were in the observation room connected to Interview Room One looking in on Bruce Hamamy. He might have been a handsome man at one time, but the passing years and the boozing had taken its toll. His skin was pitted and blotchy, and he had bloodshot eyes. When they turned up at his work with a squad car and told him they needed to take a drive to Central, his boss had called out behind Bruce that he was out of chances and not to bother coming back. Another job down the drain, but that would be the least of Bruce's worries by the time they finished with him.

Bruce had his elbows on the table and was leaning forward, cupping his face.

"Let's nail this guy to the wall," Amanda said and led the way next door.

She and Trent sat down across from him without saying a word. Bruce quickly lowered his hands.

"You got me fired!"

"Sounds like you did most of that yourself," Trent volleyed back.

"Whatever. I'll get a new job."

"I don't think that's something you'll need to think about," Amanda said firmly.

He met her eyes, and the tough exterior evaporated. "I never should have... never..."

"Never should have what, Mr. Hamamy?" she asked.

He fidgeted with his hands, cleaning under his nails. "I can't live with this anymore. Coming clean might be the only way I get peace."

Amanda shifted in her chair, glanced at Trent in such a way she didn't want it to be plainly obvious. She let the silence expand, not daring to say something that would stop Bruce from speaking to them.

"He held power over me. He said if I didn't help him, he'd tell my wife. I should have just let him. My life is shit anyway."

Amanda laid out a photograph of Sadie Jackson as she appeared in the wall, then set a picture of her the day she was taken. She pushed a finger to that one. "Sadie Jackson was eight years old when she was kidnapped from a Florida amusement park." Then she transferred her finger to her remains. "Eight years later she was put into the walls of the church. Did you put her there?"

Tears filled his eyes, and he nodded.

They were getting close to throwing this monster in prison. "Did you beat and murder this girl with Doug and Winnie Cofell?"

"What?" Bruce met her eyes, and some tears fell. "No, I never did that."

"DNA was found under her fingernails and on the dress she was buried in," Trent pushed out with force.

"No. How...? Oh, shit." He wiped a hand down his face. "This is a... nightmare."

Amanda crossed her arms, tried to wrangle her temper. But he hadn't even noticed the subtleties in Trent's statement. He'd just said *DNA*, not *Bruce's* DNA. After all, they didn't know that yet, but Bruce's reaction sure was telling. "Why, Mr. Hamamy? Because you're caught?"

"No, it's just how it looks... like I had a part in killing her, but I swear that I didn't."

She shook her head. "You'll need to do better than that. The evidence is against you."

"You don't get it. I wasn't just afraid that he'd talk to my wife. Doug and Winnie were psychopaths. The world's much better off now they're gone. Trust me."

"So that's why you took part in beating and killing that girl?" she volleyed back.

"No, I didn't. I shouldn't even have been there that night."

Amanda had taken Bruce's initial reaction to them to mean they'd have his written confession in no time. He hadn't even requested a lawyer. But now he was slipping into denial. "Detective Stenson just told you that we have evidence you were with Sadie."

He was sniffling, making a lot of noise, unable to keep up with the huge amounts of snot dripping from his nostrils. She ducked out of the room for a tissue box and tossed it on the table in front of him.

He blew his nose.

"Prints were on the crate you moved her body in." She'd phrased it so he'd assume they were *his* prints when, in truth, that was yet to be determined.

"I... I helped Doug move her, but that's all. The rest was on him."

Guess the prints will match... "I'm having a hard time believing that."

"It's the truth!" But partway through his adamant claim, he lost steam. "I received a call from Doug. He was yelling into the phone that I needed to get over to the farm immediately. He wouldn't tell me why."

"But you went anyway?" Amanda weighed Bruce's expressed fear of the Cofells with Linda saying Bruce clung to Doug and Brenda's statement that he hated the man. Both fit, after all. Bruce kept his enemy close.

"Yeah. Biggest mistake of my life. I always knew Doug and Winnie were *off*."

"How so?" Amanda could list many ways that she and Trent had discovered but wanted Bruce's take.

"It's just their house had this feeling to it. It's hard to describe."

Amanda could come up with a few. Creepy, suffocating, possessed by evil energies...

"I don't think they were good to that boy. Cameron." He put his name out there. "I believe everything he claimed. And Father Linwood would have known what they were doing to him, but he didn't report them. I wish that I had gone to the police with my suspicions, especially after learning what they did to Sadie."

"Regrets are pointless without a time machine," she said drily. "What do you think they did to her?" She wasn't sure if she wanted the entire gambit of horrors drilled into her head. She had enough imagery in that regard.

"I found out too late with her, but they beat her and Doug raped her. Winnie knew. She even watched sometimes."

Amanda stiffened. "Yet you did nothing," she hissed. "You talk about the priest, but your inaction made you an accomplice."

"No. You don't understand."

"I understand that you're a sick individual, Mr. Hamamy."

"I can imagine how this looks, but I swear I never touched

that girl. Not until I helped with her... body." His eyes blanked over. "And I had no idea just how evil they were until that night. When I got there, I heard them saying something about how she'd served her purpose."

"Her purpose?" Amanda choked on those words.

"I didn't ask, as I was quite sure that I didn't want to know. Still don't."

"I think you do though." She shot to her feet and slammed her chair into the table. All her anger needed a physical outlet. She paced around the table and circled behind Bruce, his head on a swivel as he clocked her moves. She put her face in his. "Sadie gave them the one thing they could never have. Sadie gave them a baby. A son. That was her *purpose*."

"A... I don't know what to say. I never saw a baby." Bruce's entire body began to shake. "Oh my God. Cameron?" He spoke the name as if it belonged to a poltergeist that had materialized in front of him.

"Yes, Cameron. Doug got Sadie pregnant. A sixteen-year-old girl." Her statement was cold while her insides blazed with rage.

"I didn't know about that. I swear to you."

"Your swearing doesn't mean anything to us," Amanda pushed back.

"You didn't find it odd that all of a sudden they had a baby?" Trent asked.

"They said they adopted him."

"Even if you believed that, you saw what they did to Sadie. You had to know he wouldn't be safe in that home." Her heart was pounding despite her cautioning herself to detach, remain objective. She paced some more, hoping that would calm her.

"I told you. I was afraid of Doug."

"Doug died three years ago. Plenty of time has passed for you to come forward and unburden yourself, let Sadie's parents gain closure. But you didn't do that. Instead, you kept quiet to protect yourself, so don't try to feed us the line of being paralyzed by fear."

Bruce cried into his hands, but his emotion wasn't moving Amanda. He'd known. He'd participated. He was guilty. "Tell us everything that happened that night." She pulled out her chair and sat back down.

Bruce blew his nose again, and then spoke. "Doug called, said I had to head over to the farm immediately."

They'd heard this part, but she wasn't going to interrupt and jinx the flow.

Bruce continued. "I got there, and he and Winnie were in the kitchen screaming at each other. I heard what I told you a moment ago, and Winnie also said, 'she deserved it.' But they clammed up when I knocked on the door and let myself in the house." Tears fell untouched down his cheeks. "They tried to tell me that Doug had hit the girl with his car, that she'd come out of nowhere. I asked where she was and told them we should call the police. They said that wasn't happening. I should have left right then. But it was just how they were looking at me. Sent the fear of God through me." He took a few breaths and continued. "Doug said that I owed him and Winnie because they kept my affair secret."

"The one with Brenda Witherspoon?" Trent said during the natural pause.

"Yeah. My wife would have left me and taken my boys away from me. I wouldn't have survived that back then."

Amanda pressed her lips into a firm line to prevent herself from instantly lashing out. Sadie hadn't survived. "You said they were in the kitchen. Did you see the hidden room?"

Bruce's eyebrows furrowed. "Hidden room? Don't know anything about it."

She wasn't inclined to believe a word out of his mouth, but said, "Continue."

"Anyway, they took me to her body. Doug had it in a

wooden crate. When he lifted the lid, the girl... the girl..." Bruce started crying again.

"What happened, Mr. Hamamy?" Amanda prompted, her patience drained.

"She wasn't dead. All of it happened so fast. She lunged up and reached out, scratched my cheek and drew blood. Doug intervened with this wild roar and punched her hard in the face. She... she went limp and fell back. I knew then that he hadn't hit her with his car."

"Yet you still did nothing," Amanda deadpanned.

"What was I supposed to do? I was already in too deep. I saw all the bruising on her body. Clearly something dark had gone on."

"Then you should have excused yourself, called the police, and explained what happened," Trent put in.

"Would you have believed me?" He let his question sit for a few seconds. When neither of them answered, he continued. "Yep. Just as I thought. I'd have gone to prison even though I'd done nothing wrong at that point. And that's if Doug or Winnie hadn't caught up to me and killed me."

"Go on," Amanda said.

"I did challenge Doug, though. Chalk it up to pure adrenaline at the time. I accused him of not hitting her with his car. He didn't respond to that. He just told me to help him get rid of her and we could forget about all this. But it was the way he looked at me. Like if I didn't help, he'd kill me. And I saw his face when he hit that girl. Like he enjoyed it."

Amanda's empathy was tapped out, but she could understand that if his story was true, he would have been intimidated. It still didn't justify him remaining silent all these years. "Then what?"

"We loaded her into the bed of Doug's pickup, drove out to Herald Church... I'm sure you know the rest."

"I'd rather hear your account." She was curious if he'd dare mention Audrey Witherspoon.

"We put her in the wall, screwed up some sheets of drywall to cover her." Bruce's emotions seemed to have run cold, or he was in shock, transported back in time.

If he was telling the truth, his DNA could have gotten onto Sadie's dress during that process. "And that's all? You got in and out with no one the wiser?" She was giving him a chance to come clean about Audrey. Would he take it?

"Huh. You know about her, that neighbor lady, don't you? She ever come forward?"

She slightly hitched her shoulders.

"Well, I thought for sure we were busted right then and there, but Doug came up with a convincing story about us delivering supplies for the renovations."

"Well, she didn't buy it," Amanda said. "She thought you were up to something bad, but her husband talked her out of saying anything back then. He tried to make her think she was making something of nothing. Good thing for you is she didn't know who you were. But you knew who she was, didn't you?" She slapped a photograph of Audrey from the crime scene on the table.

Bruce's gaze landed on the prone form of the older woman. He paled. "Brenda's grandmother. Is she dead?"

"Murdered. This week. Thursday evening. So how did you do it, Mr. Hamamy? How did you convince her to let you inside her home?" She was running on an unsupported theory that Audrey may have had tea with her killer, but there was nothing to suggest she had company for that.

"Hold up, I never laid a hand on that woman." His earlier histrionics were gone.

Amanda sat back. "You must understand that we're having a hard time believing you. "Why did you kill her now and not twenty-three years ago?"

"I swear that I never touched her. Brenda and I were over, but I'd have no reason."

"You just said it yourself. She saw what you were up to that night. It's all over the news about Sadie. You wanted to make sure she didn't resurrect the past and expose you."

"No."

Amanda carried on. "As you said, Audrey was your mistress's grandmother. Your close relationship with her afforded you the knowledge that she was on pain medication for her arthritis."

"I swear I have nothing to do with her death." He pushed Audrey's photo away, and Amanda pushed it back.

"She was killed by a lethal cocktail of oxycodone and lorazepam." She said the latter drug slowly and watched familiarity wash over his expression. "Your wife was prescribed lorazepam for her fear of flying, but the bottle and the pills are missing. Do you see where I'm headed with this?"

"Since you don't seem to be listening anymore, I think it's best I request that lawyer now."

"That might be a good idea." She stood and left the room with Trent, but Bruce's claim was niggling at her. He'd admitted to his wrongdoing when it came to Sadie Jackson, so why not own up to killing Audrey?

They joined Malone in the observation room.

"I don't think there's any question of his guilt," he said.

"None whatsoever," she said, disappointed they hadn't gotten around to asking about Jane Doe. "We'll need his prints and DNA."

"No problem getting a warrant for those."

"We should get a search warrant for where he's been living since his wife kicked him out," Trent put in. "We might find the wife's prescription bottle among his things."

"That's if he hasn't thrown it out," Amanda said, but that

didn't stop the feeling that Bruce might not have killed Audrey. But if he hadn't, who had?

"And there's that. All right, well, I'll leave you to it." Malone gave Amanda a tight smile as he left the room.

"Things *are* better between you," Trent said.

"Did you think I'd lied about that?"

"No, I just hoped you weren't sugarcoating things."

Amanda didn't know what to say to that or make of it, but she had more important things to concern herself with. Primarily, those warrants. She pulled her phone and couldn't believe how fast the time was going. It was already into the early afternoon. But she noticed that she had a missed call while she was in with Bruce. It was from Brenda Witherspoon, an hour ago, and she hadn't left a message. She hit the number to call it back and landed in voicemail. "Huh."

"What is it?" Trent asked her.

"Could be nothing. Probably is nothing."

"Don't keep me in suspense," he teased.

"Brenda Witherspoon called while we were in there, but she didn't leave a message. Now her phone's ringing to voicemail."

"So she's on the phone, or it ran out of battery. You're pale, like you think she's in trouble. The person she needs to be afraid of is in that room we just left."

He was right. Brenda had probably called about something she'd remembered, but if that was the case why not leave a message? And why not try again after one failed attempt? None of this was sitting well with her doubts about Bruce killing Audrey. "We should just pop by her place and make sure she's all right."

"The warrants?"

"They can wait a minute. It's just to support our case at this point. We know Bruce Hamamy's guilty." *Of helping to hide*

Sadie Jackson's body at least... She swung by her desk for her coat and waited while Trent grabbed his and they headed out. If her instincts were right, Brenda Witherspoon was in grave danger.

FORTY-ONE

Amanda banged on Brenda's apartment door. No response from inside, but a neighbor woman popped into the hall. Amanda rushed over to her. "Do you know the woman who lives in this unit?"

"A little. What's going on? Is she all right?"

"Have you seen her today?" Amanda served back.

"About an hour ago. She was leaving with a man when I was coming up."

Amanda took a few beats to process that. It could mean absolutely nothing. "A boyfriend?"

"I've never seen him before, and he wouldn't look me in the eye. I don't care for those types."

"Did she appear distressed at all? Like she was being forced to go with him?" Amanda's instinct was screaming at her.

"He was holding on to her arm, but she looked at me and said 'hello.'"

It could be that Brenda wanted the woman to read her eyes. "What did he look like?"

"He was young, late twenties, early thirties. Good-looking.

If it wasn't for his shifty eyes, I'd say Brenda was a cougar and netted herself a catch."

"Okay, thanks," Amanda told her.

The woman retreated back into her apartment, and Amanda headed toward the elevator.

"Amanda, what are we doing?" Trent asked her.

"There's something wrong here, Trent. I feel it in my gut."

The elevator arrived, and they got on and headed down.

With the doors shut, Trent turned to her. "Are you going to share?"

"What are the chances Brenda tries calling me and doesn't leave a message, but then she leaves around the same time with a man the neighbor's never seen before?"

"I doubt that woman sees everyone who comes and goes."

"Fair enough, but she said the man had a hold on Brenda's arm."

"Then you think this guy was forcing her to go along with him? But who and why? We have Bruce in custody."

"I don't know, Trent. Something here just isn't adding up for me."

"Forgive me for saying this, but maybe you're seeing what isn't there?"

She met his eyes, thrown back by his comment. He'd never questioned her before. "I'm not losing it."

He held up both his hands. "Oh, I never said that."

"But it's the insinuation."

"I know this case has been hard on you, but we have our killer in custody."

The elevator reached the ground floor, and she wasted no time unloading and heading for some fresh air. His implication hurt, as if he thought she was emotionally compromised and incapable of doing her job. "Fine, I don't deny what you're saying, but it doesn't change the fact that I feel Brenda is in trouble. A man in his thirties, avoiding eye contact while Brenda does the opposite?"

"Brenda was being neighborly."

"Damn you."

He cringed and stepped back.

"Please, just talk this out with me." She waited a few seconds, and he didn't say a word. She'd take that as acceptance. "It's possible that Brenda has a younger man in her life, but it's the confluence of things that isn't sitting right with me." She tried Brenda's phone again, and it went straight to voicemail. "Still no answer. I'm telling you, something is off."

"Clarify for me."

"If Brenda was calling with something she thought of after our last conversation, she would have left a message or called again. She did neither. Then her phone keeps going to voicemail. As you said before, there could be an innocent explanation."

"But you don't think so."

"I don't."

"Let's say Brenda's in danger. Who else besides Hamamy would have a reason to go after her? And what's their end game?" His forehead bunched up and he switched direction, going toward a vacant spot and not their car. He bent and picked up something off the ground.

"What is it?"

He faced her, and he was holding a smashed cell phone in his hand. "Could it be Brenda's?"

"If it is, this isn't good at all."

FORTY-TWO

Digital Forensics, a branch of the PWCPD for all things technology, confirmed for Amanda and Trent that the damaged phone belonged to Brenda Witherspoon.

Amanda called the building manager of Brenda's apartment complex about the video cameras mounted under the eaves. She was told they weren't functional, removing a chance of getting a look at the mystery man that way. A BOLO was issued on Brenda's car, which was missing from the lot. The other parked vehicles were registered to tenants. Whoever the guy was, he'd found some other way of getting here. Whether that was public transit, walking, a car service, or a blend of options, it was impossible to know. An APB was issued for Brenda Witherspoon.

And Amanda had run every one of those steps past Malone before acting. She even got some credit for following her gut. Little compensation. For every minute that passed, Brenda was who-knows-where with who-knows-who.

"There must be something we're missing here." She and Trent were back at Central, and she was pacing around the warren of cubicles for Homicide. No one else was in, or she'd likely be driving them crazy.

"We need to figure out who else would have reason to go after Brenda," Trent said. "We do that, we're on our way."

"Starting at ground zero. You do agree this is about the Cofells and the disposal of Sadie's body?"

"Agreed, and along those lines, something to do with Audrey witnessing part of that act."

"Just how does any of this gel with a man of only thirty-something?" Then she had an epiphany.

"If your eyes get any wider, they might pop out of your head."

"I think I know who he is, and with the Cofells at the center of this mess, I also believe I know where we can find him and Brenda."

"Oh, I don't like where this is heading."

"You really won't, but we've got to go anyway."

FORTY-THREE

Amanda shared her suspicions with Malone and Trent, admitting she wasn't certain about motive yet. Malone cleared them to check things out anyhow but gave them explicit instructions to report back if her hunch was confirmed. He'd added under no circumstances were they to proceed beyond that unless it was cleared past him.

"I can't believe we're back at the haunted farmhouse," Trent groaned as he parked down the road. Then if Brenda was being held in the home, her captor would be less likely to be alerted to their presence.

They set out, and the evening breeze was a cold one. As they got down the drive, Amanda saw Brenda's car was behind the house.

"That's it now. We turn around," Trent said.

"But we might be able to save her." She crept toward the house, keeping low, mindful of the windows.

"Amanda, stop."

She did and turned toward him, despite every part of her instinct compelling her forward. Looking at him, she catapulted back to her conversation with Malone. Her promise.

Her word meant everything. "Fine, you're right. We call it in."

"Thank you."

They ducked behind some overgrown shrubbery that was bare of leaves but thick with bramble. She called Malone, and when he answered she got right to the point. "Brenda's car is at the Cofell farm. Permission to move in?"

"No. I'll get SWAT out there. You hang—"

A chilling scream pierced the air.

"What the—?"

"Sarge, please, just let Trent and I move in. Otherwise it might be too late for her by the time everyone arrives."

There were a few seconds of silence. "Go. Just watch your backs."

Amanda nodded at Trent, who was watching her intently. "We will." She pocketed her phone. "He said we can move in. We just watch our backs."

"You don't need to tell me."

They said no more as they continued toward the back door. The window in it had been smashed, and Amanda slowly twisted the handle. It gave way. She and Trent pulled their guns and slipped quietly inside. There would be no announcement in this situation, as the element of surprise was in their favor. Being familiar with the home's layout was to their advantage. Same too for knowing that many of the floorboards creaked and that they were best to take cautious, slow steps.

They stood and listened. Brenda was crying, and they followed the sound down the hall toward the kitchen.

Amanda's heart was pounding, thinking about her being holed up in that hidden space behind the fridge, but as they reached the living room, they found her in there.

She was bound to a chair with a bloody lip and swollen eye. She startled when she saw them, and Amanda held a finger to her lips.

Trent nodded for Amanda to go to her. He'd watch the door.

Amanda entered and holstered her gun. She was only a few feet away from the chair when Brenda's eyes widened. Then Trent called out, and Amanda turned to see his crumpled form fall to the floor.

Her heart was pounding in her ears. Each jagged inhale and exhale sliced her lungs.

She reached for her gun, but before she could take it out, a figure emerged from the shadows and butted into her with the speed of a poltergeist.

She was knocked backward, hitting the floor with a loud smacking noise, the figure on top of her. A blinding pain radiated through her body and turned her vision white. She gasped hungrily for air, but the weight of this person straddling her was suffocating. She slapped at them, tried to knock them off, but her strength began to seep away.

All became black.

FORTY-FOUR

Birds were singing. *Somewhere...* Their chirps traveled to Amanda's ears like they were a million miles away. Her head was throbbing. What the hell had happened? Where was she? She'd lost all orientation and detested the vulnerability. She tried to open her eyes. Found it nearly impossible to do. A sharp pain bolted through her back and that worked to pop them wide.

Her vision was hazy. It wasn't aided by the fact she was immersed in relative darkness. Only faint light filtered into the space. She looked around and found the source was a window. Then as her eyes adjusted, she began to make out some indistinct shapes. Her mind was still having a hard time making sense of them.

Everything around her was silent, and as she tried to process the meaning and remember where she was, tidbits of memory rose up. She was in a house, but it wasn't hers. It wasn't familiar enough, and there was a different energy running through it.

Another jab of electricity punctured her back and provided

some clarity. The Cofell farmhouse. Brenda was here... tied to a chair... in this room.

Was she one of the indistinct shapes? Amanda strained to see and plucked out more detail. Brenda was still in the chair.

Amanda tried to speak, but her voice felt locked in her throat.

Then there was Trent. He'd been struck. He'd called out and fell... in the doorway.

She looked in that direction, at another indistinct shape. Slowly, her mind made sense of it, interpreting what she was seeing. It was Trent, splayed out on the floor.

After he'd been hit... Then what? She must have hit her head.

That's right! She was plowed backward by a shadowy figure. She'd hit the floor with force.

That explained the pain in her back. But what the hell had happened? How had the suspect gotten the upper hand on them?

The silence was mocking, criticizing. How long had she been out? Was the man even here anymore?

The more questions she asked, her head cleared bit by bit. She came to realize her wrists and ankles were bound with duct tape. She considered screaming. If only she could get her voice to work. But would anyone hear her? If the man was still around, she'd bring more trouble. It was already a miracle she was still alive.

She looked at Trent again. *Is he still alive?*

A sob rose in her chest, churning up a deep fear that tasted bitter and burned like acid. What would she ever do without him?

Still on her back, she carefully turned over. Each movement was agony, but she tamped it down, placing it into perspective. It was just pain. She would survive.

She crawled across the room to Trent, stomach to the floor,

using her elbows and the tips of her shoes to move her forward. Her head continued to swim while jabs of pain assaulted her back. Trent couldn't be more than ten feet away, but her discomfort made it feel like a hundred. It was inner drive pushing her forward, the need to know that he was okay. She tried to focus on his chest but couldn't tell if he was breathing.

When she reached him, she saw a small puddle of blood on the floor next to him and nudged him with her shoulder. She could tell now that he was bound too, and his eyes were tightly closed. Was he unconscious or... No, she couldn't even consider the alternative. When he didn't budge, she put her ear to his mouth and heard him breathing.

She whispered in his ear, "Trent."

No reaction.

Tears carved hot paths down her cheeks. But as long as he was breathing, there was hope. She had to cling to that. Trent needed her, and so did Brenda.

Amanda now made the journey back to her. Once she reached the chair, she shuffled her legs beneath her and got to her knees. Brenda didn't respond. Her eyes were closed, but her chest was rising and falling.

Amanda worked to unravel the tape on Brenda's wrists, only able to take one at a time. She couldn't find the edge with her eyes or by touch. And just as she thought she had, she froze at the sound of footsteps behind her.

"I'd think twice about doing that."

At the man's voice, her cop instincts were awakened. She twisted, reaching for her gun but found her holster was empty. He'd taken her weapon, probably Trent's too. She looked over her shoulder. In the dim light, she made out a man holding a Glock on her. She also made out something else. She'd laid eyes on him once before. It had been in a photograph of his college graduation. Her hunch had been right. "Peyton Hamamy." It took mustering all her strength to project her voice.

"So you know who I am, not that it matters. We're all going to be dead before this is over."

"It doesn't have to be that way."

"Don't patronize me." He waved the gun.

She recoiled, fear seeding in her gut. But she couldn't back down. She was Trent's and Brenda's only hope of survival. *Where's our backup?* "Why are you doing this? What about your mother? What would she think?" He must have taken Linda's lorazepam...

"Just shut up! She has nothing to do with this." His voice was plump with rage, but there was also something sad in his tone. Grief. Regret.

"You don't need to do this. Your father told us everything."

"He... *No*." His hold on the gun faltered. Just briefly.

"We know it was your father, Peyton. He killed that girl."

"No, he didn't! Dad did what he had to do to protect us!" Peyton shoved one of his hands through his hair, giving the image of lunacy.

"Talk to me, Peyton. Tell me how he protected you." She winced as another shot of pain fired through her.

"I heard him talking with Doug Cofell. He said he's not a killer and wouldn't cover for one. But Dad was scared, and I don't blame him. Doug was a scary son of a bitch." With that last statement, Peyton's demeanor changed. It shrunk, giving Amanda a horrible suspicion.

"If that's the truth, let us all go, and we can end this now. We can talk with your dad again and set the record straight." She'd say what she must to deescalate the situation. It would take more than this to believe Bruce's account of that day twenty-three years ago, even though she was quite certain he told them the truth about Audrey Witherspoon. He hadn't killed her. She believed that had been Peyton, but his motive for that and taking Brenda wasn't clear.

"Nah, it's too late for that." Peyton rushed toward Brenda but had to pass Amanda to get there.

She swiftly kicked out her legs, and Peyton flew forward. He pinwheeled his arms but couldn't catch his balance and fell hard, the gun skittering across the floor.

Even as pain tried to claim her, Amanda scurried to get the weapon. The Glock was closer to her, but being bound at wrists and ankles slowed her down. Intense waves of pain also churned her stomach.

"Stop right there." Peyton's voice was chilling, but Amanda didn't listen.

Her fingertips grazed the handle, brushed over the trigger, accidentally pressing it as she picked it up. A round fired into the wall.

Trent groaned across the room. A part of her softened with relief.

Then Peyton pulled another Glock, likely Trent's. "You stop right now, or I will shoot all of you."

"Please, don't do that, Peyton," she said. "Your dad wouldn't want you to do this. He loves you. He did what he had to do to protect you." She recycled his earlier words.

Time seemed to stop.

She continued. "You're a victim in all of this. You were just a boy and have had to hold on to this secret all your life."

"I was just a boy!" Peyton wailed and cried into his hands.

She could take advantage of this moment, grab the Glock on the floor and shoot him. It was probably the safest choice, the *smarter* choice. It just didn't feel like the right one. While Peyton continued to cry, Amanda's fractured mind pieced together the image in front of her. This man was broken. His words, *I was just a boy*, rang through her head, and she had a sickening suspicion that Peyton was another victim claimed by the Cofells.

She slowly got to her feet, talking soothingly as she did. "I'm not armed, Peyton. You're safe, and so are all of us. Everything's going to be all right. Please trust me on that." She hoped like hell that Trent would be safe, Brenda too for that matter. *But Trent...* Again, emotion balled up in her chest.

She put her hands over Peyton's, the one that held the gun. "Hand it over to me, Peyton. It will be all right," she repeated.

He released his hold on the gun just as stomping boots moved into the house.

With the Glock in her hands, she shuffled back from Peyton. She looked at him while she called out to SWAT to let them know where they were, and the situation was resolved.

Officers paraded in to assist. One stopped and helped Trent sit up.

We're all saved. Even Peyton Hamamy.

As the thought fired through, a blinding pain seized her back and had her legs buckling out from under her.

FORTY-FIVE

The next day, Amanda's back was still messed up from being pushed to the floor, but an ice pack and a trio of pills made the pain tolerable. Trent and Brenda had been taken to the hospital too, and like her were released not long afterward with instructions to take it easy. But she certainly wasn't staying home today. She wanted all her questions answered.

She only figured out one last night. How Peyton had gotten the upper hand on Trent. He had ducked to the side of the door after hearing them come in and had hidden there. Amanda made it past him, but even though Trent was backing into the room to cover her and Brenda, Peyton sprung out and struck him unaware. Admirably Malone hadn't pointed out that he had warned them to watch their backs.

Amanda nudged her head toward the one-way mirror. Peyton Hamamy sat at the table in the interview room alone. He'd declined a lawyer. He was arrested last night, but the questioning was left for a fresh day. That being at Malone's direction. "You ready to go in?" she asked Trent.

"You bet."

They left Malone in the observation room and joined Peyton.

"I did all of it for my dad," Peyton volunteered as she and Trent sat across from him.

"All of what?" She needed him to say it for the record.

"To start, killing that old lady."

She'd circle back to kidnapping Brenda. "You say you did all this to protect your father? Help me understand that." A soft approach would likely work best with him.

"I was so young at the time, eight years old. I'll never forget the fear on Dad's face or in his voice. Doug was over like he and his wife always were. We never went to their house. But I overheard them talking. They didn't know anyone was around, but Dad was really worried. He said that he'd been having nightmares ever since they'd put that girl in the wall. That he never should have helped. Doug told him if he didn't keep his mouth shut or if he turned him in, he'd ruin his life. He'd tell my mother he was running around with Brenda, and she'd take us kids. I only ever knew one Brenda. A lady from church, and I knew her relative lived next door. I'd noticed that Brenda and Dad were chummy, but I hadn't thought more of it than that. Dad said he couldn't lose his sons. He said we meant the world to him."

"What happened after that?" Trent asked.

"Well, Dad was really worked up. He said that the lady next to the church had seen them with the body. Doug corrected him that she saw them with *supplies* and laughed. Then he said, 'We could kill her too, but that would be more trouble than it would be worth. She's batty and arthritic, for heaven's sake. Not much of a threat.' He also told Dad if he kept his bitch under control, her grandmother shouldn't be a problem."

It was somewhat surprising how much of the conversation Peyton had remembered. Though it would have been a shocking one to overhear, even at that young age. But was there more to it that made it easy for Peyton to recall all this so clearly? Was it linked with her suspicion about Peyton suffering abuse, possibly from the Cofells? She'd get around to that shortly too but wanted to stay on track while he was talking. "Is this how you knew Audrey Witherspoon was the eyewitness? You knew she was Brenda's grandmother?"

"Uh-huh. The fact she'd never moved was how I knew where to find her. But Doug did more than threaten to *expose* Dad, he threatened his life. Dad promised to keep quiet. I was so angry, but what was I supposed to do about any of it? I was a kid. And I did my best to put all this out of my mind, but Dad started drinking all the time and losing jobs and he was fighting with Mom. I'm surprised they patched things up as they did all these years. Despite all that, I moved on. But when that girl was found last week in the church, I did the math. I knew it must be what they were talking about that day, and I figured it would only be a matter of time and you'd be coming after my father. There was a chance the old woman might go to you and identify my father, even after all these years. I was surprised she hadn't already. But I guess she didn't know his name. Not until I gave it to her."

"Can you tell us about that?" she said. "We assume you showed up at her door, but can you walk us through it?"

"I talked myself inside. I presented all nice and sheepish. I told her I knew what my dad did and knew she did too. She asked my name, and I told her my name and my father's. I saw the look on her face, like she was recording that to memory. I knew there was no going back. I excused myself and used her washroom. That's when I saw her prescription for oxy. I had Mom's lorazepam."

That sounded more opportunistic than premeditated. "Did you go there intending to kill her?"

Peyton shook his head. "I was prepared, but only if it

seemed she was going to point the finger at Dad. I remembered she had arthritis from all those years ago, and I figured she'd be on a strong painkiller or anti-inflammatory. If it was oxy, I knew that if it was taken with lorazepam, it would be a lethal combo. I took some med courses," he added as an afterthought.

"What did you do when you left the restroom?" Trent asked.

"Well, her kettle had just boiled. She was in the sitting room, and I offered to make up her tea and bring it to her. She thought I was being kind." He at least had the decency to look ashamed.

"What would you have done if she wasn't having tea?" The question was prompted more out of curiosity than anything.

"I'd have found another way to get the pills into her. If only she'd forgotten about what she saw..."

"You would have let her live in that case?" Amanda wasn't sure he'd take that chance.

"Maybe."

As I thought... "You certainly gave thought to her murder. Even bringing the pill case along with you. That was you?"

"It was, and I typed the suicide note after she passed. I thought if I was convincing enough, you wouldn't think any more of it. You wouldn't track down my father."

"Why go after Brenda?" she asked. "How did you know where to find her?"

"The internet makes it easy to find anyone. But I swear I had no intention of killing her, not unless I had no other choice, but I couldn't take a chance that Audrey had mentioned my father's name to her. I just planned to question her, but she was being so difficult and started freaking out. I needed to get her somewhere isolated, so we could talk. That's when I had her drive us out to the farmhouse."

"I saw her busted lip and black eye," Amanda began. "You did more than talk."

"I have no excuse for that besides being angry and frustrated by that point. I'd killed a woman, kidnapped another one."

"So why the Cofell farm? Just for the isolation?" She was working her way around to her suspicion.

"Why not? I knew it was abandoned and out of the way."

Amanda angled her head. "Is that all?"

Peyton's eyes welled with tears.

"You told me you were 'just a boy.' What did you mean by that, Peyton? What happened back then?" She approached this gently.

"Doug... touched me." His chin quivered at the admission, and fat tears beaded on his lashes. "It was the same day he threatened my dad. Moments before."

This explained why the conversation from that day was so deeply embedded. He'd also lied to his mother, Linda, when she asked if he knew about abuse in the Cofell home. A victim himself, Peyton had kept quiet. "I'm sorry for all that you suffered, Peyton, and thank you for being so straightforward with us."

"It's just time I put it all behind me. He destroyed every relationship I've ever tried to have. I've had a problem with intimacy all my life, and I blame Doug Cofell for that. But my dad, he's my hero because he protected his family by keeping quiet. He kept us together for a long time."

There would be no point arguing that his father was also an accessory to murder. "Are you willing to put all that you told us today into a written, signed confession?"

"Yes. As I said, I just want to put all this behind me."

Amanda and Trent left the room, but her heart was heavy and conflicted. Peyton would never be able to put the past behind him even if he thought that's what his admission would do. Soon he'd be locked up with nothing but time to think about it.

"There you have it. Two more homicides tied up with a bow." Trent was smiling at her. "I don't know about you, but I'm exhausted."

"Oh yeah."

"How's your back?"

"Sore. Your head?"

"Sore. Aren't we a pair?"

"That we are, but it's not *all* tied up. There's still Jane Doe." The unidentified girl in the photograph found in the Cofells' attic haunted her when she closed her eyes. "We still don't know who she was, where she is..."

"We don't always get all the answers or close every case."

"It still bugs me."

"I'm just not sure what we can do without more to go on."

She wasn't sure either. "Maybe you're right. Either way, we better get some coffee in a cup because now it's paperwork time."

He laughed. "The only downside to closing cases."

They got some coffee and hit their desks to shuffle through the massive number of reports. Bruce Hamamy's DNA and prints implicated him in the Sadie Jackson murder. They were charging him with accessory to murder. His actions and his silence brought him that. They couldn't prove beyond a doubt he had a hand in killing Sadie, but he was complicit. Even if his claims and those of his son were factual, that Bruce had been coerced into cooperating, it changed little. And someone had to go to prison for Sadie Jackson. Peyton was being charged with one count of murder, one of kidnapping, and two counts of assaulting a police officer.

There was satisfaction that came with every report she knocked off, but the toll each case took was never far from her mind. The drain on emotions, mental and physical resources, the impact on her personal life, keeping her from Zoe. But despite all that, the ones who sacrificed the most were the victims. Tonight, she would honor the memory of Sadie Jackson.

FORTY-SIX

The crowd that gathered at Herald Church overflowed onto the front steps and the walkway. That afternoon, the news had hit with the truth of Sadie Jackson's disappearance and the people responsible. Now the whole world would be reminded of a young girl who was loved and missed. And here tonight it would be about letting her go.

Amanda had gone home to spend a few hours with Zoe before heading over. On the way, she had received a phone call that set a somber tone. Cameron Cofell had hung himself in his jail cell. He'd left a note saying that he didn't want to be his father.

She wiped an errant tear from her cheek. She thought he'd have wanted to know the truth about Sadie, and that he would have been able to handle it. She'd never know now, and there was no going back. A sad truth she was reminded of all the time.

Just like the reality there may never be justice for Jane Doe. Amanda had scrutinized her picture, zooming in to see if she could pick out any distinguishing markers. She'd met with luck. There was a small brown mole near her throat on the right side of her neck, and a slightly lazy left eye. But even taking those markers to the Missing Persons database would be futile. Where would she even start looking? Searching the entire United States would be unreasonable. Even breaking the search down by state or county would take forever, certainly far more time than she had. Trent was right that some cases didn't get closure. She just hated it when it was one that passed her desk.

Amanda made her way into the warm church and lit a candle for Sadie Jackson, and then backed out to allow others to do the same. As she was leaving, she bumped into Trent with a pretty woman on his arm, who was likely the infamous Kelsey.

"Hey, Amanda," Trent said, and he and the woman stepped to the side of the doors.

It felt like an inappropriate occasion for this introduction, but she held out her hand to the woman, noting her smooth chestnut hair and delicate facial features. "Amanda, Trent's partner."

"Kelsey, Trent's girlfriend." She smiled, but the expression was watered down due to the somber occasion.

Chet Solomon cut in with an announcement the memorial was going to start in three minutes in the church's lot, due to the size of the turnout.

"We'll all talk again soon?" Amanda said, latching on to the excuse to move on.

"Yes, I'd like that," Kelsey told her, while keeping her eyes locked with Amanda's until she stepped away.

Trent and Kelsey entered the church, while Amanda made her way to the back of the gathered crowd. Everyone was handed a lit candle, after which Father Linwood gave a brief speech, offered a prayer, and called for a collective moment of silence. By the time it was all over, everyone had shed tears.

As she turned to leave, she caught sight of the Jacksons. Rosemary came over, with her husband following. The woman wrapped her arms around Amanda and squeezed her tightly.

She drew back a moment later, and said, "We can't thank

you enough. Her body was released to us, and we're having her funeral next weekend in Hagerstown. We'll finally be able to lay her to rest. Again, thank you"—her voice cracked, and she sniffled—"for finding those responsible."

The Jacksons hadn't asked any more about Sadie's child, and Amanda hadn't told them Cameron was their grandson. It wasn't her place to volunteer such information, and she saw it as a mercy to spare them the pain of grieving a man they never had a chance to meet. "You're very welcome." Amanda delicately slipped away then, savoring that she brought the Jacksons closure while trying to squeeze out the families she failed.

She got behind the wheel of her car and pushed the gas a little past the speed limit on the way home. Or maybe more than a *little*. Zoe was waiting for her.

A LETTER FROM CAROLYN

Dear reader,

I want to say a huge thank you for choosing to read *Hidden Angels*. If you enjoyed it and would like to hear about new releases in the Amanda Steele series, just sign up at the following link. Your email address will never be shared, and you can unsubscribe at any time.

www.bookouture.com/carolyn-arnold

Writing this one was a rush! I felt so inspired after returning from a trip across "the pond" to meet my publisher and editor there. One touristy thing my husband and I did was tour Westminster Abbey. I knew royal weddings and coronations took place there, but I didn't realize there were so many people buried and memorialized within its walls! Looking it up online, it shows over 3,000. Most are entombed in elaborate crypts rich with symbolism. It was all quite fascinating really. An interesting side point was I had pitched the idea of a body in a church wall before even booking this trip. But having been through the abbey, I had the associated *feels* to reference when I wrote.

I hope you enjoyed the journey, even if you might have picked up on the fact I took creative liberties. These are much the same as many authors have done over the years to make crime fiction fast paced. There's always a showdown at the end between the detectives and the bad guy. There's satisfaction and a thrill in seeing the killer get their comeuppance. In real life, it's unlikely to be quite that exciting and heart-pounding every time.

You may have noticed differences in how I depicted Woodbridge, VA, Prince William County, and the PWCPD itself. Also, if only DNA results came back in real life as quickly as they did in this book! In the real world, it can take weeks and months to get results. An interesting fact I've learned recently is the labs are so backed up that law enforcement is limited in the number of samples they can even submit for testing. It's not like fiction, where *everything* is tested.

If this book had you flipping the pages, you can get excited, because more Amanda Steele is on the way! Also, did you enjoy meeting FBI Special Agent Sandra Vos? She's getting a series of her own where she'll shine as the smart and experienced negotiator you met in this book! In fact, by the time you have reached this letter, you may even be able to get started reading that series.

I'd like to thank everyone who helped me with this book. George, my husband and best friend, is always my first mention. He helps me keep balanced and sane. My editor, Laura Deacon, and I have come a long way, and we had a shared vision for the book. There are many others, too, and I appreciate everyone. And you, my beautiful reader, thank you for your support.

Speaking of, if you devour books, you'll be happy to know I offer several bestselling crime fiction series for you to savor, as well as series in other genres. One of these features Detective Madison Knight, another kick-ass female detective like Amanda, though Madison might speak her mind a lot more... But she'll stop at nothing and risk it all to find justice for murder victims.

If you enjoy being in the Prince William County, Virginia,

area and like dark serial killer novels, you must read my Brandon Fisher FBI series. He lives in Woodbridge but it gets even closer than that to Amanda. Brandon's dating Amanda's best friend. We could call this the expanded PWC Universe, or some other catchy name. I'm still deciding. If you have an idea, email me!

And before I sign off, please, don't underestimate the power and influence of word of mouth. Talk to your family and friends about my books, your local bookstores and librarians, your neighbors, the people at the checkout counter, your dentist, your... Well, you get the point. Thank you!

And last but certainly not least, I would love to hear from you if you're inclined to drop me a note! You can reach me via email at Carolyn@CarolynArnold.net. You can also follow and interact with me on social media at the links below. To investigate my full list of books, visit my website by following the link below.

Until the next time, I wish you thrilling reads and twists you never saw coming!

Carolyn Arnold

www.carolynarnold.net

facebook.com/AuthorCarolynArnold
x.com/Carolyn_Arnold
goodreads.com/carolyn_arnold

PUBLISHING TEAM

Turning a manuscript into a book requires the efforts of many people. The publishing team at Bookouture would like to acknowledge everyone who contributed to this publication.

Audio
Alba Proko
Sinead O'Connor
Melissa Tran

Commercial
Lauren Morrissette
Hannah Richmond
Imogen Allport

Cover design
Head Design Ltd

Data and analysis
Mark Alder
Mohamed Bussuri

Editorial
Laura Deacon
Sinead O'Connor

Copyeditor
Fraser Crichton

Proofreader
Becca Allen

Marketing
Alex Crow
Melanie Price
Occy Carr
Ciara Rosney
Martyna Młynarska

Operations and distribution
Marina Valles
Stephanie Straub
Joe Morris

Production
Hannah Snetsinger
Mandy Kullar
Jen Shannon
Ria Clare

Publicity
Kim Nash
Noelle Holten
Jess Readett
Sarah Hardy

Rights and contracts
Peta Nightingale
Richard King
Saidah Graham

www.ingramcontent.com/pod-product-compliance
Lightning Source LLC
La Vergne TN
LVHW090154200225
804157LV00004B/51